CRAWL

A DARK STALKER ROMANCE

AUDREY RUSH

Crawl: A Dark Stalker Romance by Audrey Rush

Independently Published

Copyright © 2021 Audrey Rush
All rights reserved. No portion of this book may be reproduced in any form
without permission from the publisher, except as permitted by U.S. copyright law.
For permissions contact: audreyrushbooks@gmail.com

Cover Photography from DepositPhotos.com
Cover Design by Kai

Amazon ISBN: 9798783154157
Barnes & Noble ISBN: 9798881153441

Author's Note

This content notification may contain spoilers.

This book follows the romance between an antiheroine with a traumatic past and an irredeemable serial killer. As such, this story contains extremely graphic violence, disturbing content, as well as harmful contact between family members. Furthermore, the serial killer always takes what he wants without remorse, and the couple indulges in dark games featuring torture, weapons, and blood.

This is a *dark* romance. Reader discretion is advised.

CRAWL

CHAPTER 1

CASH

FIRST, I SEE THE TAWNY GLOW OF HER UPPER ARM. HER THICK bicep twitches, then her fingers pinch at the fabric. The shirt flutters to the ground. There's barely any room to move, but I shift my eye against the peephole, the inner surface of the plaster scraping my cheek. She crosses the room again and I get a glimpse of the tattoo on her back: two rib cages pressed together, the phalanges clutching each other like they're afraid they'll fall apart. But I've seen the piece in full: skeletons embracing, teeth against teeth, dark eye sockets turned toward one another. As if the only promise we can rely on is our base instincts.

These old houses weren't regulated during construction, and occupants expect things like holes in the plaster. Some of these homeowners don't even know that they have wall cavities. Itching to see her again, my hands scratch the inner wall, and suddenly, it's deathly still. I can imagine it already; another complaint about rats sent in a work order. Pesky little things. The foul scent of decaying palm trees fills the air, a dampness heavy on my shoulders, like a mouth breathing down on me.

Then the artificial moans shriek through the wall. The adult actress squeals, backed by creaking wooden furniture, and I instantly know the video Remedy is watching. It's the same one every time: a man with bloodshot eyes towering over a woman with a rope around her neck while he takes her from behind. She always comes back to this one.

It's only midday and she's already going at it. My kind of woman.

I lean back against the outer wall, inching a hand into my pants, but I'm compressed between the two walls, and it's hard to get a hand on my shaft. There's a layer of fabric between the hard inner wall and my hand, but my forearm grinds against the plaster. I press my eye against that tiny hole, shifting in each direction to get another peek of her. Remedy Basset. What a name. Medicine. Treatment. A substitute for what's needed. And my favorite little cure.

Blood fills my bulge, but it's no use with a hole this small. I can't see anything. I'm lucky if I catch a flash of her shoulder, and yet, I still prefer this vantage point. An associate back in Missoula had helped me hack her webcam so that I can see everything: every twist of her lips, every scrunched eyebrow, every pant that escapes her purple lips. But when it comes to my free time, before she goes to sleep, I prefer to spend it as close to her as possible. And that means being pressed between her wall cavities.

Her bare foot props up on the desk, her toenails nude and unpainted, but I can picture the webcam footage now: Remedy with her legs spread, a bobby pin falling out of her hair, hands clutching at her holes. Perhaps she'll have clamps on her nipples, with the rubber guards removed this time, so that it's metal teeth on skin. The clamp's chain will dangle between her purple lips.

The computer chair squeaks with each thrust of her hips. My dirty girl doesn't take her time; she knows what she wants. I stare at her twitching foot through the peephole and imagine us in that video: my ropes around her neck, watching as her face turns a beautiful shade of plum that complements her painted lips, mascara staining her cheeks, blood racing down her chest and hips, slashes from my knife marking her like a torn bag of cement, her velvet walls constricting around my shaft like she's taking the life out of me.

And then, on the other side of the wall, a moan erupts from Remedy's lips like a lamb who knows it's about to be slaughtered, a sweet cry that lets the last notes hang in the air. With that image of her mouth twisting in release as she rips the clamps off of her nipples, I rub my length, my knuckles ramming into the wall. She gasps. Her computer chair creaks as she quickly stands up. A ruffle of commotion, like things being pushed around her bedroom. Perhaps she's searching for a weapon to defend herself against a rather big rat. And that fear pushes me over the edge; my hot spurts of release soak my boxers.

After a few moments, she gives up, and this time I see the tips of her brown nipples, raw and red, as she crosses in front of the hole. I'm hard again. But she's distracted; this is my chance to move. I inch between the inner and outer wall, not wanting to disturb her this time. After all, I enjoy watching Remedy and want to keep doing so. As an expert in my field, my job gives me access to houses all over Key West, and I've gotten to know her well over the past few months. I know the jasmine scent of her hair that lingers on her lumpy pillow. I've sniffed the sweet and tangy musk in her dirty panties. I know exactly the kinds of dirty videos she watches on repeat. And I know that her full name is Remedy Elise Basset and that she's a personal assistant to the wealthy. I even know that she uses the password *Bones1934* for practically everything.

The doorbell rings and I freeze in place. There's never been a visitor before. Curious, I slide back to the peephole. There's a loud clatter—she's probably hiding those clamps—then an aerosol room spray puffs into the air. She flickers in front of the hole for a moment. Once she's gone, I press my nose to the hole, using that single moment of solitude to take it in: the nauseatingly ripe stench of fruit punch, synthetically saccharine. It beats the hell out of plaster, rotting trees, and come.

Another body passes in front of the hole. Pale soft arms, the strap of something—probably a purse—hanging from a shoulder. She doesn't live here, or she would have left her purse in the other bedroom. This is a good thing; I prefer my little cure by herself.

"You should have had me pick you up," Remedy says. Her words are muffled by the wall, but I can still hear the coarseness of her voice. I can't wait to hear that raspy gasp when she screams for me.

"You're one to talk," the friend laughs, her voice high like a runty little puppy.

"I took the self-defense classes; you didn't. A serial killer is out there."

I hold back a chuckle. Like a groin jab or pepper spray will stop a serial killer.

"Peter escorted me," the friend says.

Remedy scoffs under her breath; even through the walls, I can hear the disdain in her voice. Whoever he is, she doesn't trust Peter like her friend does.

"So you finally got the transfer?" Remedy asks, changing the subject.

"Starting on Monday at this old lady's house on Duval."

"But did you tell LPA what Winstone did?"

The friend hesitates. And if I know my little cure, the longer the seconds drag on, the antsier she gets. She likes tapping her fingers on her sides, flicking them open and close, to keep herself under control. Straining my fingers, I match her movements behind the wall. I'm a big man squeezed into a tight space, like stuffing a king-sized mattress into the back of a golf cart. I can't get comfortable, and it's hot as balls, but it's worth it. With these motions, I try to get inside of her head. Is it sadness? Perhaps. Anxiety? Anger? Why does she keep it locked inside of her rib cage?

Whatever happened doesn't have to do with Remedy. It's her friend's problem.

"I just want it to blow over," the friend says.

A faint sigh escapes Remedy's lips. The lock on her bedroom door crunches, and the blinds over her windows shift up, then down, like she's checking to make sure her windows are locked. It's a nervous habit, one she does often even when she's alone, to make sure she knows exactly who can get in and who can get out.

"He backhanded you," Remedy says, anger in her raspy voice. "Slapped you. Spanked your ass like you were a child." She groans, and I imagine her throwing her hands up in the air, but in the hole, I only see the empty spot next to her desk. The two women must be sitting on her bed. "Someone *has* to do something."

"But that doesn't have to be me," the friend says. "Or you."

A slight pause passes between them. I shift my weight, angling myself toward the bed, but now, all I see is the wall.

"I'm not going to let it happen again," Remedy says, a warning in her tone.

"This isn't about your—"

A phone vibrates, rattling on a hard surface. The two of them scramble for the device, but it beeps and Remedy answers it.

"This is Remedy Basset," she says. The taps of her feet are light on the hard floor as she paces the room. A bare shoulder passes in front of the hole, a lace-lined camisole sits on her frame. I rub my fingers along the inner plaster of the wall as if I can feel her smooth skin, and I imagine stroking the intricate black lace tattoo sprawling over her supple stomach. She turns around, pacing the other direction, and I suck in a breath.

"You mean Mr. Winstone at the Winstone Estate, correct?" Remedy asks the caller. She whispers to her friend, then clears her throat. "Absolutely. I'll be ready. Thank you."

As soon as the phone beeps again, the friend wails.

"What the hell, Remedy?" she asks. "This is bullshit."

"It's a job," Remedy says, her tone matter-of-fact. "Since the Johnsons left, I've been out of work. You know how hard it is in the off-season."

Another pause stretches between them. There must be some truth to that statement, even if it is convenient that the personal assistant agency assigned Remedy to the same job her friend recently left.

"But you took a job with *him?*" the friend asks. "You encouraged me to transfer, just so you could take my job? What's up with that?"

"It's luck," Remedy says. "Bad, bad luck. But this way, he can't hurt you or anyone else anymore."

"So what, he'll hurt you instead?"

"I'm going to hurt him too."

A pause shifts between the two women. "Remmie," the friend says.

"It's fine. It's a short assignment. Temporary until they find a better match."

"Temp for a month, right? Then he'll sign you for a year. That's what he did with me."

"So?"

"Like you said. It's fine at first. He left me alone, right? Like I was a meaningless staff member. But then he physically assaulted me. And you want to work for him? What if he does it to you too?"

"Then I'm going to get it on camera."

"He's got his surveillance under tight control."

"I'll install my own."

"I'm telling you, he'll *know* about it."

"And if I have to, I'll kill him."

Kill him?

The friend gasps. My groin tenses with sudden pressure. She's so damn hot. Maneuvering between the walls, inch by inch, I take my phone out of my pocket, careful not to make any sudden movements. I don't want to stir the two women into a frenzy. My associate, the same one who hacked Remedy's webcam, gave me an app to see her webcam on my phone at any time. I want to see her face. The thick, dark brows, her shiny black hair. Her eyes beaming down her nose as she looks at her friend. So sure of herself, like she knows she's going to kill him.

Most people say that in bluster, confident until the knife is in their hand, then they can't do anything. Not because of the guilt at the life they're stealing, but at the fear of getting caught. But others? We can look each other in the eye and feel it. Murder is an action and death is the result. And Remedy?

Perhaps that's why I haven't killed her yet.

But when I click the app, it says: *Webcam Offline.* She must have closed her laptop when she finished that video. Damn it.

"I'm not going to let Winstone go unpunished," Remedy says, her voice stern.

"He's not your stepdad," the friend squeals out, then gasps

again, like she immediately regrets it. "Winstone is more like your stepbrother than your stepdad. And you said so yourself: Brody didn't even bother you that much."

This time, Remedy says nothing. I press my eye to the hole, but the desk is all I have. The nail polish stains. An empty water bottle. A peel of an orange.

"I shouldn't have said that," the friend stammers.

This time, Remedy walks past the peephole, and I catch a glimpse of her hand—black nail polish, always chipped, her fingers clutched around the other arm like she's holding herself.

"I have to do this," Remedy says. "Or I won't forgive myself."

"You don't know what he's capable of."

"I've dealt with people like him before."

"Brody was still your family. Winstone isn't. He can really hurt you, Remmie."

"I'm not going to let anyone get away with it again."

There's a boisterousness in those words that silences the both of them, an emphatic declaration that Remedy knows what she wants. The friend groans, but Remedy doesn't offer anything to placate her. She's not going to give up on this. I like that.

"You have to be careful," the friend says.

"I will."

"You're doing this alone. That means he's got more power over you."

"At least he's not getting us at the same time," Remedy chuckles.

"That would almost be better. I could distract him while you take him on."

"Yeah, right!"

The two women laugh, and finally, I zone out. The conversation wanders into monotony, droning about work, school, family, topics I care little about. I don't understand the term 'best friend,' but with the way these two talk, I imagine this is what it is.

Eventually, the friend leaves, and Remedy sighs. She's relieved, and I let out a breath too. The friend's voice is like shredding eardrums on a cheese grater. The lock shudders in the front of the house, the bedroom door slams shut, and then the computer chair squeaks with Remedy's weight. The keyboard clicks. She's using her laptop, then. I check the phone app, switching to the mirrored screen. She flips through the usual social media pages, even searching for the Winstone Estate and Mr. Winstone himself.

She hovers over an old headline: *Cassius Winstone, owner and CEO of The Winstone Company, reclusive developer of the Southeastern United States, discusses his new projects in Key West.*

At least they got the 'reclusive' part right.

Her phone pings, and as she checks it, I switch to the webcam view, her hand resting on the keyboard, her eyes on her phone in her lap. She smiles, then gets up, walking out of the room. The plumbing shudders through the house like an old machine stumbling to wake up. She must be starting a shower. Usually, I prefer to wait until the residents are sleeping to leave, but this is my queue. I take long, careful side steps through the wall cavity. With the gradual, stroking movements of my chest and legs against the inner walls, it's less likely that she'll hear anything, especially with the shower running. Once I bend into the crawl space, I emerge from the floor hatch. I brush my hands over my clothes, wiping off the dust from inside the cavity, then exit out the back door. She never hears it.

I relax behind the wheel of my truck. The pale moon breaks up the bright blue sky, and I nod my head at the tourists on the sidewalk: drunk, comfortable, completely unaware. A few police officers roam beside them, more than usual especially during the day, but the civilians seem fearless. A gruesome murder like the Key West Killer's victims won't keep them from enjoying their afternoons out. They hold on to the belief that it'll never happen to them.

A woman in a red lace leotard and a thin sweater skips in front of one of the spring breaker bars, bumpy winter goosebumps covering her thighs. My mind wanders to Remedy. The tattoos of lace on her chest, dipping between her legs, like she can never truly be bare again. The way she answered the phone call from her agency was amusing, so formal and polite, like she's completely trustworthy, not a deviant who yanks off toothed clamps from her nipples to get off. No. To everyone else, she's

Remedy, the angel willing to take a job working for a man who had committed *terrible* crimes against her best friend. She's doing it to protect her friend and the rest of the world from him.

Queue applause. This, my friends, is Remedy Basset.

Inside Mike's Home Supply, the closest hardware store in the area, the cashier bows his head, shrinking behind his shoulders, like a dog that's been kicked too many times, but he's not as innocent as he looks. I click my teeth at him, making sure he knows I see him. The owner emerges from the back.

"What're you doing back here already?" he asks. "You still working?"

"I was one batt of fiberglass short. You got any?"

"Twenty-three by ninety-three?"

That's the one. I nod. "Same rate as yesterday?"

"I'll send it upfront."

I wander for a moment, always keeping myself in view of the cashier. I want to cut off his fingers, just to see his expression when he realizes that every suspicion he has about me is true. But if I kill him, then I won't be able to see him squirm.

The owner drops the fiberglass batt onto the counter and I walk languidly up to the cashier.

"Cash again today?" the cashier asks.

I slap the correct amount on the counter, never leaving the cashier's eye contact. He's always wary when it comes to our interactions. Begging for a card to keep on file. Asking for my name, in case they need to contact me about a new shipment. 'Cash' is enough. I know my place and there isn't any reason to waste time with meaningless interactions.

But my shaft twitches. I love knowing that he's afraid of me. I tilt my head toward the register. He hasn't liked me since I helped cover his ass for stealing from the store.

"Don't worry, kid," I say. "You're stuck with me for a while. At least until I finish these projects."

"Thought you said you were moving soon?" he asks.

Ah, he remembers then. "Eventually."

In truth, I don't give a shit about stealing. I first stole lunch meat from a grocery store when I was nine years old. But I enjoy having power *over* someone. If you have a person in a corner, then they have to do whatever you say. And Remedy likes it dirty. What will make her finally crawl to me, begging for the sweet release I can give her?

I wink at the cashier, then grab the fiberglass batt. "You take care now."

Outside, the sea air brushes my cheeks, the salty, mildly fishy scent hovering in the cold humidity. I suck in a breath. I always enjoy the winter here. The high sixties to mid-seventies. A light, constant breeze. Clear skies. And enough of a population to keep me entertained. Tourists. Locals. The rich bastards who visited their third homes for the winter. They all have their place here. And usually, I keep myself in check, only killing one to three every season. But this time, the itch is growing like my hunger for Remedy. I'll have to do it again soon. And that will be my fifth this year.

I decide to walk, leaving my truck on the street. I can have someone pick it up later. The occasional pedestrian passes and we exchange nods. The mayor has urged people to stay home after dark, but no one seems to think it can happen to them. And why would they? It's not like they'll pass a killer on the street. I like it that way. Dressed in jeans and a long-sleeved button-up shirt, I look unimportant. The shock on their faces always amuses me when they realize how wrong they are.

I find my way to the estate, right off of Queen Street. Six bedrooms, four bathrooms, two offices. Navy blue shutters on a crisp white exterior. Enough palm trees surround the property to give it a natural barrier of privacy beyond the white fence. The Winstone Estate. My home.

A black cat slinks up to my side. Her fur is matted, twigs tangled in the strands, but she purrs at my ankles, not giving a damn. She gazes up at the estate with me.

"Do you have a home?" I ask. She purrs, and as I stroke her neck, I check for a collar, but her neck is bare. My mind shifts to Remedy's dirty video, the rope around the adult actress's neck.

The image of Remedy sprawled out on that squeaking computer chair fills my mind: those light brown nipples strapped into the clamps, her moan of release when she rips them off, the tiny beads of reddened skin.

I'm supposed to move soon. Get the hell out and keep law enforcement off of my back.

But what if I stay?

If I pin my crimes on Remedy, perhaps killing everyone she loves, to prove that *she's* the one who did it all, it'll be *new.* A way to pass the time. A bigger challenge than simply moving away.

The idea is enticing. I can't kill her yet, then. But it'll be worth it.

The cat purrs against my leg, white patches around her eyes and nose and mouth, like the reverse image of a skeleton. *Bones.* Remedy's favorite password. Those boney tattoos on her back fill my mind. Tattoos are a way to control your body, to show owner-ship over the canvas you're given. But she doesn't own that skin anymore. I'll cut her up, leaving my scars, and my knife won't be as forgiving as the tattoo gun.

I gesture to the side of the house. "Let's go home," I say, and the black cat and I disappear.

Chapter 2

Remedy

"All finished up," a male voice, like a smooth, aged scotch, startles me. I quickly dash up, but as I spin around to see him, I only catch a glimpse of him in my mirror: a button-up shirt, sunlight flashing across his face, casting ripples of shadows on his eyes, the sockets dark and cavernous.

"I thought you finished last Tuesday?" I shout, racing to the hallway. But he's already gone.

The maintenance men are awful at actually notifying us like they promise. You'd think that living in a place like Key West with a high influx of tourists would guarantee adequate maintenance. But when it comes to the *local* dwellings, those of us that live year round in the older buildings, the opposite is true. Despite Mr. Winstone being an obsessive and wealthy real estate developer, he's a cheap bastard with his long-term tenants. He gives us the absolute bare minimum, not caring whether we tenants have a life or need privacy. I *hate* that the maintenance men get keys from our 'gracious' landlord, but what can I do? Winstone controls practically everything in Key West, and the man barely leaves his house. Years ago, he fired the entire house staff for incompetence; he's *that* kind of billionaire. He only works with one personal assistant, and now, that's me.

Back when we were in high school, Jenna was the only person

who immediately believed me when it came to my stepdad. I owe her this. And luckily for me, no one wants to work with Mr. Winstone.

I park my car on the street, then stare up at the house. It's massive compared to its neighbors. The spiky edges of saw palmetto trees fan-like blades, splitting off the estate from civilization. Drooping skinny edges of the lilies hang down, like an omen, to warn onlookers that nothing *nice* lives here.

The plaque on the white fence establishes the historic significance of the building: *The Winstone Estate, built in 1889.* I roll my eyes, huffing out a breath. He thinks his home is old and refined. I open the white gate, taking the stairs up to the front porch. I make sure my hairpins are fixed in place, keeping the hair out of my eyes, then I adjust my blouse, making sure my cleavage is ample, everything set to attract his attention. Slipping the key from underneath the mat like the agency instructed me, I let myself inside.

Light streams in through the open windows on the first floor. Chills pebble over my skin. Winstone's a recluse, not someone who lives with open windows, and yet the scent of the ocean, salty and sweet, lingers in the air. It's brighter than I expected, and the openness makes my senses heighten. Everything is accessible, nothing is locked. Winstone must know about the Key West Killer. Why is he keeping everything open? Isn't he afraid?

I run my fingers across the clean marble countertop. Though the home was built over a century ago, it's been renovated every few years, as that is what Winstone does best. Rumor has it that he even did some renovations himself.

I scan the countertop for instructions like the agency directed, but it's empty, so I explore. Three rooms and an office downstairs, three bedrooms and another office space upstairs. But *every* window in the common area downstairs is open. My insides burn, my fingers itching at my sides to close them, but it's not my place. It's Winstone's. And if he suddenly prefers open windows, then I'll let it be.

Except it seems strange. Jenna, my best friend, said that he kept his windows covered with newspaper and the blinds drawn. Why is everything so... open?

Maybe it's better this way. Even if I can't hear someone coming, there are more ways to get out.

In the kitchen, I check the stainless steel refrigerator. A mechanical device hisses above me, the camera lens following me as I walk. I open the doors to the fridge—fresh-squeezed orange juice, organic health-prepped meals, protein shakes—then turn, letting my eyes scan the ceiling carefully. Every few feet, there's another small black camera in the shape of a half-sphere. My skin heats. Jenna mentioned that he likes to watch.

But at least I can use that as an excuse.

I pull out a small home security device I brought with me, setting it up with the Wi-Fi password the agency provided. Most of the assaults happened in his office, so I go to the downstairs office and place it on the fireplace mantle, in between a miniature globe and a set of old books.

"Remedy Basset," a male voice calls, deep and reverberating, a fluidness to his tenor. My skin flames and immediately cools. My new boss. I bring my eyes to his.

He's a full foot taller than me, with broad shoulders and a firm chest. Stubble on his face. But his skin is smooth and unblemished like he's still too young to be a self-made billionaire developer. He can easily pass for his late thirties. Almost like Winstone has a son, an heir he doesn't talk about. His black hair has a tapered fade on the sides, with a side-swept textured mess on the top, the kind of style where you can tell he knows how good he looks. Then I notice it—the touch of grey at his temples. Maybe he *is* older but looks good for his age.

His dark brown, almost black eyes, peer at me. A dark uneven circle blemishes the outside of one pupil, and a line crosses the outside of the other: freckles on the whites of his eyes. A vein tenses by his temple. His sleeves are rolled up to his elbows, his muscles veiny and thick. Calloused, tan hands.

The recluse gets out, then.

He steps forward. I stretch my fingers at my side, biting the inside of my lip. I bow my head curtly like I was trained at the agency, and extend my hand. He's just a man. Just my new boss. It doesn't matter if we're alone. I can handle this.

He takes my grip, both of his hands swallowing mine, and I force my lips into a smile. But inside, I'm seething. He has the nerve to humiliate and bruise my best friend, and thinks he can shake my hand like I'm just another waiting victim?

Not this time.

"Cassius Winstone," I say, matching his words.

"Call me 'Cash.'"

I nod politely. "Cash."

"What brings you to Key West?"

There's a familiarity to his tone, a polished effortlessness that makes me swallow hard, but I push those thoughts away. He reminds me of my stepdad and stepbrother; he's full of smug grins and even tones, like he can do nothing wrong.

Trying to hold in my anger, I purse my lips together. "I grew up here."

"Which part?"

I tilt my head. Why does he care? "Did you ask your last assistant these questions?"

"I didn't have an interest in her like I have an interest in you."

Everything inside of me is on fire, the sensation roiling in my gut. I don't know how to take those words, so I level his gaze like I'm not afraid of him. Those dark eye freckles study me with laser-like precision. I press my chest forward, arching my back, trying to get his eyes to move to my chest, but he doesn't flinch.

"Why Key West?" he asks.

"My mother found a good position teaching. And my stepdad did glass-bottom boat tours for a while."

"So you never made it out?"

My fingers ball into fists. The prick.

"Why leave when I was lucky enough to find this position with LPA?" I ask, a hint of sarcasm in my voice. "We thank you for the low rent agreement you have with our agency. We're indebted to you."

"I'm keeping you chained to this rock, then."

My teeth clench together. Why is he asking me these questions? Winstone ignored Jenna for months, but now, it's like he's hunting me.

"Look at me," he orders, his voice full of iron.

My body tightens, but I instantly meet his gaze. His dark eyes burn, those brown freckles on the whites captivating me. Like blemishes that make him beautiful in his imperfections. A ball in one eye and a thin string in the other. Like bait and a fishing line. Two eyes that haunt me, waiting to drag me out.

I pat my hands against my sides. I have to keep myself under control. Revenge is best served cold, and this asshole is going to choke on my icicles.

I force my lips into a wide grin. "Mr. Winstone—"

"Cash."

"*Cash,*" I repeat. "I'm honestly very grateful for my position. Whatever you need, I'll make it happen. And if I can't, I'll find someone who can."

And I'm going to make you pay for what you did to Jenna.

"Good," he says, his lips curved down into a sour expression, like he can read me somehow. I have to be better at this. Play along like I'm a good little assistant. Someone he can take advantage of. Just like Jenna.

But I can't stop myself. I *want* him to know that I hate him. I want him to understand my rage.

"I simply ask that you don't cross any boundaries with me," I say plainly, my voice louder than before. I shrug, covering it up with pleasantries. "I want to be the best assistant you've ever had, but I can only do that if I trust you. And that means knowing the expectations both ways and *respecting* those boundaries. Right, Cash?"

A smirk spreads across his lips. He steps closer, his footstep creaking on the hardwood floor. My stomach stiffens, but I stand my ground.

"Right," he says.

I glance around as he takes another step closer. "The agency mentioned that you don't often leave your room," I say, nerves fluttering into my tone. "Thank you for meeting me down here. It's very nice of you."

Another step forward. We're only a few feet apart now. The scent of his sweat drifts underneath his piney cologne, and it's like we're lost in the woods. I close my eyes, trying to stop my head from spinning.

"What else did they tell you?" he asks.

He steps forward again, the distance between us disappearing. I clear my throat.

"They said that you don't like associating with people often. That I may not be meeting you for a few months. That I'll be getting most of my instructions through email and notes." I lick my dry lips. He takes another step forward. My shoulders fill with weight. I raise my chin, forcing myself to be brave. "That I will do most of your in-person meetings for you."

He gives a slight shake of his head. "They forgot the rest, then."

I open my mouth to ask questions, but a black cat pounces out from the hallway, curling at my feet. I bend down to pet her; her rough fur catches on my skin. It seems like she's only recently become a house cat.

My brows squish together. "The agency didn't mention any pets."

"That'll be your first task. Bones needs a good diet." He tosses his head to the side, and I realize that his cat's name is Bones. Weird. Where did he get her name?

He hands me his black card. "I have only two rules," he says. "Recently, I've taken to leaving the windows open. Do not close them. And if any of my doors are closed, *do not enter.* Otherwise, you may come and go as you please, even if I'm occupied. My space is your space." He turns to the stairs, and I scrape the hair at the back of my head. *My space is your space?* It's a lie to make me comfortable and let down my guard.

"And Remedy?"

I lift my head. His palm rests on the volute handrail fitting, an expensive watch on his wrist, his face angled to the side, as if he can't bother to address me directly.

"Button up your shirt," he says down his nose. "You're not going to control me that easily."

I suck in a quiet breath, my fingers fumbling with the buttons on my shirt. The stairs creak as he ascends. Yeah, the cleavage was a cheap move, but he noticed. That means he feels something toward me, even if it's only irritation.

I purse my lips, letting out a calming breath. Pet food. I can do that. As a personal assistant with the agency for the last few years, I've done a lot worse than ordering pet food.

I set up my laptop at the long, grey-washed wooden table to the side of the kitchen, then use his black card to order some expensive gourmet pet food that costs more than a week's worth of my groceries. Bones circles at my feet, and I find a bag of dry food in the cupboards. I pour some into a dish, and as I lower it to the ground, the cat acknowledges me with brief eye contact before nibbling at the hard pebbles. How is Cassius Winstone a cat lover? Had I missed that in Jenna's stories?

As I put the bag back in the cupboard, I grab one of the kitchen knives and imagine holding it to Winstone's veiny neck, slicing across his stubbly skin until blood cascades down his white shirt like a red sunset over a white, sandy beach. Usually, I imagine my stepdad, but there's something enchanting about picturing Cash right then. His angular, harsh jaw, his smooth lips, his dark, spotted eyes, bloodshot like his red-stained shirt.

Maybe it's good that my stepdad left Key West. He's still alive, and I'm not in jail.

But jail doesn't scare me. If I can stop someone like my stepdad, it's worth it.

Cash is another bad egg.

Still carrying the knife, I step up the stairs, careful not to let them creak. At the end of the hallway, his office door is open, and so are the two bedrooms and the bathroom across from them. But the room on the left is closed.

Which is precisely why I want to open it. Screw his rules.

I open the door as slowly as I can, holding my breath, but it stays silent. I let out a breath. Light from the hallway spills into the room. Wet concrete covers each space where there should be a window. Like he wants to keep something, or *someone,* inside.

What the hell?

His desk chair squeaks, the sound drifting down the hallway, and I jump, closing the door behind me. I bound down the stairs, no longer trying to keep my presence a secret. I have no idea what he's doing with that room, but it seems like his compulsion with blinds and newspaper coverings on overdrive.

But why is it fresh if he's 'taken to leaving the windows open'?

My phone buzzes in my pocket, erasing those thoughts from my head. On the screen, a picture of my mom and me illuminates the screen. It's from before she divorced my stepdad, and in it, I'm tattoo-less and have pink lips. I check my surroundings; the stairs are empty and the place is silent. I answer the call.

"Hey," I say in a quiet voice.

"How's your first day so far?" Mom asks.

"It's only been an hour," I wrinkle my nose. "You don't have to worry like this anymore. I'm twenty-five. I'll be fine."

"I just know how you get sometimes, sweetie."

My gut twists. This is how she acknowledges it, with these strange, subtle questions and statements, like it physically hurts her to directly address the fact that my stepdad abused me and she didn't notice.

Which is why she doesn't know the reason I wanted this job so badly.

"How is he?" she asks.

He's an untrustworthy jerk with creepy eyes and a cocky attitude. Basically, he's like every rich asshole in the Keys.

"He's fine," I say. And if it weren't for what he did to Jenna, it would almost be true. "I'm ordering cat food right now."

"He has a cat?"

"Yep. And the boss-hole wants the best for his little puss," I say. Bones lifts her head and jumps into my lap. I scratch behind her ears and she purrs, nuzzling my stomach. I like her. It's not her fault that she's owned by a jerk.

"I met someone," Mom says. My fingers stop in Bones's fur, and I breathe through my nose, waiting for Mom to explain. "I was thinking we could get together soon, so you could meet him too. Maybe a double date."

My head pulses. "Who?"

"He's new to town. Why don't you see if that boy from the police department wants to join us?"

I roll my eyes, screaming inside. What's with Mom's and Jenna's obsession with him? That 'boy' is the *picture* of a good man, and that's why I don't trust him. A cop. A mama's boy. A supposed protector. People in power always take advantage of everyone below them. I mean, *everyone* takes advantage of everyone, but *especially* people like them. People like my stepdad. Men with power over others.

Men like Cash.

I almost considered 'that boy from the police department,' after he promised to investigate my stepdad years ago, claiming it was why he wanted to become a cop: to bring people to justice. But it was a lie to cover up the guilt. Everyone knows he drugged and raped that girl from our high school.

Still, my mother and Jenna hold on to him like he's the best thing to happen to Key West. They believe him.

"I'd rather not," I say, a sourness in my words.

"Are you still seeing that professor, then?" she asks. "He's nice."

She only likes him because he's a teacher too. "I broke up with him almost a year ago."

"But I thought you two stayed friends?" she asks, a hopeful lilt to her voice. "I was hoping you'd get back together."

I groan. Not *him* again. The ceiling creaks; Cash crosses from his upstairs office to another room. Honestly, Cash is an option too, but dealing with him outside of this estate makes my head hurt. The maintenance man from this morning fills my mind: a nameless, faceless stranger with rippled eyes. If I ask *him* out on the double date, *that* is the best option. Hell, I can even pay him for getting my mother off of my back for once. Maybe I can even screw him afterward. A one-night stand with no feelings attached means there's a better chance that he'll be willing to give me what I want.

How is it that I can fantasize about a faceless maintenance man screwing me while I'm tied to a chair, but when it comes to my boss, an actual fairly attractive, wealthy businessman, I can't stand the thought of him touching me?

"I date around," I say.

"Hooking up is not dating," she says.

I laugh. "I'll keep that in mind. Anyway, I got to go. Boss is coming," I lie.

"Remmie, wait—"

I hang up before she can say another word, my limbs heavy with exhaustion. She still believes there's hope out there for me, and maybe there is, but I'm not going to search for it. Why waste my time on that when no one watches out for you anyway?

And besides, I have enough to deal with right now. Cash. *Cassius Winstone.* A man who can do horrible things without any fear of punishment. Jenna is the last person to deserve what he did, and I hate him for it. He may be more like my stepbrother in his assaults, but his mindset is *exactly* like my stepdad's. My stepdad ran away, but Cash won't be able to leave. Not with me around.

I flip open my laptop. A message comes through my agency email: instructions from Cash on delivering a proposal to the city council. So far, work is easy enough, but the hard part will be putting him in jail where he belongs. Jenna won't be ruled by his presence anymore.

And if I have to kill him, I will.

CHAPTER 3

REMEDY

THE PHONE VIBRATES ON MY NIGHTSTAND LIKE A JACKHAMMER. Jenna's selfie—all bright red lips and bleach-blond hair—illuminates the screen. I focus my eyes, squinting at the bar on the top of the screen; it's past eleven o'clock. She never calls this late. My heart races. Something is wrong.

"Hey—"

Her sobs interrupt me, and a sharp pain impales my chest.

"What's wrong?" I ask as tenderly as I can.

She heaves between each word: "Are—you—home?"

Her sobs ricochet through the front door, practically blasting it from the hinges. I swing it open as fast as I can. Her hair is matted to her face, a crop top and leggings on like she's been crying since she left the gym. Sweat beads her brow, mascara streaking her cheeks, her eyelashes practically glued together. She smells faintly like body odor and cheese fries, which means she probably visited her mom at work; it must be really bad. I pull her close, holding her as she cries, her small frame trembling against me, and I bring her inside, sitting her down on my bed. My throat tightens. I hate seeing her cry. She's my rock. It's not supposed to be like this.

"What happened?" I ask.

She opens up her phone, clicking her call log. Her last few

received calls are *Lavish PA*, but the most recent call is from hours ago. Has she been crying this entire time?

"They don't believe me," she says through each breath. "They need proof."

I close my eyes. Of course they do. That's what my mom said when I tried to tell her about my stepdad years ago. *It's hard for me to believe that,* she said. *He loves you, sweetie. Just because you don't like him, doesn't mean he's hurting you.*

My ears pounded, my heart squeezing in my chest. Why don't they believe Jenna?

"What about your arm?" I ask. She lifts it up, but it's flawless now; the bruises have healed, the evidence of Cash's assault gone with them. "Damn it," I whisper. This is a complete and utter mess.

"What do we do?" she asks. She shifts to the edge of the bed, her palms clutching the comforter. "They said they can't do anything with him. If they say anything, he could drop the contract. And then what will we do about rent? It'll be full price, and you know none of us can afford that." Her breaths are shallow, the veins on her neck throbbing with each word, like her body can't quite figure out whether to fight or retreat. "They told me I could either keep my new placement or find a new agency, letting go of the contacts I've made within LPA."

Her words jumble and my vision tunnels as my mind focuses on him.

Cassius Winstone thinks he can get away with this because he's rich. And he will do it again, and again, until someone forces him to stop.

Jenna is locked into place. But me? I'm his current personal assistant and the only person allowed on his property.

"I can't do anything," she says.

"I can."

Her tears stop. I stretch my fingers, keeping them close to my sides. One way or another, I will bring Cash down. For both of us. For everyone who has been manipulated by disgusting alpha filth.

"Don't do anything you'll regret," she warns.

I smile evenly, my mind filling with visions of ripping Winstone's teeth out with pliers.

"He's got surveillance cameras everywhere, right?" I say. I flick a hand to the side like she's silly to question my intentions. "All I have to do is get access to the recorded footage of him assaulting you. Then we'll have undeniable proof. We'll sue LPA *and* that asshole."

Jenna bites her fingernails, her cheeks redder than her lips. "But what if you get caught?"

I don't care if LPA fires me. It's a good job, but I don't get attached to anything anymore.

"I'll find somewhere else to work," I say.

I stand up, moving one of the blind slats to check the weather. Gray clouds sail across the sky. I pull out a black cardigan from the hall closet, my eyes stopping over a wooden hatch in the flooring. A small metal loop shines in the dim light. The door is big enough for a person to fit through, but I don't remember seeing it before. Has it always been here?

"Is that from the new insulation?" Jenna asks, peeking over my shoulder.

"Hell if I know." I grab my purse from the desk, the house keys jingling in my palm. "Must have been the maintenance guy."

"What maintenance guy?" Jenna's eyes widen as I pass her. "You're leaving *now?*"

I tilt my head. "Why not?"

"You literally just scolded me about going out during the day with the Key West Killer, and now you're going to a man's house, alone, *at night?*"

A random killer isn't important; I'm used to dealing with people who lack morals, like my stepfamily. Besides, *Winstone* is my enemy. If I happen to stumble upon the Key West Killer, I'll ask him to help me get rid of Winstone.

"I'm fine," I say. "But call Peter. Make him escort you home again." She nods, happy to rely on a cop. And to be honest, right then, I'm glad she is too. "Stay inside here until he gets here, all right?"

She bows her head. "Be careful."

I hop in my car, taking the short drive over to the Winstone Estate. Most people keep their master passwords near their computers, and though Winstone is—I regret to admit—*smart*, he seems too complacent to be protective over his security. He seems to think he's invincible.

And I'll prove him wrong.

I park a block away, then quietly get out of my car. The palm branches rustle against one another, like a tranquil current. It's quiet tonight, almost like the PSAs running on cable television are actually working; people are too afraid to go out, knowing that the Key West Killer doesn't have a pattern when it comes to his victims. Young, old, woman, man, black, white. Everyone is fair game. My stomach flops, but I clench my fists. Fear of an invisible killer isn't going to stop me.

I open the front door as quietly as I can. The red lights from each of the security cameras glow like monster eyes. My pulse races. There's no way I can avoid surveillance, but I *can* make up a lie. I go through ideas in my head:

I forgot to clean the litter box.

I left my phone in the kitchen.

I wanted to make sure you closed the windows, because of the serial killer, you know?

The sea breeze blows through the house, goosebumps bubbling my skin. I slip off my gym shoes, using my socks to move noiselessly through the house. I check each open door, trying to establish where he is, but the door to the downstairs office distracts me. The surveillance footage has to be in there.

I check his personal computer, typing a few passwords that other clients have used, including the password to his Wi-Fi. I even try his address, then *WinstoneEstate1889*, but nothing works. What am I supposed to do now?

Screw it.

I crawl under the desk, unplugging the hard drive, then carry the electronic brick to the front door. Once I have both hard drives, I can hightail it out of Florida until I find someone to hack the footage. Getting the footage is the hardest part, and I'm so close to finishing.

I hold my breath as I stop in the kitchen. The refrigerator hums, and those cameras hiss as they follow me. Still, I run my fingertips over the handles in the knife block. Winstone has anger issues that he exposed to Jenna, but does he carry a gun? What if he thinks I'm a random intruder? Can I make him believe that I'm not trespassing before he realizes that I'm stealing his hard drives?

Just in case, I put a knife in my back pocket. Then I scurry across the room, back to the stairs, those red, mechanical eyes watching me in the dark. My gut rolls as I lift my feet. I don't care about breaking and entering. I don't even care about stealing, because I know that what I'm doing is the *right* thing. But will proving that Cash is an abuser do *anything* in the long run? It will take an infinite amount of time and money to put him in prison, and even if he is convicted, there's a chance he'll end up under house arrest in his glorious estate because of his wealth.

That's not justice to me.

But I keep going, unplugging the upstairs hard drive, creeping with it to the end of the hallway. As I reach the stairs, my body boils over. I set down the hard drive.

Then I tiptoe back down the hallway.

His bedroom door is ajar. In the open crack, there's a sliver of visibility: the moonlight shining through the newspaper-covered windows in dull beams. And there he is: a large lump in the shadows. My chest expands as my stomach churns, but I swallow it down, then push open the door, crossing my fingers that it won't creak.

No sound.

No movement from the bed.

He's still asleep.

I bump into a table next to the door, but quickly steady the lamp sitting on top of it. The base of the lamp is pure bronze, with a stained-glass shade decorated with red flowers amongst a green background. I gnaw the inside of my lip; if I had knocked into it, he would be awake, and finding me in his bedroom would be a *lot* harder to explain than being downstairs.

But the lamp is solid. Heavy enough to put someone out cold. It can even kill him.

I'm supposed to be getting the footage. But a man like Winstone—a man willing to lay his hands on someone smaller and weaker than him—will never change. Once a man like that gets a taste of the power, they never let it go, no matter how much they promise or apologize. No matter how much they swear they love you. They will keep hurting everyone in their path until it's too late.

Adrenaline rushes through my body. I'm not going to let it happen again.

I unplug that gaudy, awful lamp, using both hands to carry it. With each step I take closer to his blurry black figure, my heart pounds, each beat banging in my ears, my skin prickling with knives. I raise the lamp in the air, my muscles straining, the cord dangling to the side of me like a leash. I grit my teeth.

Instead of Winstone's shadowy form, I see my stepdad's light brown hair and blue eyes.

It should be you, Daddy, I think. Then I swing the lamp down onto his head.

The base lands, a dull thud behind it, dust rising to the sides like his soul is leaving his body. The silence envelops me, my limbs shaking as I bend closer. There's no movement. But the room is dark and it's hard to see anything. Resting the lamp on the pillow, I touch his chest to see if he's still breathing—but it's cold and hard like he's already dead. I pull back the sheet.

White bags of different sizes lie on the mattress, full of dry cement.

"What the hell?" I whisper.

The ceiling fan's light flickers on, the leafy blades whirring into motion, like a circular saw ready to slice me in half.

"What a performance," a deep voice calls from behind me. I spin around. A handheld camera covers half of Cash's face like a mask. His button-up shirt is undone, his chest chiseled with his hair groomed, his sleeves rolled up. Keloid scars splatter his toned stomach like he was burned or even stabbed repeatedly. What the hell happened to him?

No. He doesn't deserve sympathy. He's an abuser. His past doesn't make that okay.

"Was that your plan? Use a lamp to kill me?" he asks, amusement leaking into his tone. "How original."

"Fuck you, Winstone," I mutter.

"How many times do I have to tell you to call me 'Cash'?" He lowers the camera but keeps it focused on me. His tongue runs over his teeth. "Let me give you a hint, little cure. Playing nice may keep you out of jail."

"I'll *never* play nice with you," I snarl, my palm squeezing around the lamp's base again.

"Ah, little cure," he chuckles, a bemused smile curling his lips.

"Don't call me that."

"*Remedy,*" he corrects. "This isn't what I expected of you." He taps his lips, faking bewilderment. "Now, here's the situation. You tried to kill me. I caught the attempt on film. That's quite a predicament; don't you agree?"

I glare at him, meeting his gaze, not letting him back me into a corner. I'm not afraid of him. Even if he's a foot taller than me and at least twice my muscle mass, I have more anger than Winstone can handle, and you don't mess with that.

He sets the camera on the table by the door, the lens still haunting me. Patting the top of the device with a smug air, he flicks a finger at the red light, reminding me that he's still recording.

"I can turn you into the police. Give them this video. Get the surveillance footage of you putting that steak knife into your pocket right before you hit my body double with the lamp. Oh, and how about stealing my hard drives? That will be fun to explain." He drums his feet against the floor. "Coming to my estate in the dead of night for a second-degree premeditated attempt at murder—I'm sure the jury will love to hear your defense on that one."

My fingernails dig so hard into my palm that the pain buzzes to my skull, but the adrenaline numbs everything. I don't feel it.

"What do you want?" I ask.

His chin juts forward. "Be my assistant and fuck doll."

My jaw drops, my stomach twisting into knots. "*Your fuck doll?*"

"I have it on good authority that you like it rough. So do I."

"Who told you that?" I gasp. "Jenna?!"

"Let's keep it simple: I get to play with you however I want, whenever I want, and I'll keep this footage safe. Disobey me? And you can find your safety behind prison bars."

I huff out a long, hard breath. He's insane. Did he do this to Jenna too?

No. She's never been in a situation like this. I asked her repeatedly and she promised that he never touched her sexually. Instead, she made small mistakes—jamming the printer, ordering the wrong type of protein shake, being ten minutes late to a meeting on a construction site—and he hit her. She kept it a secret until I noticed her bruises.

I'm not going to let Jenna live in fear because of some jerk like Cash.

Which means that I have to be smarter than him. Always two steps ahead. But right then, I can't help but let it out.

"You are a sick bastard," I mutter.

"Oh, sweet cure, you flatter me," he snickers.

"Is this what you did to Jenna?" I straighten my shoulders, readying myself to take him head-on. "You slapped her for mixing up files, and spanked her for being late to a meeting? Then you bruise her arm because the printer jams, like it's her fault that your printer is crap? And now you're blackmailing me!" I point at the cameras. "*This* is on camera too. You're as guilty as me, and you know it."

He glances at his watch dismissively. "Blackmailing someone who is trying to murder me. I'm sure the judge will make sure that I'm *justly* punished. Oh, and by the way?" He widens his smirk, his sharp teeth in full view. "I sold one of my properties to the judge at a discount. He owes me."

My fingers twitch like I can't control myself any longer. I ball my hands into fists. The knife is still in my back pocket.

"You hurt Jenna," I hiss. "You ruined her life. She will never be able to trust men again because of you. She will never be alone with a man without thinking of the fastest way to get out—"

"Jenna was never my concern," he says. He steps closer, his body blocking the view of the camera. "But you, Remedy. *You* are my concern. You think killing me will somehow eradicate your demons, but I'm not the devil you're after, and we both know it."

My lips open, gawking at him.

Does he know about my stepdad?

But how is he *not* the person I'm after? If he didn't hurt Jenna, then he *knows* who did. And he's protecting them.

"Who am I after, then?" I snap.

His lips press into a thin line. "How can I say?"

I shake my head. "You are an egotistical, power-hungry, son of a—"

"I'm giving you a choice," he says. "You can leave. Come back to work tomorrow. Pretend like everything is fine. And do exactly as I say. Or," he pauses, running his tongue across his bottom lip like a snake, "you can go to jail. A simple, but necessary consequence for what you've done. Perhaps the judge will give you ten years. Or do you think you deserve twenty? A life sentence?" He taps his lips. "How lenient will the judge be for a pretty woman like you?"

I clench my teeth harder, staring at his thick bottom lip. If I bite hard enough, my teeth will slice through it.

He's trapped me this time, but this is far from over. I'm not done.

Screw it.

I run forward, aiming the knife from my back pocket at his face, but he grabs my wrist, twisting it around my back until my shoulders strain so badly that the pain shoots through my entire upper body. I whimper, tears forming in my eyes, and he pulls my arm harder until my fingers finally loosen, dropping the knife on the floor.

"Little cure, little cure," he says, clicking his tongue. The scent of chemicals, pine needles, and sweat lingers on his skin. His cock twitches against my back and a shot of energy rams through me at the contact. I try to move, but I can't. He presses into me, his body weight holding me down like a helpless animal. And though I hate him with every fiber of my being, a heat flutters in my lower belly. The pain in my arms and back, the scent of his natural odor and expensive cologne surrounding me, the pressure of his cock, every part of him completely devouring me.

I bite the inside of my lip, reminding myself that he's the enemy.

"I have the footage," I say as my last stab at him, pointing toward his office. "I can take that to the police too."

"I already put my hard drives back in my offices."

Shit. A headache roars in my forehead, a throbbing sensation stretching over my skull. I suck in a breath.

"This isn't over," I say.

"That's only true *if* you agree to my terms," he says, clacking his teeth together. "If you go to jail now, you won't have another chance to kill me."

My cheeks flame with anger. He lets go of my wrist and the flush of relief spreads through me. I stretch my arm, rubbing my shoulder from the ache. I grab my purse off of the floor; it must have fallen off. I leave the knife on the bed.

"I'll see you tomorrow, Mr. Winstone," I say, shoulder-checking him as I pass. He grabs my arm, whipping me around and shoving me against the wall. My head bumps into the plaster and his lips pull back, baring his teeth.

"What did you say?" he growls. His sweet, metallic breath brushes my cheeks. Fear barrels through me and I pant. His body heat pulses, caging me in. He can do anything to me right now. He can rape me. He can even kill me.

My stomach tightens. "Cash," I whisper.

He lets go, adjusting his button-up shirt like nothing happened, his jaw harsh. I steady myself too, gnawing at my inner lip. I pause at the door. He steps closer, but I stay still, holding my position steady.

I know what I have to do.

"One day, I'm going to kill you," I say. His pupils beam into my soul. Those dark brown freckles on the whites of his eyes are like dark clouds hovering over me. He pinches my chin between his fingers, forcing me to look up even higher, and I grimace, my lips flinching, but I don't shy away. I've done this before. I survived then, and I *will* survive now.

"I hope you do," he says in a low voice. "And I hope you enjoy it."

CHAPTER 4

CASH

WARM SATISFACTION RIPPLES THROUGH MY CHEST AS REMEDY GOES through the filing cabinets. The television buzzes in the background, but it doesn't interest me. Remedy's straight, black hair swishes from side to side as she peels through each file, separating them into categories by the style of development, then further by year, always sticking the folder back onto the cart, keeping her back to me. It's a menial task, and yet *that* is the fun of it. Remedy's mind is too rapid to zone out when she has her back to me. She can't escape, and *that* amuses me.

She had been at these types of tasks all day.

It's been years since I messed with someone like this. Getting close to a victim is never as fun as it seems; they always have irritating habits that get in the way. And once they're dead, there's one less loose end to think about. But Remedy isn't like that. She isn't annoying me yet, but each time her fruity scent—like peaches and mango roasting in an oven—crosses my nose, my dick hardens and her words fill me.

One day, I'm going to kill you.

She said it with such conviction that after she left, I choked my dick until I came, picturing the venom in her eyes as we fought each other to the death. Our hands crushing each other's throats.

Blood soaking our skin, matting our hair, so that we resemble the monsters we truly are.

It's why I'm attracted to her, and why six orgasms the night before didn't satisfy me. It's why I needed to feel someone's heart stop to finally get her off of my mind. Perhaps Remedy can entertain me for the last time.

I kick my feet up onto the desk as I peer at Remedy, her juicy ass jiggling in her trousers as she works. A skirt on her first day, and pants today. Like that will protect her from my attacks. I pinch my lips together. *It doesn't work like that, little cure.*

"Is Jenna your best friend?" I ask. Remedy stills for a moment, and with that, I know the answer. "How long have you known her?"

I give her a minute, adjusting my sleeves, making sure they're properly rolled and out of the way. Still, Remedy doesn't answer.

"I can fuck you until you're raw right now if you'd prefer that to a conversation."

Her muscles tense, her clothes shifting across her body back as she struggles to hide her reaction. Her body knows what she wants. But she lets out a sigh, holding a file in midair like a dagger.

"We've been friends since we were kids," she says. That's a long time.

"And your parents. Are they still together?"

"No."

"You said your mother is a teacher?"

"Yes."

"And you didn't want to follow the family business?"

Her tongue pokes her cheek, holding back her words.

"LPA is a better fit for me," she finally says.

"Even if you wind up working for people like me."

"Yes," she mutters. "Even with people like you."

A gong chimes on the television screen, the volume suddenly louder. *Breaking News!* plasters the screen in bright red text. A blond reporter fills the frame.

Another body has been found in the Key West murders, the reporter says. *Again, in the flooring underneath the Dry & Clean on Ernest Street. Though the official report hasn't been released, our insider states that this victim follows the others: the bodies have been mutilated in different manners, painted white and encased in foam, then crammed into the building's crawl space.*

The image switches to the police chief. *A copycat murderer can't be ruled out,* he says. *It's paramount that you stay indoors at night. Your safety is more important than a drink at the bar, people.*

The blond reporter nods deeply. *The name of the latest victim will be released after the family has been notified.*

Remedy's fingers stretch at her sides as her teeth chomp her bottom lip, worry painted on her face. She flicks her chipped black fingernails over the two bobby pins holding back her hair. Once she got home the night before, I logged onto her laptop through the hacking app. She accessed articles about the serial killer. Perhaps she realized she should truly be afraid of strangers after interacting with me. Smart woman.

"Does that scare you?" I ask, tapping my fingers together.

"Key West is so small," she says. "They'll find him."

"How do we know it's a man?" I tease. "It could be *you*. After all, you tried to murder me last night. Might have succeeded if I hadn't been ready. Perhaps you took care of someone else when you couldn't get me." I grin. Her shoulders curl around her. "How would you have mutilated me?"

"I'll make you eat your own dick."

I laugh, and she cringes at the sound.

"I know a cop," she says. "He's my friend."

I raise a brow. There's a confidence about her with those words, like she *wants* him to protect her.

"And?" I ask.

"He's a guy from my high school. He's older than me. He became a detective a few years ago." She crosses her arms. "He'll find him."

"And what if he doesn't?"

Her knees tremble, but when her eyes meet mine, she locks her legs, forcing the nerves out of her system.

"Peter is strong," she says.

So the cop friend has a name. *Peter.* And Peter is strong. And she's proud of it. She even *believes* in his abilities.

He isn't the only person who is strong.

"You say that like he's going to protect you," I say. She narrows her gaze, but her fingers twitch. No matter how much she denies it, the situation scares her. "Don't worry, little cure," I chuckle. "I'm sure the killer only hunts at night. You're safe, for now." I wink, then grab an envelope off of the top of my desk. "Drop this Offer to Purchase off at Dry & Clean," I say.

She stares at the envelope, then looks up at me. Her body tenses as she lets that information sink in: Dry & Clean, the final resting place of the latest Key West Killer victim. The primal fear is getting to her. Her bright green eyes dampen, and I want to yank her by the hair to force her to her knees. I want those tears to fall.

"Oh! What a coincidence," I tease, knowing it will unnerve her. I pull the steak knife from yesterday out of my desk's drawer. "Here." I hand it to her. "Take this with you. I encourage you to protect yourself. After all, it's only self-defense."

She scowls at me, then stomps toward the door.

"Better hurry," I say. "They close in about twenty minutes."

The truth is that I don't care about buying the dry cleaning shop. With my status, I can develop anything I want, transforming the crappiest, oldest buildings into pure gold. But I enjoy messing with Remedy. Seeing her pissed off. Panicked. Frustrated. There are so many things you can do to a person's physical body, but the mind? The mind is harder to break. And so far, she's an exceptional challenge.

I'm supposed to head to a project site to meet with the lead contractor, but I text him: *Emergency. Reschedule?* Then I drive to Dry & Clean, speeding to catch up with her.

Remedy pauses outside of the door and glances at the road; the shop is only a block away from her rental house. Her focus reaches the horde of people lingering on the side of the building, trying to catch the glimpse of the corpse. She lifts her nose and walks inside like she doesn't have a care in the world. She acts like the killer doesn't faze her because she could be a killer too. And that interests me: she's drawn to violence. She's even willing to kill to protect her friend. But I know, deep down, that she *wants* to kill, even if it has nothing to do with vengeance.

My primary phone buzzes, knocking me out of my trance. *Rescheduling again?* the lead contractor texts. I ignore it, stuffing the phone back into my trousers with my other phone. But what am I doing watching her anyway? This is why it's annoying to get close to victims. You think they're intriguing until you realize you're wasting time watching them going through the motions of daily life.

I need to get out of here.

The drive to Miami takes three and a half hours without traffic, but I don't care. As long as I'm out of Key West, I won't follow Remedy or be tempted to show her exactly where I left the body.

By the time I arrive in the heart of the city, the club lights flash to each side, women in slinky long dresses with big asses prance down the sidewalks, tan muscleheads chasing them like flies. It's so different to Key West lately; with a killer on the loose, fewer and fewer tourists ventured out. In Miami, they have other worries, but no serial killers. I maneuver the car out of the main stretch, then find the strip mall. Most of the storefronts are empty. The building is a couple of decades old, but the rent is too high for most to occupy. A place that's perfect for the Winstone Company to take over.

But at the far end of the lot, *Spa and Massage* is lit up on one side, *Rebecca's* on the other.

I slip inside of the massage parlor, swarmed by the floral fragrance of lotion.

"Hello, sir," one of the workers says, giving me a knowing smile. I pass her, immediately using the door to the side, weaving between the dimly lit cubicles. In the darkness, the slap of hands cracks through the murmurs of conversation. I take an unmarked door in the back.

A two-way mirror covers one wall, a bench seat on the other. Gray and white tissues scatter the floor, crumpled and sticky. Burnt hair and semen waft through the air. I slump down onto the bench, the wood digging into my ass, then I palm my thick dick.

On the other side of the mirror, a red-headed sex worker rides one of her clients on top of a massage bed.

In the past, I participated myself. Transactional interactions are what I prefer. It's better than fucking a victim; the physical stimulation with a sex worker does the job, letting me focus on what truly excites me: *killing*.

But now, I enjoy the detached nature of watching. Any glass barrier will break with the right amount of force, and those two on the other side—the red-headed sex worker and the old john under her—they know voyeurs are watching. And yet they have no idea that someone like me sits behind the glass. The only reason I'm not killing them right now is because it's a hard situation to clean up. There are too many witnesses. Otherwise, I would let them fuck each other to death while I jerked off.

But that's an idea for another day. Perhaps with Remedy.

At the realization that the redhead is *not* my dark-haired Remedy, my dick falls limp in my hand. I squeeze the head until my dick swells with blood and turns purple. Then I stare at the sex worker, but instead of her red hair and beady black eyes, I see Remedy. Green eyes full of venom. Her breasts swinging as I pump my cock deep into her cunt like one end of a spit roast. Her thick, tawny hips reddened from my firm grip. The lace tattoos sprawling across her chest gleaming in the light, all the way down to her furry pussy, drenched with sweat. The blood vessels popping in her eyes as she strains against a noose around her neck, wanting more of my cock, knowing that the closer she gets to coming, the sooner it will be over.

A sourness fills my throat, the lust getting to me. I need to wait before I see Remedy again. Make her think that I'm not that bad. That our fuck-doll arrangement is only to watch her. Until one day, I'll make her so hot, she'll beg for it. Then, I'll let her take the blame for those deaths, or I'll kill her.

But my dick twitches, ignoring that logic. In my mind, Remedy's body weight slams into me as she rides me, her neck circled with a rope, the blood rushing to her head, painting her in such pretty red and purple hues. I can't stop fucking myself. *Come for me*, I'll demand as I fill her up with my come. Because I own her. A knife against her throat. A gun to her temple. Her nails piercing my flesh. I own her even as her pussy constricts the blood out of my cock, threatening to dismember me.

I zip my trousers, then head out, pounding a hundred on the front desk before disappearing into the parking lot. It'll take hours to return to Key West, but the convenient part of having a personal assistant is that they're always on standby. Even in the dead of night.

———

Remedy

"In here," Cash calls from upstairs. I swallow, then rub my eyes, still groggy with sleep. Even though it's past midnight, the windows are open. A light, salty scent filters through the house. A car rumbles by, but it's quieter than usual for the nightlife in Key West.

I tuck loose hair behind my ears, knowing that Cash apparently does not care about the Key West Killer, but at least with the two of us, there's less of a threat. Each step up the stairs shakes me into lucidity. What am I doing here anyway? Is he finally going to force me to be his fuck doll?

I have it on good authority that you like it rough. So do I.

He irritates me. He thinks he knows me just because he heard some rumor.

A rumor that is true, yes, but that's beside the point.

Upstairs, the bedroom door on the left is still closed. A magnetic force draws me to it, beckoning me in my half-conscious state to *just freaking open it.* My heart races as my fingers land on the handle, the grip cold and smooth. It jiggles, but it doesn't budge.

He locked it.

I pull a bobby pin from my hair, bending it into an 'L,' then quickly flatten the other pin and remove the rubber tip. I ease the second pin into the keyhole, finding the first locking pin—

Cash clears his throat and I stuff the bobby pins in my purse. I'll have to resume picking the lock later. I move toward his office with dread in each step. It's like walking to the executioner's block, where one day, he'll have my head. Recessed lighting illuminates the office from the corners. Though the downstairs office is decorated like an old, rich person's library, the upstairs office is modern. White walls with large pure black canvases. Curved, black furniture. Yet the windows have newspaper plastered over them, just like in his bedroom. Why does he insist on keeping some windows open, and others completely cut off?

His eyes hold me, wrapping around me like a chain. And though I hate the way he looks at me as if he's starving and I'm a bloody steak, that same hunger simmers in my lower belly, his words echoing in my head: *I get to play with you however I want, whenever I want.*

"Your hair is different," he says.

I roll my eyes, but inside, I'm surprised that he actually has his head out of his ass long enough to notice someone else. It's the missing bobby pins; I always have them in. And hell, I hope he's offended that I'm in an oversized t-shirt and leggings. You want business professional? Act like a damn professional.

"It's called bedhead," I say. "What can I do for you tonight, Mr. Winstone?" I expect him to sneer, but his face stays blank, and somehow, that scares me more than any other reaction. It's like he knows what I'm going to say before I say it, and he already has a punishment planned. Nerves getting to me, I correct myself: "Cash. What can I do for you on this very late night, *Cash?*"

He gestures to the side of his desk, his calloused hands bigger than I remember. They can take my entire neck in one palm.

"Stand there. Eyes forward. Chest out." He taps his watch. "I'm waiting, Remedy."

I suck in a breath, then position myself, pushing down that fluttering sensation in my pussy. The sooner we get this over with, the better. His piney cologne is stronger now, like he sprayed it right before I arrived. Dark circles surround each of his pupils, those freckles on the whites of his eyes like blots of paint. He looks wired like he's been up for three days straight, and though he ignores me and continues to type, I can feel his tension, the way his eyes shift like he's barely scanning toward me, to make sure I'm where I'm supposed to be. His fingers click on the keyboard and he switches between the different open windows on his monitor. He stays focused on his work like I'm another piece of furniture, nothing more. An object. *Damn it.* Why do I like this so much?

I grit my teeth, biting my inner lip. Just because I'm giving in now, doesn't mean that this is over. If he thinks I'm his *obedient* fuck doll, he'll let his guard down.

Then, I'll strike.

"Hands behind your back," he says. "Chin up."

Tension seizes my stomach. I scowl but move my hands behind my back, sneaking a sideways glance at him as I keep my chin *down*, to emphasize the fact that I'm looking *down* on him. A spreadsheet is open on his wide monitor, but I can't read what it says. His hands travel down to his lap, and he strokes his length through his pants, his cock growing and pressing hard against his trousers.

Holy hell. It's as thick as a baseball bat, and he doesn't even look full yet.

But he's ignoring my defiance. My nostrils flare and I drop my hands to my sides, testing his boundaries even further. Is this part of being his fuck doll?

It's hard to remember what my goal is when nothing feels real and it's so late. As much as I deny it, I *want* him to punish me. I hate him so much, but somehow, I know screwing him will be even better like that.

Suddenly he lurches forward, grabbing my arms and moving me closer to him, and my stomach prickles with pins and needles. Then he fixes me: my chin up, my hands behind my back. He even pushes between my shoulder blades until my tits are out. Everything inside of me tingles, knowing that he *wants* me positioned like this. He relaxes back into his state of ambivalence. Eyes on his computer. Fingers on the keyboard. His cock still thick and heavy on his leg.

Ten minutes pass like this. I lean to the side, drowsiness getting to me. One of his hands roams my chest absently, while his other hand stays fixed on the keyboard. His touch is gentle, reminding me of furry handcuffs, and I cringe.

Are you sure you want this? my ex-boyfriend had said. He held the fur-lined handcuffs like they were the devil himself, and the belt was limp in his other hand, like a poor dead snake.

We're just having fun, I said, trying to convince him. *I trust you.*

Yeah, but this isn't— my ex stopped, unable to find the words, his posture sagging even lower. *I don't want to hurt you, Remedy.*

I'm asking you for it, I said. *I'm consenting.*

He stroked my cheek, the touch tickling my skin, goosebumps erupting, reminding me of my stepdad even more.

It's not normal to want something like this, my ex said. *This has to do with your stepdad, doesn't it? You don't need this, Remedy. You need help.*

I blinked back the tears. No matter how many times I explained that my stepdad was gentle with me, my ex couldn't believe that I wanted cruelty. Those soft touches are what I hate most. Whether or not I want it, my body reacts and I can't enjoy it, because I always think of my stepdad. I need pleasure to be ripped from my soul like it doesn't belong to me anymore.

Instead, when my ex was like this, I floated inside of my head, like a buoy off the coast.

Just like now, with Cash.

Cash's words echo around me. A question. Or is it a demand? His fingertips skim my stomach, then go under my shirt for my bra.

My ex-boyfriend was always sweet to me, and in theory, I wanted that. That's what a survivor should want. But when goosebumps rippled over my flesh at his every touch, I couldn't hold back anymore. I had to force him to understand me.

I slapped my ex. A red handprint formed on his cheek. His jaw dropped, completely stunned, but there was sympathy in his eyes. No—it wasn't sympathy; it was pity. Like I was an injured bird he needed to rescue.

Let me love you, he said. *Please, Remedy.*

It wasn't until I broke up with him, knowing that he'd never be able to give me what I needed, that he convinced me to go to the sex addicts recovery program. As if that would save us.

In reality, he wanted to fix me.

Fingernails pinch my nipple then twist my skin until I gulp on dry air. I gasp, holding my tits.

"What the hell?" I ask.

"Where did you go?" he asks. His brows pinch together. "That vacancy in your eyes. Your mind went somewhere else." He swivels his chair and fixates on me, then palms both of my breasts, forcing my hands out of the way. His fingernails turn into clamps, sucking the blood from my nipples. A sharp sensation curls through me and I hold my breath. "If pain is the only way I can keep you tethered to this earth, then, by all means, let's keep you here."

With his pinched fingers, he twists, my skin bunching up around his fingers, the pain shooting through my chest. A scream builds inside of me, but I keep it inside. He grins. The bastard *likes* the reaction. And I don't want to give in to him.

"You," I breathe instead, "are a sick, sick man."

"Tell me why I can smell your cunt, then," he snickers. My cheeks burn and my mouth opens. He licks his thick bottom lip. He gives some slack to my breasts, a hot wave of relief washing over me. "Your nipples are hard," he says as he rubs my pebbled peaks between his fingers. He takes a handful of each breast, then crushes them like a stress ball, like he's going to use my body to get every ounce of his relief. "How wet are you, Remedy?"

I bite my inner lip. No. No. No. No matter what he says, he doesn't care about my enjoyment. I'm a fuck doll to him, an object he can toss aside once he's lost interest.

My pussy clenches; those thoughts aren't helping either. I've never had sex with someone who doesn't care about how I feel in the end. And it feels like coming home.

No. This is only about doing what he wants, so that in the end, I can get *what I want.* And I want him in jail, or dead.

If I happen to like getting there, that's unimportant. I suck in a long, hard breath.

"Screw you," I snarl.

"You would like that, wouldn't you? You realize you owe me, right, Remedy?" he asks, dust clouds swirling in his brown freckled eyes, narrowing in on me. He *likes* holding the blackmail over me. The way it makes me squirm. And that proves that he's a sick bastard. Someone who doesn't deserve his life of luxury. "From the hatred in your eyes to the sweet taste of your pussy: I own you now, Remedy Basset."

My belly swirls at those possessive words, but I refuse to react. He locks eyes with me, not letting me flinch, then he twists my nipples again, my breath hissing through my teeth as I stare back at him, trying not to make a sound. But the more I struggle, the harder he twists, and my breasts are on fire, the pain coursing through me like shocks of electricity. Cash doesn't care about how much it hurts. The more I fight it, the more it fuels him. Hunger burns in his eyes. My face flushes with heat as the realization hits me like a ton of bricks.

He's the first person to do this. And I didn't have to beg him for it.

It's almost like he listened. Like he believes me.

He presses his palms flat to my breast, a dull ache rippling through me. He breathes onto my ear, each breath hot and lingering.

"This isn't enough, is it?" he murmurs. "Do you wish I would fuck you over my desk, ramming into you so hard that I bruise your cunt? So that every time you move, you'd remember exactly who owns your body?" His thumbs brush the peaks of my nipples, the skin so tender now that everything hurts, even a touch like this. My mouth drops open. "Tell me what you want, Remedy. Tell me how badly you want me to hurt you."

"You stupid perv," I mumble. "I don't want you to hurt me."

His teeth click together, his eyes roving over my body. A smirk draws the corners of his mouth up, like he knows that I'm lying.

"Then lie to me," he says, "or I will email that video to the police right now."

Keeping one hand on my breast, his fingers pinching my raw nipple, he types with his other hand, pulling up his email on the monitor. He even enlarges the text so that I can read everything. I pant. He's messing with me. He won't actually do it.

He reads aloud: "Dear Key West Police Department—"

He's bluffing. He's freaking bluffing. He won't do it. Once he does, he won't have anything over me.

He continues: "This video contains footage of Remedy Basset attempting to murder me—"

"Does it make you feel strong to make a woman beg?" I interrupt. I raise my nose higher, looking down on him, even as my legs shake with desire, knowing that he's right: I do want him to hurt me. But I can't let him win. "Nothing is going to cure your perverted—"

"You are a terrible liar," he says. He finishes typing, then attaches a file.

"I'm not lying," I say.

He hovers the pointer over the word *Send*. His finger lifts up, about to tap the button—

"I want you to fuck me like you hate me," I blurt out, and his finger freezes above the mouse. I nod eagerly, showing him that I'm ready to play. I have to do this. If I let him control the situation just enough, then it'll be easier to get him under my thumb too.

At least, that's what I tell myself.

"I want you to choke me until I pass out," I say. My face is red, and everything in my body is filling with heat. I've never expressed my desires so plainly before. A lump is forming in my throat and soon, I won't be able to breathe. But his eyes are completely enraptured with me, and those worries melt away. He's truly listening. "I want you to make me come so hard I forget who I am. To slap me and beat me and use me and show me what a whore I am for you."

He pinches my nipple, using it to pull me closer, then forces me over his lap like he's about to spank me like a child. *He did this to Jenna.* Spanked her for being late for a meeting. It's degrading and I hate it, but I like it too. Why am I so light-headed? He rips down my leggings and pants until I'm completely exposed, and I know then that this is different. He never exposed Jenna like this. Leaning down, he sniffs me, and I blush—I'm ripe as hell—and a groan erupts from his chest like he's a beast unleashed. He pulls my ass cheeks apart, exposing my dark hole. The cool air tickles my skin and my whole body tingles.

"Why do you want that?" he asks.

"Because——" I start, but I don't know why. Why him? Why this? *Why can't I be normal?* "Because——"

"Because you can't help it, can you?" he breathes, his voice low and calm, like he's teaching me why. "You want me to take what I want. To own you. To show you that you're nothing but my little fuck doll. How badly do you want it?"

His fingertips are like sandpaper, but when he dips one between my folds, I'm so wet that his thick finger glides right through. Using my arousal, he teases my dark hole with his finger, then forces a finger inside. The pressure fills me and I gasp for air, completely stunned. It's as if in that single movement, he's telling me the truth: he doesn't care what I want.

And that turns me on so much.

"Use me," I whine, "All of my holes. *Please.*"

"I'm going to use you now, Remedy. Just like I want. All of your holes are mine, little cure. *Mine,*" he growls, then he impales me with his entire finger, forcing it inside of my ass, biting my neck at the same time, and I cry out, my moan so loud that I try to stop, try to suck it back inside, but he laughs and finger-fucks my ass. I buck my hips forward, humping his leg, wanting more, *so much more,* my clit bumping up against him. With one hand, he holds my neck like he's examining a fawn for slaughter, and with his other hand, he fucks my dark hole. Another finger slides inside my ass, filling me up, and my clit rubs against his leg—the sensations so intense that I'm close to the abyss, and I hate it but I love it and I try so hard not to think about what it means. I have to remember who he is. That I hate him. That Cash stands for everything I hate about people like my stepdad and my step-brother, and so I have to stay strong.

But his fingers slide in and out of my ass, and I lose those thoughts. His thigh muscles twitch, his cock so hard it's like a rock each time my body pushes against it. His fingers tickle my ass, a light pain mixed with pressure. The tingling sensation runs through my nervous system until it stimulates my neck and cheeks.

I can't stay strong anymore. Cash is holding me over the edge, and I pant, trying to stop the pleasure, but I've never done this with anyone before, not even myself. It's overwhelming me, pushing me to the brink. My face heats, my jaw dropping, and those involuntary spasms mount inside of me—

He instantly removes his hands, reclining in his chair, then laughs. I stumble forward, resting against him, my body covered in sweat. With one quick movement, he helps me stand. Once I'm steady, he exits the message, then switches to another program on his computer.

Like he didn't just shove out of his pleasurable hell.

Like nothing happened.

My pussy aches. Each twitch of my muscles begs for his touch, but he ignores me, completely focused on work.

He's done with me.

"That's it?" I ask.

He motions toward the door. "There's a general contractor I need you to meet at the shopping center in Waterside Park."

I blink, then check the time. It's almost two a.m.

"What for?" I ask.

"An important delivery. He'll be there at six a.m."

My jaw drops. He's serious. It *is* over. His expression is completely stoic, his hands typing rapidly, and I have to accept it. He finger-fucked my ass and denied my pleasure to screw with me.

I roll my eyes, then angle toward the door.

"Take my car," he says. He tosses me his keys. "It'll be faster."

"If it's so important, why leave it to me?"

He finally meets my eyes for the first time since his hands left my body. His smooth lips turn up, and I can read it in his expression: he knows exactly what he's doing, how frustrated I am, how much I hate that I want more. And he's relishing it.

"Because I told *you* to do it, Remedy," he says. "Part of your job description includes going to meetings for me. *Learn your place.*"

Those words stick out to me. He admitted something, didn't he?

He wants me to 'learn my place' because I'm not staying in

my lane. I'm not doing exactly what he wants. I don't know what it is, but I get this feeling like I frustrate him as much as he frustrates me. And this—making me leave, giving me an order—is a reminder to *both* of us of our positions.

He's my boss; I'm his subordinate. And he's getting rid of me.

"I expect you back by eight," he says. "Clean yourself up before you leave. You don't want them to think you're fucking your boss, do you?"

There's a snicker to his words, but by the time I check his expression, he's already back to his computer. I walk slowly, my body clenching with desire, then close the door behind me.

CHAPTER 5

REMEDY

OUR PATTERN CONTINUES LIKE THAT; HE CALLS ME AT WEIRD hours—midnight, at dawn, in the late evening—then he teases my body with sensation and pain, always demonstrating how much control he has over me, never giving me release. And of course, afterward, I find the nearest bathroom and give myself that release, knowing that I'm only reinforcing the desire. He's a monster who likes wielding that power over me. But the worst part?

I *like* how he controls me. My pussy and mind know we're losing, and he's winning.

Which is why after a few days of this, I give myself a reality check. I knock on Jenna's front door—another Winstone rental house, one she shares with three other women—and my stomach fills with knots. *This is a good thing*, I remind myself. *You're only going after Winstone for Jenna.*

She opens the door in her pajamas. I raise a brow. She's usually working on makeup by now, but she hasn't even showered yet.

"Don't you start work in less than an hour?" I ask.

"I'm sick," she says. She drags her feet, shuffling inside, and I follow her to the bedroom. Her hands wrap around herself as she slides back into the covers, lying in the fetal position.

"What's wrong?" I ask, stroking her comforter.

"Haven't been feeling like myself lately."

A sharp pain grips my chest, and I'm back in my childhood. I couldn't stay anywhere in my house without worrying that someone was going to use me, and that's what Jenna is experiencing right now. She scrunches up her face, her lips pale compared to their usual red paint, her whole body weighed down with everything that's happened. Winstone *and* the agency turned their backs on her. But I ball my fists; I'm *not* going to leave her. Even before I told her about my stepdad, she's always been there for me.

And I want her to be back to her normal self.

When we were still in high school, Jenna had a crush on my stepbrother, Brody. No matter how mean he was to her, she had her soul set on him, because she swore he was a sweetheart, somewhere inside his thick skull. All I saw was the cruel stepbrother who was twice my size now but still hurt me like we were kids. And because I knew Brody and Jenna would never *actually* become a thing—Brody was and is too much of an idiot—I let it go, seeing it as a harmless crush. After all, Brody and I hit each other because we were step-siblings; he'd never touch Jenna like that.

But one day, he cornered Jenna in my bedroom and told her to 'stop being such a needy little bitch.' I found her in tears, curled up in a blanket on my bed.

That was the end of me letting her crush on Brody.

He's done, I said to her. *He doesn't get to treat you like that. Not in a million years.*

Please, she whispered. *Don't make a big deal out of it.*

She chased me, but I ignored her. I couldn't stop my stepdad, but I wasn't afraid of Brody. He might have given me a black eye before, but I had made him cry from a swift kick in the balls. And if he hurt my best friend, he was done.

Brody, I shouted. He looked up from his phone. *You want to tell me what you said to my bestie?*

He stood up, using his height to tower over me. *Sure,* he said. *I called her a sniveling little bitch.*

Apologize, I demanded. *Apologize to her. Or you'll regret it.*

He waved a hand, dismissing us. *I'm not apologizing. You're both such drama queens.*

I slammed down my foot, and he jolted, surprised that I'd actually do something. *You don't get to talk to her like that,* I said.

He shoved a chair out of the way as he stepped closer.

What are you going to do? he asked. *Cry to my daddy?*

Asshole.

I kicked him in the knees so hard he stumbled into the wall, then I grabbed Jenna's hand, and yelled, *Run!*

We sprinted through the house and immediately locked my bedroom door behind us, bursting into laughter. And that made it worth it. Jenna had her bubbly smile back, and I knew everything would be okay.

And right now, while she's bundled in blankets, that's all I want: to make her feel better again. But kicking Cash in the shins won't be enough. He deserves so much worse.

"You don't have to be afraid," I say, gesturing at the door. "I'm keeping an eye on that piece of garbage."

"I'm not afraid," she mumbles. "But it feels like I don't have control of anything anymore."

My heart sinks. My stepdad completely paralyzed me, just like Cash is paralyzing Jenna now. A heaviness falls on my shoulders. It's a weight I'll carry around with me until Cash is gone.

"I'm going to get him," I say. "I promise."

She forces a smile. "I shouldn't have gotten you involved," she says sadly. "It's my fault. I know how you get."

I grin at those words: *How I get.* I'm going to show Cash *exactly* how I get.

"Come on," I say. "Things happen. And that's what besties are for." I hold her hand. "I'm going to take care of him. I promise."

"Bestie," she says. "I love you."

"And I love you!"

I give her a hug, and eventually, she heads toward the shower. I run home before driving to the estate: a quick break to grab my laptop and pee. I twist the bathroom door handle and the *entire* door comes off of the hinges.

"Shit!" I yell, jumping out of the way. It barely misses my foot.

The door scrapes against the wall, digging a black trail into the wood paneling. Screws hang from the hinge. I suck in a breath. It's like the universe *wants* me to interact with Cash. But I'll file a maintenance order like I always do, like the owner isn't my boss. And if it comes up at work, I'll do my best to convince him to send someone *decent* this time. But my pussy aches at the thought of trying to convince him, imagining that he'll order me to get on my knees. I shake my head. My mind is constantly in the gutter lately. I blame him. The thought of talking to him any more than I have to, makes me cringe.

But there's only one way to avenge Jenna, and that's getting closer to Cash. Even if it is just a maintenance request.

At the estate, I make our coffee—mine with cream and sugar, his black—then drop his mug off on his desk without a word. Then I fix Bones's breakfast. She eats, then observes me as I pick through my agency email and file a maintenance order. In the *Additional Comments* section, I type, *Tenant requests successful service this time,* then I click *Submit.*

Instantly, Cash appears in the doorway, a gray vest pulled over his button-up shirt, the sleeves rolled up like always, showing off his veiny arms. I zone out on those blood vessels, remembering how they roll and twist each time he touches me. Like his strength can't be contained. My breath catches in my throat.

This is stupid. He's my boss *and* my best friend's abuser, for fuck's sake.

And yet I want him.

"What?" I snap. He tilts his head to the side, curious about my attitude. I swallow hard. For now, he's still my boss. I can't get my revenge unless I pretend like I'm following his rules.

"I'm sorry, sir," I say, forcing a smile. "It's been a long morning. What can I help you with?"

He presses his lips together, satisfied by my change in response. "The door. It's been fixed before?"

I keep my eyes lowered, trying to hold back my tone, but I can't help it: "I completely understand that you must prioritize the vacation rentals properties, but when it comes to your long-term tenants, we *also* have maintenance issues."

"Agreed."

That immediate response stuns me. I expected him to resist. Is he messing with me? But his shoulders are wide, his jaw stern. For a moment, his dark, cloudy eyes are clear. There's nothing tricky about him.

"I thought a contractor handled the maintenance orders for the Winstone Company?" I ask.

"They do, but anything from you goes through me first."

Those words chill me. It has little to do with the maintenance, or even the fact that I'm his personal assistant, and everything to do with our agreement.

"It's a simple fix. Let's go," he nods toward the door leading to the attached garage. "I can teach you."

I touch the base of my neck. "You're leaving the estate?"

"Is there a better way to test my limits than to assist my favorite employee with her maintenance request?"

A silvered-gold watch sits on his wrist to emphasize his status, his lips are smooth and curved, the stubble on his jaw neatly trimmed. Everything about him refined. And yet his hands are rough, like dry, bumpy concrete, and I know that his stomach is covered in puffy pink scars. He isn't just a billionaire who develops real estate and businesses, and he isn't simply a hobbyist who does his own remodeling. But no matter how I rearrange it in my head, I can't figure it out. I don't even know if he's truly a recluse, or if that's a ruse to manipulate people into doing what he wants.

Either way, I don't trust him.

He opens the passenger side of his sleek, black imported sports car, then drives us to downtown Key West.

"Your dad never taught you how to use tools?" he asks.

I wrinkle my nose. He's asking me about *this*, now? Why does he ask so many questions?

"My dad died before I was born," I say.

"Stepdad? Brother? Boyfriend?"

Maybe he's searching to see if I have anyone who will protect me from him.

"They didn't teach me stuff like this," I say.

"Then what did they teach you?"

I let out a breath, then face the window. "I don't know."

He parks the car on the street and pays the meter; I guess even a billionaire has to follow some rules. He motions at the shop. *Mike's Home & Supply Co.* is written in faded red letters across the front of the building. An older man in a baseball cap whistles as we enter.

"Look at you," he says to Cash. "Fancy *and* with a lady."

I roll my eyes. We're technically here together, but we are *not* together. Another person, a clerk behind the register, gawks at us like we're a freak show.

"Where you going tonight with this lil' thing, bud?" the older man asks. *Bud?* This man is calling Cash, a real estate developer billionaire, 'bud'?

How does he even know Cash?

"This is Remedy, my newest personal assistant," Cash says, putting a hand on my shoulder, his grip firm. And there's no mistaking it then; he's only introducing me, which means he *knows* these people. "Her door broke off the hinges. Figured I'd teach her how to fix it herself."

"Teach a man to fish and feed him for a lifetime," the owner says, his voice wistful, like he says that a lot. "You know where to go."

We find the tools we need: a couple of new hinges and screws, though Cash implies that I may need a new door too. Finally, we make it to the front of the store. I still don't understand why Cash is *insisting* that we fix it together. Maybe it's an excuse to come inside my house. A twinge of nerves spikes through me, but I push it down. We're not there *yet*.

"How's the move going?" the clerk asks as he scans the items. Cash stares at the man evenly, the tendons in his neck taut, as if the cashier has said the exact wrong thing.

Moving?

"Moving takes time," Cash says with a harsh layer to his tone, a threat simmering below the surface. The cashier sinks down, his eyes on the floor. He caught that tone too.

But something doesn't feel right. Is Cash really a recluse if he knows everyone at this hardware store, even the cashier?

As the cashier bags our items, I whisper to Cash: "I thought you didn't go out."

"I told you," he says. "I've been breaking those habits. Your friend didn't notice."

I tighten my fists at my sides. Jenna may be timid, but she's observant, and Cash is full of shit. But the door chimes and a customer enters: light brown hair and blue eyes fill the entrance, sunlight flashing around him. My heart leaps into my chest and every muscle in my body tenses with nerves.

He looks like my stepdad.

Then the man pivots to the side, revealing the differences. His nose is way bigger than my stepdad's. I exhale, but my fingers twitch at my sides, trying to get rid of the nerves. Maybe Brody is in town. The last time I saw him, he looked even more like his dad.

But Brody doesn't live in Key West anymore. And besides, the customer is probably too old to be Brody.

"What's wrong?" Cash asks. The customer studies different displays on the shelves. He's got sloping shoulders like my stepdad, the same soft hands. I know it's *not* him, but that nervous sensation flutters in my chest. I finally got used to his absence, and now, he's invading my life again. The customer disappears down the tall aisles, but I still stare at that empty spot like I can see his ghost.

Cash pulls me into his arms, his body heat blankets me, and for a second, I forget who he is, and I melt. The dusty scent of chemicals and pine trees and his subtle sweat embraces me. I blink, letting myself be taken out of those memories. Cash absorbs my world and it feels right.

"What is it?" he asks again.

This time, I don't stop myself from answering. "I thought I saw someone."

"Who?" When I don't say a word, he grips my shoulders, bending down until we're both at the same eye level. "Tell me, Remedy, or so help me, I will *make* you. I will show everyone in this store what a—"

"My stepdad," I say, interrupting him. My stepdad doesn't deserve a name. But the truth is that I can't say his name, even if I want to. His *name* shrinks me down like I have no control. I close my eyes, then let out another breath. "I thought I saw my stepdad."

Cash studies me, his eyes reading the words I refuse to say. Like how I don't want to be around my stepdad. That I haven't spoken to him for years, and how I *want* to keep it that way. My stepdad moved to Tampa after the divorce, but that doesn't mean he can't visit Key West. He still has friends here. And his son has friends here, too.

Cash puts a muscular arm around my shoulder, guiding me back to the entrance and out of the hardware store. Like he knows I need to get out of there. Like he almost wants to protect me.

But he's selfish. A user. Like my stepdad. None of this makes sense.

I let him drive, not questioning where we're going, what we're doing, or why. But when we drive past Queen Street, the turn for his estate, I perk up.

"You can go left up here," I say. "You'll still—"

"We're not going to my estate," he says. I wrinkle my nose, questioning him. "We're going to fix your door."

I don't have the energy to fix a door, nor to be trapped in my rental house with a strange man, even if the house technically belongs to him.

"Call one of your maintenance men," I say.

"I'll teach you."

"I sent in a maintenance request. I didn't ask you for your help."

He doesn't respond. His eyes are on the road like I'm not there. A tumbling sensation rolls around in my stomach; I know what I said was rude. He's trying to *help*.

But I don't want his help.

He parks in front of my rental house, and I open my mouth to question *how* he knows where I live, but I stop myself. He owns the property *and* is my employer. Of course he knows.

He hands me the plastic bag.

"Fix it yourself," he says.

I gawk at him, then tap my purse. "But what about my car?"

"I'll have someone drop it off."

He drives down the street, our last interaction eerily short. Cash likes hearing himself talk, especially when it comes to putting me in my place, and that stark difference to how he acted in the car just now unnerves me. It's almost like I offended him.

The plastic bag crinkles in my grip. I glance up at the front porch.

What happened?

As I walk inside, my phone buzzes: a picture of my mother and me fills the screen.

"Tom wants to take us on a double date," Mom says as soon as I pick up. "What do you think?"

"Tom?" I ask. He has a name now; that means they're serious. It's a losing battle.

"My new boyfriend. I told you about him." A dull tingling sensation curls my stomach, threatening to make me curl up in bed for the rest of the night. "You can bring one of your old boyfriends. How about the professor? What's his name? Oh! Or maybe Peter!"

I roll my eyes. My ex isn't an option. If we're together after dark, we will inevitably end up having sex, and I'm tired of faking orgasms, especially now that I know how good pain actually feels when it comes from a sadist. And Peter, my cop friend, isn't any better; he's worse. He drugged one of our classmates, assaulted her, claimed that she liked it, then became a police officer out of guilt. At one point, I put his past aside since he wanted to help put my stepdad in jail, but years passed. He probably doesn't remember that anymore.

"What if I brought a friend?" I ask. "Maybe Jenna?"

"It's a double *date*," she teases. "Trust me. It'll be too romantic for Jenna."

I exhale slowly, trying to keep my cool. My mind briefly wanders to Cash. His veiny, muscular forearms. Rough hands willing to show me my place, to force me to admit why I'm nervous or scared. Considering our agreement, he actually *is* an option, and if *we* happen to fuck afterward, I'd at least get some of what I wanted—that total domination—even if he still refuses to give me the final release.

But he's my boss. My best friend's abuser. My blackmailer.

And he's pissed at me anyway.

"I'll figure something out," I say.

"I can't wait!" Mom squeals.

We hang up, and the metal hinge and screws clink in my palm as I study the door. A tension fills my stomach, and as I sniff the air, I can smell his pine and sweat. Like he's already been here. His scent must have gotten on my clothes. My pussy clenches, but I can't think about him anymore.

Instead, I drop the plastic bag, rush to the kitchen, and grab an unopened bottle of wine. I'm not dealing with this right now.

Cash

The stars shine up above, my shoes tapping along the sidewalk. It's late, past midnight, but it's quiet, even for Key West. The news reports must actually be working; the mayor doesn't have to hold a curfew. People are afraid.

But not me.

I use the spare key above Remedy's back door and let myself inside. A fan whirs in her bedroom, the white noise keeping her asleep. Her chest rises and falls in a steady rhythm, a purple towel tossed on the pillow by her head, as if she fell asleep after a hot bath. An empty wine bottle sits on her nightstand.

A bath and a lot of wine? No wonder she's passed out.

I pull her blanket down carefully, the fabric skimming her body. The sour scent of spilled alcohol lingers in the air. She wrinkles her nose, like she often does during the day, then stretches back into sleep, never opening her eyes. Her lips are light pink, stripped of her usual makeup. As the blanket falls off the bed, I rub my cock in my pants. She's naked, her brown nipples erect from the plush blanket, red scabs dotting her areola from my fingernails. Her legs are spread, her pussy lips glistening. The lace design tattoos stretch across her stomach, cupping underneath each breast, then down over her mound, mixing with the silky trimmed hair on her pussy.

My mouth waters. She's natural. Vulnerable. And mine. Fuck, she's gorgeous. And this is transactional. She obeys me, and I don't turn her in to the police. It's an even exchange. If anything, she comes out ahead.

And damn it, I want to make her come.

Which is why I need to leave Key West soon. Find a colder climate. A place where I can work and enjoy my interests. In my line of work, it's not good to stay in one place for long. You stick around enough to get established, then move on to the next location.

But the idea of staying, of seeing how Remedy evolves as we continue our game, entices me. She's even stronger than I expected. Feistier. And being able to say what she wants sexually, knowing that I'm her sworn enemy? The predicament is intriguing as hell.

And eventually, I can frame her. Everyone around her will die, and soon, the police will realize that she's the last person they spoke to. Even her boss will be gone.

But right now, I want to taste her. I drape my fingertips over her calves, then between her thighs. Her skin is smooth and damp, as if she put on lotion before falling asleep. My fingertip traces her pussy lips, my cock twitching in my trousers. She soaked like she's having a wet dream marathon. I stroke my dick through my pants, licking my lips as I trace those pussy lips with my fingers. Her satin hair. Her slick skin. Her warmth radiating off of her holes.

I want to destroy her with my dick.

I lay between her legs, then take as much of her clit and pussy lips in my mouth as I can, letting my tongue run in between her folds, tasting each crevice, the tangy sweetness. I know her taste well now, from licking it off of my hands, but this is the first time I've tasted her straight from the source. My cock fills for her, desperate for her warmth. I run my tongue over that bundle of nerves, playing with her clit, swirling around and around. It engorges with blood, her sensitivity increasing. She spreads her legs more for me. In her sleep.

She's unconscious. Completely helpless. And so damn sweet. I want to keep her like this, bound by her own sleep paralysis, but I want her to wake up too. I want her to fight me.

And then I can't help it anymore. I lick her like a hungry beast, from her clit down to her asshole, licking those bumpy ridges until her tight ring clinches, then relaxes for me, ready for more. I tongue-fuck her ass, dry-humping the bed, and her arousal drenches my face like syrup. Her musky scent surrounds me, and I hastily move so that I can finger her ass with one hand and grind into my fist with the other, humping the bed. I suck her clit, swirling my tongue in sharp movements. She gasps, and that fuels me. I finger-fuck her tight little ass harder, then shove in a second finger. Her ass is smooth and fucking delectable, and my eyes roll back in my head, imagining her ass swallowing my cock whole. Her hips buck forward, then her legs wrap around my head.

"What the hell?!" she yells.

She kicks a heel into my lip, but I lurch up, pinning her to the bed with my body. Lust glazes over her expression and I can see it in her eyes: she sees her come shining all over my face, the ravenous hunger in my eyes; she feels my cock stabbing into her thighs like a dagger; she knows how desperate I am for her pussy and ass. It stuns her, and her body relaxes.

When I'm positive that she'll be compliant for now, I touch my lip. A drop of blood smears my finger. I put my finger in her mouth, and she doesn't hesitate. She sucks it clean like my finger is a cock, and her eyes disappear into her skull, devouring that drop of metallic liquid.

"The more you fight, the more I will too," I warn. "And fuck, Remedy, I love putting you in your place."

"Why are you here?" she asks in a hoarse voice.

"You want me to go?"

She's seething, but she doesn't say a word. She doesn't tell me to stop. Because she's fighting it too: she knows she wants this, that she wants *me*. Whatever this fucked up lust is between us, it owns the both of us.

And she can't lie about that.

I bend down, biting her ear. "I can't stop thinking about your sweet little cunt," I say. Her stomach tightens, but her eyes are glossy. She loves the dirty way I treat her. My filthy little fuck doll. "I needed a taste. Needed to devour every fucking part of you. Because you're mine, Remedy, and I want you. I'm going to tear you apart."

I lower my body, dragging myself along her tender flesh so she can feel what she does to me: my hard dick stabbing into her belly and thighs. I swirl my tongue along her clit, but she's limp. She's not moving like before.

I lift myself up. Her eyes are empty. Her focus is on the ceiling. Not on me.

She'll give me her attention *now*.

I bend down, taking as much flesh as I can in my mouth, then I bite down hard, my canines tearing into that deep muscle and she screams, her hips bucking me off. I growl as I peer down at her, my dick hungry for her even more now.

"Tell me you're mine," I growl. "All fucking mine."

"Cash," she whispers.

I slap her thigh, right against that bite mark, and a groan rips from her chest, primal and instinctive and full of pleasure.

"Tell me you're mine," I say, slapping her again. I lick my lips, savoring her tangy scent on my mouth. Salty and sweet. "Tell me you're mine or I'm gone, Remedy, and you'll never get this again."

"I'm yours," she shouts. Energy pulses through me and I shove my fingers back into her ass, her muscles relaxing into me. Her hips writhe against me, bucking toward me. As I take her clit into my mouth, she hisses, "I'm yours, but I fucking hate you."

I tease her clit, barely licking it, while I still finger-fuck her ass into a frenzy. She needs that clitoral stimulation, *needs* it to come right now. And I'm denying her of it. I shift to her thigh, taking her flesh into my mouth again, biting with less pressure, because I already did the work: she's raw and a nibble hurts like a steak knife. She moans, and that sound fills me with savage lust. My cock grows bigger, my dick heavy and uncomfortable. We both want the release so damn bad, but I have to hold back.

"You hate me just as much as you want me," I say.

"I *hate* you."

Her eyes leave mine, but I grab her chin hard, forcing her to look at me, to see exactly what she wants. Sweat covers every inch of me, my clothing drowning from her come and our sweat, and I'm so soaked I drip onto her, but she doesn't notice. She glares at me as if to say, *Don't you dare stop fucking me, or I'll kill you.*

"You want me to use you, little cure?" I ask.

And before I even finish the question, she's nodding, and I ram a free finger into her cunt, using both holes, manipulating her like a puppet, refusing to be gentle. I pinch her clit between my teeth, teasing that bundle of nerves with my canines, her holes clinching around me, each moan that rips from her soul mixed with delight and distress. With my other hand, I shove two fingers deep into her mouth until her tonsils grapple with my knuckles. She gags, tears filling her eyes. I let go, giving her a small breath of air, but then I lean my weight into her again, pressuring all of her holes, making eye contact with her.

"You don't hate me because of your best friend," I growl. My fingers dig into each hole, and I rub her g-spot. My fingers tease the thin walls of flesh separating her ass from her pussy, and her throat gags on my fingers. "You hate me because you love what I can give you. You need it. No one can fuck you like you want. No one can make you feel like this. No one, and I mean *no one*, can make you feel like I can. You want this just as much as I do."

Tears fill her eyes again, and this time, it's not from my fingers in her throat. It's from the truth; it disgusts her and liberates her at the same time. I fuck her holes with my hands, penetrating her with abandon. I bite every piece of flesh I can reach—her stomach, her thighs, her navel—until her legs jiggle, the pleasure overwhelming her. Once I feel her body tighten around me, I fuck her harder, biting her with everything I have, wishing I had three cocks to stuff her with until she's a mindless toy. She convulses around me like she's possessed by an angry demon, and now, she won't be able to deny that she *wants* this. I've kept her from that final brink for so long, and by delaying this gratification for both of us, she'll want everything I can give her. In the end, she'll *want* to take the blame for my murders.

She'll lose control.

She twitches around my hands, her moans vibrating across my fingers in her mouth as her orgasm dissipates. Suddenly, every single touch is too sensitive, too much for her to take. She begs me with her eyes, pleading for me to go easy on her now. I lick her thigh over the bruised bitemarks and she twitches uncontrollably. I finger-fuck her harder, *rougher,* and every touch makes her jerk around my fingers, the pleasure breaking through her soul like she's being erased from her body.

But I don't care. I *want* her to remember what it feels like when I make her come. Her velvet walls squeeze around me again, her smooth ass clenching around my fingers, her throat gagging between each panting breath.

"You can give me another one," I demand.

She chokes on my fingers as I massage her wet throat, but come runs down her legs, my fingertips wrinkled from her moisture. And still, she doesn't push me away.

"You are so fucking hot," I murmur. I suck in the sweet scent of her arousal, licking my lips. "Come for me again, Remedy. Show me what a whore you are. How much you love when I take whatever I want from you."

The tears crash down her face, and this time, she comes immediately, the spasms rocking between us, flinging our bodies apart. I pin her down with my whole body weight as she loses control, gasping and convulsing around my fingers. Her eyes roll back into her head and her body curls and contorts, her nipples hard, and I find empty skin right above her mound, biting down as hard as I can until she pulls my fingers out of her mouth and screams in pain, in pleasure, in all-consuming lust.

I breathe down on her, finally letting go. Each breath tremors through her body. My trousers are stained with her come, my pre-cum, and sweat. If she even dry-humps me, I'll come in my pants like a teenage boy, but I don't care.

Her eyes are heavy with sleep. Purple and green bruises spread across her tawny skin, like a galaxy engraved in her flesh. She's one step closer, completely exhausted, too tired to fight me. And soon, I'll make her beg for my come. She'll take the blame for my crimes willingly. All I need to do is keep manipulating her like this.

And once she's mine, she'll fall.

CHAPTER 6

CASH

THE NEXT NIGHT, I PARK MY CAR DOWN THE ROAD, FAR ENOUGH away so that she can't immediately tell that it's me, but close enough that I can watch her. Her matte red car—the shiny exterior stripped off—is on the street, and her window is lit up around the blinds. She's awake. What's she doing?

Most of the time, I keep to myself for as long as possible, sometimes even waiting until the police find the bodies before moving on to the next. Criminal justice experts preach about 'patterns' that people like me have, which is exactly what I use against them. The tie holding my victims together is that they're all in Key West, and they're left in the crawl spaces. They don't have anything else in common.

A silhouette hovers behind her blinds. I run my palm over my dick, tenting in my trousers, thinking of her wet, succulent mouth, her pink and purple lips. I'd be in Remedy's wall cavities or watching her on her webcam, but I need to hold back. A situation like this takes time. But the itch to control someone in their final moments keeps getting stronger, and the longer I wait, the more I burn to play with Remedy. And I *need* to give her time. She's consuming me, and I can't let that happen.

I glance at my phone. If she wants to play, then I'll skip a kill tonight. But if she's occupied, then I'll give her a break. *26 Missed*

Calls blinks in red at the top of my phone, the general contractor's name for each call. When is he going to realize that I'm not interested in working on that house anymore?

No calls or texts from Remedy.

I push the button to start the engine, then stare at her bedroom window.

It's your fault, little cure. Someone has to die because you don't want to play.

I put on my gloves, the leather crunching as I flex my fingers. I should be killing anyway. Remedy's schedule doesn't matter to me.

A muscle man in a tank top with a bright gold spray tan turns the corner, heading toward Duval Street. He swaggers with each step, like he deserves the street to himself, like he doesn't give a damn that there's a killer on the loose. One of my foster fathers walked like that.

By ten years old, I knew what to expect. It was my sixth home, and when it came to this particular family, if the biological kids screwed up, the father took it out on me.

You think my wife's food is shit? he had asked. I hadn't said that—in fact, I hadn't said a single word in that house yet—so I glared back, refusing to take my eyes off of him. He wasn't the first foster parent to lay a hand on me, and he wouldn't be the last. But this was a lucky night. This time, they actually invited me to sit with them.

My stomach twisted in pain, but I refused to take a bite. I wouldn't back down from his gaze. That would show weakness, and I'm not weak.

You ungrateful son of a bitch, he said. He tossed my plate, the casserole splattering on the floor like vomit outside of a dive bar. *You'll eat like a dog.*

One of the biological children giggled at the word 'dog,' a nervous lilt to her voice. But still, I didn't move, and when the foster mother said, *Chris*, trying gently to get her husband's attention, my foster father backhanded me so hard that I fell to the floor. My head spun and bile crept up my throat, but I sat upright, crossing my legs, then met his eyes again, my vision blurring.

You got anything to say? he asked.

Everyone was silent as he stood up, looming over me. The worst thing was the silence. They all hated that, and I used it like a weapon, driving them mad. Keeping my expression blank. Never letting them in on what was going on inside. With each step, he swaggered forward like his muscles were too big for his body. Like he knew exactly how much sway he had.

I could have said anything. That I hated him more than I hated my biological parents. That his parents must have hated him more than I did. That there were more important things to do than to talk to an idiot with the IQ of a potato.

But instead, I smiled, pretending like nothing mattered. That facial expression spoke the words for me.

And that's when he knocked me out.

On the street, the muscle man sways to each side, his shoulders too big for his body. He must take steroids like my foster father did. And for a moment, I wonder if this muscle man has any kids. Biological. Foster. Adopted. But that isn't my concern.

All people are fucked up. I don't need proof to kill someone. *Everyone* is fair game. Even Remedy.

I follow behind him, keeping my feet in time with his footsteps. By the time his head twists to the side, realizing someone is shadowing him, I swing an arm around his neck, a firm palm on his mouth, pulling him inside of one of my empty vacation rentals.

He drops to the floor, coughing and red, then reaches for his holster. But I hold up his gun and phone, letting my lips spread wide, baring my teeth. I roll up my sleeves, the veins in my arms twitching, itching for his last breath of life. I leave his gun on the small table beside me. He studies me, trying to judge my actions, but when he propels himself forward, reaching for the weapon, I grab it first and ram the back of it into his nose. The cartilage crunches like wet sand and he wails, holding his face, rolling on the ground like a baby.

"What do you want, man?" he asks. He reaches into his pocket, throwing his wallet at me. "Take it. It's all I've got." Keeping the gun aimed at him, out of curiosity, I pick up the wallet. This isn't about money, but I'm not the kind of man to leave cash on the table. I put the wad into my pocket, then check his license.

Donny Kent. Twenty-seven years old. Lives on Queen Street, only a few blocks away from my estate. Apparently, he's well off. A little prick that lives off of his parents' paychecks.

He could be anyone. I don't care. I simply need what a living body can give me.

"Now here's the deal, Kent," I say. I lock the front door, stowing the key in my pocket. "The front and back door need a key, a copy of which is hidden somewhere in this rental. Tempered glass on the windows and the panes are nailed shut. But if you can find a way out," I pause, glancing at my watch, "in the next two minutes, I'll let you live."

The man widens his eyes. "Please," he begs. "I'll do anything."

I set the timer on my watch. "And—"

"What do you want, man?"

"Starting now!"

His mouth gapes, but he runs through the house, stumbling through each room, nearly crying when he sees the foam insulation machine, mask, and tools I have set up in the guest bedroom. Each of his footsteps is loud and erratic, shuddering through the walls, but the perks of my profession are knowing exactly how each house is tailored. Because of recent renovations, this house won't let a sound escape.

He stumbles around. Couch cushions fly. Drawers spring from dressers. The key is hidden in the freezer, one of the most obvious places, and yet his tiny brain can't think. One minute down. The hysteria sets in. Tears streak his cheeks. He pants like a bulldog, sniffling around for anything. Finally, his eyes widen, realizing that *I* am his way out. He has to kill me. And until the timer is up, I won't fight back.

He steels himself, rolling his shoulders, then he propels himself forward, but the adrenaline pumping through his veins makes his moves unbalanced, like a teenager learning how to fight. But not me. I jump out of the way. My pulse is steady, my dick filling with blood as he loses control. Panic. Pure fight-or-flight adrenaline coursing through his veins. Volatility. He runs full speed at me again, his bulky feet plodding forward, but I step to the side, letting him crumble into the bedroom wall, a painting of the ocean waves falling to the floor.

My watch beeps and the man gulps. I lock the bedroom door behind us and pull him into my grip. I silence the alarm. Acrid body odor swims inside my nose, and I take it in. I fucking love it. I push his neck into the crux of my arm, nearly cutting off his windpipe. A tear runs down his cheek.

"P-p-please," the man whimpers, "I don't want to die."

I let him drop to the floor, and he immediately stumbles, doing his best to reach for the door, but the lock stumps him.

"I don't want to die," he cries again, his cheeks shining with tears. I stroke a finger along his skin, wetting my finger, then lick the salt off of my tip. Instead of the man's colorless eyes blinking up at me, I see Remedy's green eyes burning, her mouth open and slobbering for my cock, black tears staining her cheeks. How long will it take for her to beg me like this? How long will she last, given how depraved she is? My cock presses the seam of my pants and I step closer to the man. He cowers on his hands and knees. Is Remedy alone now? Naked in her bedroom? Touching herself so she feels safe? She wants it all—nipple clamps, knives, baseball bats—anything to help her take control of the pain, that deviance, her entire world. I pat my pocket, the chain jingling inside the fabric. I want it around her throat. Right fucking now.

My phone rings; I ignore it. Then I groan. *Fuck it.* I know what I want. I pull the chain out—the thick links end in o-rings. A choke chain for a large dog. Or, better yet, a human.

I slip the chain through an o-ring to form a loop, and the man cowers, tripping over his own feet as he crawls to the door. This chain is supposed to be for Remedy. It's supposed to be for tomorrow night.

But I can't wait.

"Put this around your neck," I order.

"Then will you let me go?" the man asks. I rub his head like a dog. People are pathetic. Once they know their lives are on the line, they'll do *anything*, as long as they can be free.

It will take Remedy a long time to reach the bottom of that desperate pit, and I intend to enjoy every second of it.

"Of course," I lie.

Compliant, he puts the choke chain around his neck. "You're into pet play?" he asks. "I can do that. I can bark. I can do tricks. I can suck your dick. I can—"

I grab the long end of the chain, then kick his chest until I lean my full weight on his rib cage, crushing him down, then I pull back with the chain, watching as he darkens with blood. I don't see him anymore. Her emerald eyes swirl in his, her body twitching for release as I fuck the last breath out of her.

He pulls at the chain and I let go. His gasps fill the air. But he's already so weak. It's irritating.

"I'll do a-a-anything," he says. On his knees, he pulls at my belt and zipper. "Please. Don't kill me."

The zipper teeth click open like the ticking of a clock. He's right; I *am* hard, but not for him. It's never about getting off or money. It's about power and control. Knowing exactly what I can do.

My phone buzzes again. But this time, when I check it, *Remedy* flashes on the screen.

I grab the chain, shoving him off of me as I answer the phone. Spittle flies from the corners of his mouth like he's gargling mouthwash, and I pull the chain tighter.

"Yes?" I answer the phone.

"Can you come over?" Remedy asks. "My door is still broken. And you're right. I should learn how to do it. And the door handle on the fridge ripped off, so yeah. Things are falling apart here."

It's almost like she needs me.

"Be there soon," I say.

I hang up, then look down at the muscle man's dark red face.

"Sorry to cut it short, but I've got an appointment to make."

I pull on the chain, standing on his chest until the man's face swells purple like an eggplant, and finally, the stress in his face relaxes, letting go, escaping into death. I wipe my brow. Sweat laces my fingers. My dick is full of pressure, and I squeeze the head through my trousers. *Soon.*

I stare at the body. I need to clean the mess. Remove the nails from the windows. Discard the extra keys. Paint his body in primer, then stash it in the crawl space, filling it up with insulation foam until he's barely there.

But all I can think about is Remedy on her knees.

I pull the man to the crawl space, then put on my protective mask. I quickly paint his body with primer. It doesn't erase the odor, but it helps to block it, especially paired with the insulation foam. I take the pump from the guest bedroom and start the gun nozzle, letting the polyurethane swarm his body in waves. In the end, only his fingers stick out of the puffy white material, but they blend in with the rest. My cock twitches, eager for my little cure. She's been waiting for too long now.

I close the hatch, sealing him inside. I pull the rug over it.

Once I clean up my mask, the primer, and the foam pump, I race over to Remedy's rental house. I don't care about the locks. The nails. The broken painting. I don't care how screwed up that vacation rental is. If the cops haven't found me yet, they won't find me tonight.

I just want her.

I dial her number from the front porch. Instantly, she opens the front door and her green eyes flutter. The short skirt around her hips shows off her thick, sunset orange thighs. Her tank top barely covers her tits. Her peach fragrance surrounds me and I lick my lips.

She's ready for me.

"I made you a drink," she says.

She points to her bedroom. Cheap lace jewelry decorates the walls. I grab a cup off of her desk, handing her the other. We clink the glasses together, but she hesitates before she drinks, and that makes me stop. I sniff the contents.

The amber liquid stinks of liquor, but that doesn't mean it's pure.

"You poisoned this," I say.

"It's just whiskey. Here." She reaches for mine and takes a sip. "It's drinkable. Don't worry."

It doesn't explain why she's waiting for me.

I narrow my gaze, but I'm slightly disappointed. I *want* her to fight me. She makes things interesting.

"What am I repairing?" I ask.

She throws a finger at the kitchen. "Fridge handle came off."

I exit her room. It's dark, and as the fridge comes into view, I see that the handle is there, and intact. Is she messing with me?

She leaps forward, jumping onto my back, the knife hitting my cheek. I growl, smacking the knife out of her hand, then spin until she falls off of me, stumbling onto the floor. She howls, then moves to attack me again, but I pin her to the tile, her wrists in my hands, small and delicate, and so damn breakable. I pry her legs open with my knees and she breathes through her teeth, rasping out each breath.

My dick throbs with blood, a lightness filling my body.

She still wants to kill me.

I like that. I like it a lot.

"You surprise me, little cure," I grin.

"You deserve to die," she yells.

I press my legs between her thighs, my trousers against her naked pussy. She grunts, baring her teeth, even as she wets my pants, writhing on them. No matter how much she wants to kill me, she can't help herself. It's so fucking hot.

"And how do I deserve to die?" I ask.

"I'll cut off your dick."

I laugh, then put a hand around her throat. My hands are so big they wrap around her entire neck. I put just enough pressure so that her mouth opens and her eyes glaze over with lust. Other people run from a man like me, but Remedy? She opens her mouth, waiting for my cock. I pull the choke chain from my pocket, dangling it above her, letting one cool metal link settle on her forehead. The light from her bedroom catches on the metal, and she thrashes against me. I tighten around her neck, waiting for her to surrender.

"The hell—" she chokes out, "—are you doing?"

"Showing you your place."

She hisses with rage, but I hold her down, forcing the chain around her head and tightening it around her neck. Her hips buck. Keeping the end of the chain in my hand, I let the rest of the links fall on her chest like a bag of cement. I'm tempted to tell her that minutes ago, I killed a man with that same chain, but I keep that secret locked inside of me. One day I'll tell her. But for now, I want her to trust me.

"We both know what you want, Remedy," I say in a low, controlled voice, "and I'm not going to let you go until I get what I want too." I pull the chain around her neck until her face turns red. She yanks at the chain, but she's not even half of the strength of the muscle man. I can take her life in seconds, but I don't want to yet. I want to drag her along. Push her closer to the edge. Make her *want* to jump for me.

I give her slack on the chain and she gasps like a balloon filling up with air. Her green eyes glow like emeralds full of fire, and I see myself in her. I let go of my hatred for the world a long time ago, but that passion inside of Remedy? I used to have that. No matter how many people I kill, that fire grows duller each day.

And yet Remedy awakens me. Reminding me of what it's like to *desire* power and control over someone specific. I can't predict Remedy. And I want to break her so damn bad.

I grip the chain, not yet choking her with it, but with enough tension to show her that *I own her.* Pulling her closer to me, like a slave on a leash, I bite her neck over the chain. Her wiry muscles shift under my teeth. I lift her skirt, cupping her pussy. Her pussy lips are covered in satin hair, drenched in her arousal, and that scent—like tangy peaches—floats in the air. I growl into her, then pull out my dick. Once my pants are around my hips, I slap her, just hard enough to watch the shock ripple across her expression. She spits at me and I lick her lips.

"Spit all you want," I say. "One day, you're going to crawl to me."

Her tank top bunches above her breast and I pinch her nipples, twisting them. She's sensitive from healing, and even the slightest pinch makes her moan. And when that sound echoes from her throat, my cock stretches against her.

"What the hell, Cash?" she cries. With a handful of her breast, I wring her flesh as hard as I can, clenching my jaw, the sensation rippling through her. My cock aches for her pussy, but I'm not going to give in yet. I tease us both, giving her the thick, purple tip of my choked cock, veiny and mean. Remedy's eyes flick back and forth between my face and my cock. She wants to gawk at my dick, but she wants to anticipate me too. Her hips wiggle, and she rides the head of my cock, trying to get it deeper than the tip.

"How does it feel to have my dick slide in and out of your pussy lips?" I breathe into her neck. "You want to feel how hard I can give it to you, how I own your pussy, don't you, Remedy?"

"Fuck you."

I tighten the chain around her throat and she whimpers.

"All you have to do is tell me to go to the police and I'll let them take care of you." I slip my cock in an inch deeper and she cries out—my girth is wide, rivaling a soda can, and with the blood surging there, it's unforgiving, ripping her apart like a virgin all over again. I release some tension on the choke chain, then breathe into her ear: "Tell me to stop. You won't have to deal with me behind bars, right, little cure?"

"Just fuck me," she cries.

I stop everything, letting the silence eat away at her. She wants me to say more, wants me to confess my dirty, fucked up thoughts that are completely obsessed with her. My dick should be rubbed raw with how much I've fucked myself thinking of her every night, but I licked every crevice of my hand, hoping for the unwashed taste of her come. I've touched her sacred, pretty little cunt with these same fingers. And now that I have her, *now* that she's telling me to *just fuck her,* I want to take my time. Draw it out. To make every painful second count.

Her eyes blink as she realizes what she said.

"I hate you," she says. "Fuck you. Fuck you, Cash."

But she can't take it back. She knows what she said. Her eyes close, and a musky, sweet scent wafts from between her legs. She swallows, then looks to the side, avoiding my gaze.

"Please fuck me," she whispers this time.

I keep my stare cold, observing her like she's an animal roaming around a test lab, waiting for the machine to give her a treat. Her begging isn't enough, and she knows it. But it *kills* her.

And it kills me too. I want my dick so deep inside of her cunt that my width rips through her esophagus. Fuck! I want to destroy her.

"Please. Please. Please," she shouts. "Just fuck me, Cash. Please fuck me. Use me. Own me. I'm yours. Please. Just fuck me."

I stab my cock inside of her, ripping her apart, her pussy straining to meet my size. Her eyes widen, she screams, and her body revolts from me, twitching out of the way, but I press her down with my shoulders, my chest, my stomach, my legs, every heavy part of my body keeping her down, keeping her compliant. Once the sensation of my big meaty dick cools and her pussy stretches for me, I pulse my hips, rocking my dick inside of her, deeper, and deeper, until I ram into the tip of her cervix. Her eyes close and I keep rocking my dick into her. She wraps her legs and arms around me, cocooning me in her scent, refusing to let go. I boom with laughter, then tighten the chain around her neck until her face bulges red, and her pussy constricts around me with each missed breath, desperate for more.

I give the chain some slack and as soon as her mouth opens, gasping for air, I spit into her mouth, letting it drip down onto her tongue. She licks her lips, swallowing it down.

"That's good, isn't it?" I say. "You can spit on me all you want, but you're going to swallow my spit like it's the last drink you'll ever have."

She moans, then opens her mouth. "More. Please," she cries. And I spit again and she swallows it down, such a needy, desperate little slut. Her velvet walls clench around me, her black-chipped fingernails digging into my back. Both of us slick with sweat. She feels so fucking good. Like my first kill. Like an adrenaline rush of almost getting caught. Like the car crash where I finally killed my foster mom after she molested me. Remedy feels like everything. Like power. Like control. Like need. Her limbs cling around me. The salty sweat on her skin. Her labored breath. As her lips part, I shove my dick even farther inside of her, then spit into her mouth again.

"Swallow it," I say. She knows what to do, but her eyes roll back into her skull; she loves hearing those demands. "Swallow it down like a good little fuck doll. Fuck, Remedy. You are so damn hot."

I lean down, breathing onto her supple lips, and I thrust inside of her like it's the last time she'll ever be fucked. She howls like prey that knows that this is the end, but every twitch proves that she loves it.

"You hate me," I say in her ear, biting down on the lobe, "but you hate yourself for knowing what I can do for you. Because you fucking love it. You need it. You need *me*. You haven't been able to come without thinking of me since I first twisted your nipples like the greedy little fuck bitch you are. Tell me you love it when I own you like this."

"Fuck. You," she hisses, sputtering out each word. And still, she doesn't tell me to go. She refuses to tell me to stop.

"Who do you hate more?" I laugh. "Is it me or you?"

"Shut up and let me come," she cries.

"I don't hate you," I say. I keep riding her cunt, splitting her apart. "No. I fucking need you like you need me. I've been fucking myself every day and every night. The anger in your bright green eyes. Your slippery pussy. Your smooth, tight little ass. The purple lipstick, matching your face when I choke you. And damn it, the smell. When you're wet or nervous, you smell like tangy peaches. Those tattoos on your stomach and pussy like you're such a bad girl. Or the skeleton tattoos on your back like they mean something. Like they're *us*. Because that's all we are. It doesn't matter who I am to you because we're just bones. And I own you, Remedy." My hips pulsate, my cock swelling bigger inside of her tight walls, her face contorting in pain. She's breathless, waiting for me to finish her off. "Now you're going to come on my dick while I choke you."

Her eyes widen and I pull the chain, her cheeks flushing red. I press into her, rubbing my body against her clit, her pussy crushing me like it's the last shot we have.

"Please," she rasps out, the words barely audible. "Please. Please. Plea—"

"Who owns your pussy?" I bellow.

She doesn't hesitate: "You do. You own my pussy!"

"Come for me," I demand, my voice vibrating through her. "Come for me. Right fucking *now*."

My dick hammers inside of her and when her cheeks turn purple, her velvet walls grasp around me, fighting back. Her nails scrape my back, the pain searing my body, making me let go of the chain for half of a second, but I don't stop pounding into her cervix. I ram my dick harder and harder until she convulses around me like a feral animal, her moan primal and cathartic.

As the last spasms of her orgasm dull, I pull out. She sprawls out on the tile, her body drenched in sweat, her legs smothered with come. My back stings like hell; she probably cut me. But I hold my dick in my fist, fucking myself as she gains composure. Her tank top is still bunched above her tits, each bell of flesh hanging to the side, her brown nipples still perked and blushing. Her skirt is on her hips like a loose belt, covering that tattooed artwork. A faint purple line crosses her neck: a bruise from the choke chain, my necklace to her. A blood vessel stains her eye—it probably popped from straining against the choke chain—and it bleeds like a red firework into the whites of her eyes, matching the birthmarks in mine. It'll take a few weeks to heal, but then it'll disappear like it never existed. But still, my dick fills with blood, knowing that she won't be able to hide that mark from anyone.

She tries to sit up, but she's defeated. Exhaustion overwhelms her, and that makes me come. My dick throbs and I let each drop fall on her skin and clothes, marking her, claiming her with my come. Like drops of primer on the side of an empty paint can. Used up. Ready to be discarded.

And what a wild ride.

Her green eyes blink up at me, hazy and heavy. She's tired, and seeing her like that makes me want to wake her up with my dick again. She's beautiful.

A drop of sweat or blood trails down my back. I ignore it and kneel, brushing the hair out of her eyes, painting her with a drop of my come. I fix her clothes as best as I can, then scoop her into my arms. She resists me, pushing against my chest, but she quickly realizes that she can't do anything, and gives up, resting in my arms. Her head finds its place against my chest, and I wonder if she can hear my heartbeat in there. If I have anything human left.

I lay her down on the mattress. She blinks up at me, but her eyes are already gone. She's barely conscious.

"Why am I so tired?" she yawns.

"Have you forgotten your name yet?" I ask.

She blinks at me in confusion, but I remember every single word: *I want you to make me come so hard I forget who I am.* Finally, recognition flashes behind her pupils, and she laughs. Her smile burns inside of me, genuine amusement behind it that I haven't seen or felt in a long time.

I excuse myself, then find the bag of screws and hinges, then grab the small toolbox I left inside of the hatch in her closet. I fix her door. I only messed with it enough so that she'd have to ask me for help, so it's an easy fix. Then I check the handle on her refrigerator. It *is* loose, but all it needs is some glue, so I fix it too.

When I return to her room, she's already asleep. Her nostrils flare. I reach down, skimming my fingertips over the purple and red marks on her neck. A warmth circulates inside of me, knowing that I did this to her. That she survived it. That I *let* her. I can't explain my feelings for her. If I want what's best for myself, I'll kill her right now. After what we did, she won't have much of a fight. It will be easy. And in some ways, it's the right thing to do. Once she learns I've ruined her life, she'll beg me to end her. They always do.

But I don't want her to die yet. She can handle more than I expected, and it's selfish of me, but I want her to live. To see how far she can go. To pry open each of her senses until she's got nothing left. Like me.

I stroke her cheek, the softness of her skin filling me with dread. But my cock ignores that. Because in the end, all I want is her.

"You're no good to me dead," I say. "Not yet."

I close the door, making sure her windows and doors are locked. Then I let her sleep.

Chapter 7

Remedy

The late afternoon light shines through the blinds, casting strips of shadows on the floor. The doorbell rings again and I wrap the black scarf around my neck; I'm not used to uninvited visitors. I squint into the front door's peephole: shaggy, reddish-blond hair, a loose shirt, and jeans on a tall, slim frame. Detective Peter Samuels. My old high school friend.

I open the door. "It's still weird seeing you in regular clothes."

Peter scratches the scruff on his chin. His facial hair is longer than usual, like he wants to reject the image of being a cop. He bends down to give me a quick hug, and I pat his back in return.

"How are you, Remmie?" he asks. He cocks a brow. "Jesus. What happened to your eye?"

I touch my face. I forgot about the popped blood vessel. "I sneezed?"

He whistles. "Must have been one hell of a sneeze."

I laugh, my cheeks burning red. I hope he believes me. "You want some sweet tea?" I ask.

"Please."

Peter stays on the front porch while I close the door behind me, fixing our drinks inside. Since we've known each other since high school, he knows I prefer to visit on the front porch. He just doesn't know that it's because I hate being alone with certain men.

And yet, I let Cash physically destroy me, and I welcomed him inside. I *invited* him.

I don't understand it.

Peter mumbles his thanks, then takes a long swig. He sighs with relief, then gestures at the scarf around my neck. "Cold?"

"It's weird. If my neck is cold, the rest of me freezes." I shrug, trying to play it off. Cars pass on the street like usual. It's like you can almost forget that there's a serial killer loose during the day. "But what's going on?"

"You heard about Dry & Clean?" he asks. I nod, looking down the street in the shop's direction; it's only a block away. "Came to see if you've heard anything. Any visitors lately? Anyone at all? Maybe like a random tourist asking to use your phone?" He counts on his fingers. "Your mom? Your stepdad? Your landlord? Something like that?"

I tap my lip, thinking over the last few weeks, but nothing out-of-the-ordinary pops up.

"Just Jenna," I say. He jots a note on his phone. A sinking feeling fills my stomach; I left one important detail out.

Cash has visited twice.

But Cash lives close enough that Peter is probably questioning him too. And if I say anything right now, he'll bother him more than necessary, and if they do that, there's a risk that he'll retreat further into his shell. He's doing well, breaking out of his reclusive bubble. I can't ruin that for him.

But I should probably say something.

"All right, your bestie. Anyone else?" Peter asks.

"My boss came by once," I say quickly. "Dropped off some paperwork." I cross my fingers, hoping that covers it up.

"Name?"

"Cassius Winstone."

"You're kidding. Winstone?" Peter laughs. "You got Winstone to come out of his tower?"

I press my lips together. "Don't be too hard on him."

"I'll go easy on him," he winks. "Anyone else?"

I shake my head. "You think the murderer is someone local?"

He angles himself closer to me like he's ready to tell me a dirty secret, and instinctively, I scoot back. Then I steady myself; I need to be able to hear him, and I don't want him to think that I'm uncomfortable. I pretend like I'm fixing my scarf, then lean closer to him.

"It's someone who knows Key West," he says. "We think it's one person. Every so often, there's a slip. This guy thinks he's smarter than us, and yeah, he's making us work, but eventually, even if it takes years, they always get caught. He isn't *that* smart, you know?" I nod, pretending like I understand what that means, but my skin prickles, like the killer is watching us right now, choosing us as his next victims. "The mayor is considering a curfew," Peter says, wiping his nose on the back of his hand. "You're being safe, right?"

If by being safe, he means that I'm keeping to myself and staying out of trouble, then yes. But when it comes to Cash, I haven't been safe at all. And yet that's what I expect from Cash. I know what I want from him, and he knows how to tear it from my soul. We work well that way.

And somehow, with Peter, I don't actually know what to expect. His badge promises protection, but he reminds me of my stepdad. My mom swore up and down that my stepdad was a good man, great with kids, that I would love him, and she's said similar things about Peter. A dull ache fills my stomach as I force a smile. Even as I study him now—his boyish red hair, his light blue eyes, his gentle demeanor—I can't let it go. Those rumors from high school never left my head; who drugs a girl and becomes a cop, if he's innocent?

"Safe as I always am," I say, which is almost the truth. "This one is troubling you guys, huh?"

"We think the murders are connected to the crawl space murders in Montana a few years ago," he says. "You remember that?"

I don't pay attention to the news. I never have time for it, unless my boss—whoever I'm assigned to at the time—specifically asks for a recap. But it makes me cringe. This is bigger than Key West? Nausea twists in my stomach. I steady myself, resting against the exterior of the house.

"Not really," I say. "How do you know it's a 'he'?"

Peter glances toward the street like he knows the killer is right there, under his nose. "It's a man," he says. "I can feel it."

I roll my eyes. As if I need another reason not to trust any of the men in this town. Peter lifts his shoulder and taps the house.

"Well, be safe about it, you know?" he says. "That's all you can do. By the way, how's your mama doing? I saw her on Duval a couple of days ago. New man?"

The double date! I completely forgot about it. For a second, I consider bringing Peter as a friend. Mom would be over the moon, and maybe if we have enough time together, I can convince him to *really* start looking into my stepdad. But if I tell Peter what I need—that I truly enjoy the darker, depraved side of sex—he'll try to fix me, like my ex.

Peter isn't an option, no matter how much Mom tries to plant the seed.

"I haven't met the new man yet," I say.

"Tell her I said 'hi,'" he says. He squeezes my shoulder, then keeps his hand there to comfort me. "Are you okay? You look a little pale."

I sink under his weight, and he's pushing me deeper into quicksand. My fingertips graze my cheek. Peter is a friend from high school. His job is to protect Key West. But when he touches my shoulder again, I bite the inside of my lip. He smiles at me, and I see my stepdad in him, hiding behind a trustworthy smile.

Is Peter a protector, or is he the Key West Killer?

I close my eyes, then open them slowly, regaining my composure. Forcing myself to act like everything is fine.

"Just a little tired," I say.

He slurps the rest of his tea, then pats my shoulder. "I'll let you rest, then. Thanks for letting me stop by. See you around."

I wave as he drives away. All I want is to call Cash. It's my day off; I'm not supposed to think about him. But that urge grows inside of me, and I see his face: those dark, spotted eyes, hunting me.

Even though he practically tried to choke me to death the night before, I want to see him.

As I dial him, I tell myself that the only way to sabotage, or even kill him, is to make him trust me, and to do that, I need to be clever. And that includes having sex with him. It may be an excuse, but it's a good one. I leave a voicemail with another repair request.

Ten minutes later, Cash calls me from the porch. As soon as I open the front door, his expression shifts like he can see something inside of me that I don't see myself. His shoulders tighten, his mouth sours, and those ominous eyes capture me.

"What's wrong?" he asks.

"Nothing," I automatically say. I motion inside. Why is he still standing out there anyway?

"Tell me what's wrong," he demands.

I tilt my head. "Aren't you worried about being out in the open like that?"

"What's wrong, Remedy?" he asks, his voice stern. He glares at me like it doesn't matter if he's out in public. But I pull his arm, yanking him inside. An overwhelming chemical odor permeates the air, and his clothes are lightly dusted like he's been working on a construction project. I don't remember anything like that on his schedule. I guide him over to the round table in the kitchen, and we sit down a few feet away from where he fucked me on the floor. My belly tingles at the memory. And I realize something.

He's been out of the estate a few times, so standing on the porch probably won't bother him. And yet, I still made him come inside with me.

His cloudy eyes simmer with demands. He hasn't let go of his concern over me.

"Something's wrong," he says.

"Nothing's wrong!" I laugh. "You're worse than my mom."

"I'm not playing, Remedy," he growls. "Tell me what's wrong, or I will fuck the words out of your right now."

I crunch my teeth down until the pain surges in my skull. How does he read me like this? I almost want to give in to that threat, but I also want to tell him the truth. It has everything to do with Peter touching my shoulder, how he reminds me of my stepdad. I can't bring myself to tell Cash about my stepdad yet, but I can tell him about Peter.

"My friend came by," I say.

"Jenna?"

"Different friend. The cop friend I told you about." I try to read Cash's facial expression, to see if he's jealous that a man came by. But he doesn't shift at all. "He asked about the murders. Wanted to see if I knew anything."

"And those murders scare you?"

We always try to fix these rules and connections between the criminals and these horrific deaths, to assert meaning when there is none. And a killer like that isn't going to be interested in someone like me. In the end, it comes down to luck. The wrong place at the wrong time. No one can prevent something like that.

I shake my head. "I just don't trust cops."

"Who do you trust?"

I blink. Cash is asking about Peter, but he's also asking if I trust him. And I don't know. I'm supposed to hate Cash more than anyone in the Keys, and yet I keep drawing closer to him. I'm like an insect chasing his sugary scent.

I can't answer his question, so instead, I ask, "Why don't you hate me?"

The corners of his mouth lift, but then he drops back into his stoic expression. It's almost like he doesn't appreciate that I've caught him off guard by asking questions he doesn't know the answer to, but I don't know what else to say.

"I've tried to kill you multiple times now," I explain. "Shouldn't you hate me? Or at least fire me? If anything, *you* shouldn't trust *me*. Why do you care if I feel like crap when I'm around cops?"

A real grin forms on his face, dissolving the cold, detached expression, and a strange warmth washes over me. Cash is a billionaire real estate developer, my best friend's abuser, my black-mailer, and the only person who has ever made me come. But he also seems like the only man who listens to me, who actually tries to understand where I'm coming from. And I can't wrap my head around it.

"Your murder attempts were an act of passion," he says in a matter-of-fact tone, a subtle emphasis on the word 'attempts,' almost like he's teasing me for failing. "Why should I hate you for doing what you want? I do what I want too."

"But you've stayed inside of your estate for years," I blurt out. "Isn't that being *caged* by your desires?"

He bares his teeth, and for a split second, he looks like a wolf. I'm his red riding hood, but this time, there's no one to save me. I'm alone with my wolf.

The anger dissipates, relaxing his shoulders. "That passion is the real side of you," he says, ignoring my question. "Not much interests me anymore. But when a person has passion like that, a desire that drives them to murder?" He licks his lips. "That interests me. I like that about you."

My cheeks flutter with heat, burning under his gaze. I clear my throat, tossing my hair over my shoulders, then quickly adjust the bobby pins. But the question flashes in my mind: is he *encouraging* my emotions?

He's so different from my mom, my ex, even Peter. And though I like that about him, it confuses me. What does it mean when you're actually *seen* by a man who assaulted your best friend and trapped you in an arrangement where you're his fuck doll?

I can't figure it out. In a panic, I change the subject.

"What are *you* passionate about?" I ask.

"You."

A chill runs through me. *I'm just his fuck doll,* I tell myself. *This means nothing.* But he's not talking about our arrangement anymore, and he knows it. Every nerve in my body tingles like butterflies trapped in a net. It's like he's been planning this for a long time, even before we met.

But he's been a recluse until recently. I would've remembered those freckles in his eyes, like wrinkles on the surface of a dark pond.

Before I can stop myself, I blurt out: "Go on a double date with me." I smack my hands across my mouth, realizing my error. He's my boss. My blackmailer. My enemy. What am I doing? I shrink behind my shoulders. I don't want to take it back. "Please," I whisper.

His lips curl in amusement. "A double date?"

I suck in a breath. "My mom has been bugging me to meet her new boyfriend, and if I go alone, she'll keep insisting that we arrange a double date until I finally give in. My guess is that it has something to do with proving that her new boyfriend isn't that bad. Like, as long as my date doesn't see red flags, then nothing can be wrong." I sigh to myself. That's probably too much info, but I don't care. "It'll be at her apartment. Game night and pizza. We'll be inside. It'll be a good step to—" I raise my hands, "—reintegration?"

He lifts his chin, actually considering the idea. But that nerve in the back of my skull pokes me. How can someone go from newspaper-covered and concrete-covered windows, to being okay with anything, even standing on a front porch? Would he actually be okay with a double date at my mom's house?

"What's in it for me?" he asks, like we're bartering goods.

"That's not enough?"

"Reintegration is a chore, not a desire."

His nostrils flare as he studies me, and I try to think of something I can offer him. It seems so stupid to invite him—but *if* he comes, mom will let go of the idea. *And* Cash will be out of his element.

I may be able to get revenge. I can poison him like he assumed the other night. And if it comes down to it, my mom will have my back.

"What do you want?" I ask.

"Think of your biggest offer, then triple it."

"Why?" I snicker. "What's so hard about a double date?"

"I've never cared to meet family."

I squint at him, trying to read between the lines. His eyes darken, knowing that I have nothing to give.

In the long run, Cash and I are business. I just need someone to tag along.

"It's not like we're getting engaged," I insist. "I'll tell my mom that you're my boss, not my boyfriend. She won't care."

"That's an add-on, not an exchange."

I flatten my palms to my sides. I try to think of what a supposed recluse billionaire wants. He likes tormenting me, but apparently hates double dates and family. What's the best mix of both worlds?

"You can see how awkward and awful it is for me to meet my mom's new boyfriend?" I offer.

"I don't care."

My face reddens. He's serious; he doesn't find my joke funny at all.

"You can screw me in my old bedroom," I say.

A twist of lust crosses him like he's considering it now.

"I can fuck you right here if I want."

A chill runs through me. "It's hard for me to be in my old room," I explain, trying to appeal to his twisted side. "You like seeing me squirm? Trust me; I don't want to be in that bed." And yet the thought of being in that bed *with Cash* makes my thighs part. Maybe he can help me take back those memories. "And after that, you can embarrass me in front of my mom and her new boyfriend, making innuendos and bawdy jokes. I don't care. I just *don't* want to suffer through this alone."

A few seconds pass between us. I clench my sweaty palms, then rub them against my pants. *Please*, I beg internally. *Please. Just give me this.*

"Honestly, Remedy, I don't care about any of that." He tilts his head, a hint of irritation in his voice. "Is that why you brought me here? To be your accomplice?"

My stomach seizes with nerves. "I just thought—"

"Meeting your mother, sitting through a family dinner, shit-talking about her new boyfriend? That doesn't appeal to me any more than going to a zoo. The only way I'd be interested is if I get to fuck you over the dinner table in front of them."

Everything inside of me is on fire. The image of him fucking me over the round dinner table in my mom's apartment flashes in my mind, the vision real and enticing: Red cheeks. The choke chain around my neck. Cash holding the chain tight enough to make me struggle, but not enough to keep me from talking. *Tell*

87

them that you're mine, he'd say. My chest banging into the table as my mom stares at me, jaw dropped, her only daughter writhing like a whore. But in that vision, I'm doing it to prove that I can control my body. I can indulge, even if it means my destruction.

It almost sounds nice.

Cash stands from the table, then squeezes my shoulder in the exact place that Peter did. But with Cash, his touch doesn't bother me. I lean into him, and his hand moves to the back of my neck, rubbing my tender muscles. Shivers travel down my spine.

"Think of something better to offer me, and I'll consider it," he says. "Or bring your cop friend." There's a subtle hint of jealousy in his voice, like he can read my thoughts and knows that I actually considered Peter *before* him. My stomach drops with nerves. He rips the scarf from my neck until it's loose in my lap. "And when you're around me, lose the fucking coverup."

I touch my neck, blinking rapidly, completely stunned. But in an instant, he's gone and I'm alone again.

CHAPTER 8

CASH

ANOTHER DAY PASSES AND THE SUN BEATS DOWN AS IT GETS READY to set, letting everyone in Key West forget that it's winter. Lush palm trees hang over the narrow pool, shielding the back porch of the estate from the rest of the street. Moisture clings to my skin, the salt drifting in the air. But no matter how much luxury or beauty surrounds me, I only think about her.

Remedy with my blood striping her nose. Her cheeks rust-red. The purple bruise on her neck. The popped vessel in her eye, matching the freckles in mine. The lacey tattoos covering her like armor. The skeletons on her back, mocking the world.

I need to establish boundaries between us. For fuck's sake, she wants to play house, like I'm her fiancé, and even though going on that god-forsaken double date will give me a clue on how best to frame her, it's the exact opposite of everything I stand for. The only family dinners I remember from the foster care system ended in blood, and I'm not willing to relive that because Remedy has an intriguing penchant for violent lust.

Bones lazily weaves herself in and out of my feet, her body vibrating with purrs. I scratch behind her ears before she hops up the wooden stairs leading to the master bedroom's balcony. Just like Remedy, Bones is supposed to be gone by now, but she keeps sticking around. Giving her food doesn't help. It's like Bones *and* Remedy are my newest pets, and they both think they have more autonomy than they actually do.

Am I going soft?

I follow Bones up to the balcony, then settle down on the cushioned wicker sectional, propping my feet on a throw pillow. When it comes to Remedy, the thought of fucking her in front of her mother intrigues me, and I know, without a doubt, that I can make Remedy do it. But it can also derail my plans. I can't push Remedy too far if I want to keep manipulating her. In a situation like this, you have to move with careful deliberation. You have to make her think it's her own volition.

Perhaps there's something else I can do, showing her that as much as she wants to believe that it's blackmail, she *wants* me. Even if she wants to kill me too.

Just like I want to frame or kill her.

But not until I'm done.

I roll the cuffs of my shirt, concealing my tan lines. I may as well go to that stupid dinner date; I can use it against her.

I dial Remedy, sucking in a full breath. The phone rings then goes to voicemail: *Hi, this is Remedy Basset. Leave a message and I'll—*

I hang up. It's not like her to miss a call. What's she doing?

She got off of work an hour ago, but her LPA contract dictates that she has to be available at *all* times to ensure her bonus at the end of the year. She never ignores my calls.

I tap my fingers on the woven armrest. With some effort, I find a loose reed and yank it up, sewing it in and out of the fibers until I finally snap it off. I check the app that's connected to her webcam, but her laptop is closed; there's no image. My temple pulses. *I'm* the one who ignores phone calls. *I'm* the one who makes those decisions. *I'm* the one who controls her.

I dial again.

No answer.

I glance in the direction of her home. There's always another option.

I park my truck a few blocks away from her rental house. As I approach, my blood boils: another car, one I don't recognize, sits behind her red sedan. Another fucking truck. Once I confirm with a quick check that she's in her bedroom with whoever the hell it is, I find her spare key and go through the back door. I keep the locks on the properties well-oiled; it helps when people can't hear you enter.

Inside of the hall closet, I close the door behind me, then let myself into the hatch and inch across the crawl space to the wall cavity, bumping up against the hard foam insulation. In the peephole, I see her desk. Her closed laptop. A bottle of lime soda opened next to it.

Remedy doesn't drink soda.

Then I hear a male voice.

Who the fuck is that? And why is she *alone* with him?

I snap my jaw together so hard, my teeth grind. *I'm* the one who gets to be alone with her. Not this garbage. I strain closer, pressing my ear to the inner wall. I need to hear everything.

"But you quit SAA, right?" he asks.

Does he mean Sex Addicts Anonymous? If Remedy quit, then that means that she was a member for a while.

"I told you: just because I like it rough doesn't mean I'm an addict," she says.

My stomach hardens. I want to pinch the bridge of my nose, but in the wall cavity, I can't do anything. I'm stuck listening.

"You don't like it rough; you like it brutal," he chuckles.

The fact that he knows that means they're close. That he knows her intimately. Spots flash in my vision as I strain to see through the peephole, to get one peek at that bastard so I can commit his image to memory. I swear to the world that if he lays a hand on her, I will cut him up on top of her.

I'm losing my mind.

"So?" Remedy asks.

"So, that's what I'm saying. I've been thinking about it. Maybe it's a phase you're going through. We can have fun, even if it is a little—" he pauses, "—weird. Everyone's weird, right? We can help each other out."

A slight beat passes, then I see his hand—long fingers wrapping around the soda bottle, a fraternity ring on his finger. But I need more than a frat organization, or the Key West Killer's list of victims is going to get very long, very quickly.

"Are you going to actually choke me this time?" she asks.

I clench my fists. I'm going to kill him.

"Choke you? Let's do something a little more mainstream. I don't know. I could spank you?"

Remedy sucks in a breath, and I scrape the inner wall with my knuckles, wishing I could touch her. To run my hands over her bruises and scabbed skin, telling her she doesn't have to fall back on this poser. She knows he'll spank her ass like he's tapping her shoulder in a library, the kind of man who politely asks for what he wants.

Fuck. That.

"You mean like a love tap?" Remedy asks, her tone irritated. Heat rushes through me. *That's my girl.*

"Come on, Remmie. Give me more credit than that."

"What am I supposed to say? We broke up over a year ago because you thought I was too—" I can imagine it now; she's raising her hands, struggling to find the right words, "—too perverted!"

Silence lingers between them. I flatten my palms at my sides, trying to get into Remedy's head, that nervous tick she has when something makes her uncomfortable. But my fingers keep curling into fists, knowing that *he's* in there, with *her,* my little cure.

"We always said we'd give it another try if we worked through our issues," he says. "And Remmie, I've been working hard to learn. To make things better. To understand why you need that." His footsteps creak against the floor, getting closer to her. "I may never understand, but I want to, Remedy. And I know we can work through this phase. You know we're good together."

Instinct tells me that they had sex even after they broke up. Even with SAA and the lack of a stable relationship, the ex convinced Remedy to settle for his passable dick. I don't blame her for that. I've done similar things in the past.

But not anymore. For either of us. I will cut off his head if I have to.

She crosses the bedroom, pacing past the peephole. A white scarf coils around her neck. He passes in front of the peephole too, his hand reaching out to touch her.

My blood boils, but I don't understand it. Why do I care?

"Dean," she whispers, her voice distraught. Dean. Dean. *Dean.* Perhaps he's a banker. An accountant. A dentist. Someone who can provide for her, but will never get dirty. A man her mother probably *wishes* Remedy would marry. Dean is the person who is supposed to take Remedy to dinner.

Dean. What a name.

And that's all I need to hunt.

"You haven't been dating. I know you're waiting for us," Dean says. "I've been waiting for you too, Remmie. You don't wait for someone unless you love them."

As earnest as his delivery is, I doubt it's true.

"First you say you want to hook up, and now, you're pretending like we're waiting for each other?" Remedy forces a laugh. "It's been over a year, Dean. I'm over you."

His voice softens: "I know we're good together, Remmie."

She sighs, then crosses the room again. "Just because I haven't been dating doesn't mean I'm not fucking someone."

Ah. There she is. My little cure.

"Who have you been fucking?" he asks.

"Whoever I want."

He leans on the desk, and I can see him now, that angled chin, his cocky attitude shot down.

"Damn it, Remedy."

"You don't own me. You *never* have."

He's probably shaking his head like a wind-up toy. But her words stop me.

Dean doesn't own her. *But I do.*

"You promised you wouldn't do stuff like that anymore," he says. "SAA was supposed to—"

"I've been seeing someone," she says, interrupting him, a

jarring confession to get Dean to shut up. And he does. My chest tightens, my breathing hoarse, waiting for her explanation. Will she claim me, or will I have more victims to kill?

"Who?" he finally asks.

"Cash."

Saliva gathers in my throat, a sour taste on my tongue.

She's claiming me.

What the fuck does that mean?

"What kind of name is 'Cash'?" he asks.

"Cassius Winstone."

"Your *boss?*"

"What? You screwed your student!"

"*After* she passed my class. Before I met you. It's different when you're fucking your boss."

His shoes crunch across the hard floor, meeting her on the other side of the room. I can sense their presence past the inner wall. In my mind, I see him staring into her bright green eyes, giving her his practiced look of adoration. My palm teases the knife in my pocket. It's been a long time since I gouged a person's eyes out.

"I just want to make love to you, baby. Isn't that enough?"

Baby? The word crawls down my spine like molasses dripping down a tree trunk. *Baby?* What the fuck is that?

"Why are you his assistant anyway?" he asks. "You could be doing so much better. You could be *running* LPA if you wanted right now."

The walls breathe with her weight. She's so damn close.

"I'm right where I want to be," she says, her voice vibrating through the walls.

"He'll never see you as more than a secretary."

The walls shift again, and I know she's walking away, because she knows it may be true.

But I'm trying to accept her double date invitation, for fuck's sake.

"What is your problem?" she asks. "You had enough time to be jealous. Now get out."

He follows her, his footsteps thudding across the room. "Come on, Remmie."

"Leave."

He crosses in front of the peephole, reaching for her.

"Don't touch me," she hisses.

Their voices murmur on the other side, but I'm done listening. I'm not going to watch her take her ex-boyfriend's bullshit anymore.

No one is going to take her away from me.

I kick the hatch closed, then slam the closet door behind me. Each of my steps pounds through the rental house.

"What the hell is that?" Remedy shouts. A man with shit brown hair and shit brown eyes fills the doorframe to her bedroom. His shoulders puff up like he thinks he can actually do something.

"Get the fuck out," Dean says, his fists up in the air, ready to box. "Stay back! I'll call the police!"

He's tall, but I'm slightly taller. And he *looks* muscular underneath his button-up shirt and sweater vest, but strength alone isn't enough to beat someone like me.

I glare at him, daring him to fight me.

"Call the police," I say. "I'm not trespassing."

His jaw hangs open. Remedy appears behind him, her eyes wide and her mouth gaping.

"Who are you?" Dean asks.

I'm Remedy's landlord. Her boss. Her fucking savior.

But he's not worth my answer. Only she is.

I turn my full attention to her.

"My little cure," I say. I lick my lips, her peachy scent enveloping me like drizzling rain. Dean shifts, trying to get between us, blocking me from her, but I reach for her hand, and she takes mine as if Dean isn't there. Her fingers are small and cold. The chipped black nail polish reminds me of her scabs on my back, and my muscles tense, stretching the healing skin. She's marked me too. Her bright green eyes hold me like I'm the truth she's been waiting for, and I let my fingertips travel up to the back of her neck, the scarf scratchy on my rough palm, hiding our secrets from him. She doesn't want him to worry about her. And that unnerves me. Why does she care what he thinks?

But then it comes to me: the scarf is to protect me too. So that no one knows that I'm hurting her.

Because she doesn't want to be saved.

"Cash," she whispers.

CHAPTER 9

REMEDY

MY HEART BEATS LIKE A HUMMINGBIRD SKITTERING AWAY FROM A feral cat. Cash's dark freckled eyes gaze down at me, like he knows that he's caught me in the middle of his trap. He's the owner of the house, but how did he get inside? Did he bring his own key, or does he know where I keep my spare? Why is he here?

And why am I relieved?

"*This* is Cash?" Dean asks, gesturing at him. "Your *boss?*"

My eyes flicker between the two of them. Dean's fluffy brown hair, light eyes, and the 'kindness' he always gives me, are so different from the darkness that consumes Cash. His black hair. His rolled-up sleeves showing off his strong, muscular forearms. His dark, spotted eyes, like inkblots melting together on a page, blurring the meaning of any message. The veins in his neck constantly throb, like he's always ready to fight. Like he wants to kill Dean. But why would he kill Dean?

And what am I supposed to do with my ex-boyfriend and my current boss-with-benefits in the same room?

"Introduce me to your friend," Cash says, his voice low, a hint of contempt boiling in the word 'friend.' As if *that* is a betrayal in and of itself.

Is Cash jealous of Dean?

"Cash, this is Dean," I say, swallowing hard as I make eye

contact with Cash. He holds my gaze. "And Dean, this is Cash Winstone."

"Mr. Winstone," Cash says. My chest tightens at that correction, and I lean back as the two of them shake hands, clearly sizing each other up. Dean broadens his shoulders like he's going to protect me from Cash, but Cash's eyes stay unmoved, like he knows exactly what he's going to do to Dean. My heart palpitates. Dean gawks at the freckles marking the whites of Cash's eyes.

"What's wrong with your eyes?" he asks.

"What the hell, Dean?" I ask, smacking him in the arm. "That's rude."

Dean rubs his arm, ignoring me. "I thought you were older," he says.

"Plastic surgery works wonders," Cash says, almost like a threat.

Dean angles his body in between us, to block Cash from my bedroom. "What can we do for you, Mr. Winstone?" he asks.

Cash's brows perk up, noticing *that* word, like I do. *We.* But Dean and I haven't been a 'we' in a long time. Why is he trying to protect me from Cash?

In a way, Dean's instincts are right. Cash is a manipulative, power-hunger asshole boss. But he's not going to hurt me like *that.*

Not before I hurt him first.

"Where's your phone?" Cash asks, his attention focused solely on me. My cheeks flush. *Damn it!* I forgot to take my phone off silent. I grab it out of my purse and quickly check the two missed calls, both from Cash. Sweat beads on my body, a dank odor coming from my armpits. I'm always supposed to be available, or I can lose my bonus or even my job at the agency. LPA has a huge contract with the Winstone Company, and I can't afford these errors.

And Cash *still* has that blackmail video that he can hold over me.

"It's off of silent, now," I mutter.

"I tried to warn you I was coming by. You wanted me to check on your maintenance order?"

I blink rapidly, trying to figure out what he's referring to.

Maintenance order? Cash licks his teeth, and I realize that he's trying to give me a cover so that Dean doesn't know why he's really here: our arrangement. Maybe he's even trying to get Dean to leave.

I tug the scarf around my neck; it's too hot to wear clothes like this indoors, especially with Cash, but I have to wear it around Dean.

"Yeah. About that," I say. "Thanks for coming by."

"Maintenance order?" Dean asks.

"I told you about my fridge door, remember?"

Dean shakes his head, but before he can say a word, Cash interrupts: "When my time allows it, I make personal visits to ensure everything is satisfactory in my properties."

"This is Remedy's house," Dean says. "You have no business being here."

"Dean," I snap. What the hell is he doing?

"It's her rental, actually. One of mine," Cash says.

Dean's jaw drops and I lift my shoulders. "The agency has a deal with the Winstone Company. Cheaper rent for access to the workers."

"And I like to make sure everything is to my standards," Cash says. He checks his watch. "What do you do, *Dean?*"

Dean scratches his jaw, his posture rigid. "I teach at the community college."

Cash nods like he expects this. "It's the same situation with tenants. You understand the importance of creating bonds with your students, then. If you're just another nameless, faceless person who pushes another faceless person's ideology around—if you don't *listen* to your students' needs, and truly understand what's important to their experience—then how will they trust you to teach them anything of value?"

They stare at each other, and though Dean bows his head to agree, I know he's pissed. But Cash has the upper hand, and Cash isn't talking about teaching community college or rental properties. He's talking about *me.* Like he knows Dean will never truly understand me.

Does Cash know that Dean is my ex?

"Let me walk you out," Cash says. He puts a hand on Dean's shoulder, gripping him hard enough that his knuckles turn white. My stomach twists. There's violence in the way they're approaching each other, and for some stupid reason, I know if anyone wins, it'll be Cash. And that scares me for Dean.

"Cash?" I ask right as they reach the door. Cash waits. "Be nice," I say, pleading with my eyes. Cash nods and I sink inside of myself with nerves. Dean keeps his shoulders straight like he's ready to fight Cash, but he couldn't kill a fly, and I know Cash will do anything to destroy Dean. I bite my inner lip.

What's going on?

Cash returns shortly without Dean. Dean's truck rumbles outside, and I let out a sigh. I'm relieved. Dean is gone and Cash didn't have time to do anything to him.

Cash enters my bedroom, settling himself on the wall opposite of me, crossing his arms. The stubble on his face is slightly longer than usual, like he forgot to trim his beard this morning. He's been losing sleep. I want to hold him and thank him for being there for me.

And I want to slap him. Why is he here anyway? Even if this is his house, it's *my* rental.

I throw up my hands in exasperation. "What are you doing here?"

Cash tilts his head toward my phone on the nightstand. "You didn't answer my calls."

"So you break into my house?"

"Not your house," he says, locking his eyes with mine. "I was in the area, and I'm sure you've read the rental agreement. Owners can come into the house at any time." He doesn't budge, like he's daring me to challenge him. I don't know if he's lying about the lease, but I know the real reason he's here: he doesn't like that I was unavailable.

"Everywhere in Key West is 'in the area,'" I mock.

"Not necessarily."

"How did you get in?"

"Spare key on top of the doorframe in the back." He checks

his cuff sleeves. "If you don't like that the spare key is so obvious, then hide it better."

I narrow my eyes. "Do you have a copy of the key at the estate?"

"Of course."

This is the second time he's shown up in my rental house without an invitation. It's like he's infiltrating my life.

But part of me is glad. Dean won't hurt anyone to get what he wants, but sometimes, he's so nice that he's hard to push away. And after a while, I get so mad that I give in, because I want to connect to someone for a while, even if it is a disappointment. And I don't want to do that anymore. I have Cash. I know what I deserve.

Still, that doesn't give Cash any right to barge in like that.

"Why didn't you knock?" I ask.

"I did. You were too focused on your ex."

How does Cash know Dean is my ex? His lips press together, reading the questions in my mind, like he's ready to hunt me until I surrender. Every muscle in his body tightens. It's like he wants me to think that he's amused by all of this, but it's obvious that he's not. He's jealous.

"Why were you calling anyway?" I ask.

"You went to SAA?" he asks, completely disregarding my question. I run a hand through my hair, my fingers catching on the knots.

"How long were you listening?" I ask.

"Long enough."

I exhale, the breath long and strained. I don't want to have this conversation, but I don't want to avoid it either. I *want* to tell him. Keeping my face forward, I sit down on my bed. Cash stays rooted against the wall, waiting for me to speak. If there's anyone I can tell, it's Cash. He's twisted like me, and he won't judge me.

Still, I don't like the memories. They stir up a lot of unwanted emotions.

Will the truth finally scare him away?

But my instinct says that he'll stay.

"What's there to say?" I lift my shoulders like it's nothing. "I thought I might be a sex addict."

"Are you?"

"Not to sex."

He clenches his jaw. It's the only sign of emotion he gives, a hint of impatience as he waits for me to explain. I kind of like knowing that he's capable of a reaction. That I can stir that in him.

"Then what are you addicted to?" he finally asks.

"It's a long story."

"I've got time."

I check my phone. He has a digital appointment with a contractor in half an hour.

"You've got a meeting soon. You should drive home now. Get the webcam running."

He types on his phone, then stows it. "Cancelled. Now, tell me: what is this long story?"

A lightness blooms over me. Cash isn't only curious; he *wants* to know my story, and he's even willing to cancel his appointments to hear it. His jaw strains, his eyes darkening, and I know he's never going to give up. He needs to know.

"Dean thought I might benefit from it," I explain.

"Why?"

"He thought—" I stop myself, unsure of how to say it. Dean doesn't understand my desires, nor does he share them. But he's still a good person. We just aren't compatible.

I change my wording: "I knew I had problems."

"With?"

I huff out a breath. "You know what."

"Tell me, Remedy."

"That I like pain."

His eyes darken like he's reading the hidden meaning behind my words, confirming what he already knows. Cash is the only person who's gotten to me like that, and we both know it.

"He couldn't cut it, then," Cash says.

Relief swells through me. "You don't think I'm crazy?"

"Come on. I'm the one who choked you until you bruised," he

says. He puts a finger through my scarf, tugging it until it pulls off. The air cools my warm neck, and I blush. It's like exposing the most authentic side of myself. I hold the scarf in my hands, stretching the fabric. I'm not sure what I'm supposed to do with it now.

"He always asked if I was okay. If he was hurting me. If he should go easier on me. That kind of thing," I say. "Finally, he convinced me I needed to go to therapy or SAA."

Cash nods. "How long did you go to SAA?"

"I didn't keep track."

"Did it help?"

"I was celibate for a while."

"Why?"

"They said it might fix me."

Cash sits on the bed next to me, the mattress dipping under his weight. Our thighs touch, his body warm against mine, and his presence comforts me. I thought he would leave when he heard my story, dismissing me as his insignificant fuck doll assistant, but instead, he's closer to me than before. And for once, I don't feel the need to kill him or to run away. Because if Cash wants me underneath him, I'll be underneath him. And that reassures me.

And it's clear that he's here to listen.

"Did it fix you?" he asks.

I twist a loose thread from the scarf, then ball between my fingers. "No."

He puts a hand on my knee, and heat pulses through my veins. I let out a breath, trying to calm myself down to a simmer. I don't understand why my body reacts like this to him, like I'm only safe when I'm tucked inside of his violence. But it's like some primal energy inside of me *knows* that he'll do anything to protect me, and that means we're safe.

He puts a hand under my chin, forcing me to look up at him. His dark eyes envelop me.

"You don't need to be fixed," he says.

Those freckles in his eyes make it so painfully clear that he's focused on me, and *only me*. No matter how rich and powerful he may be or the violence he's capable of, he *wants* to talk to me. To see me. To know me.

I huff through my nose. His words are nice, but they're not true. Everyone has issues, and my issues are about as big as they come.

"Now you're messing with me," I say.

He subtly furrows his brows. "He's a judgmental idiot."

That I can agree with. But my shoulders sink, my gaze flicking back to the scarf in my palms. I pinch the fabric and try to understand myself. Why did I think a relationship would work out with Dean?

Why does everything feel better with Cash?

"He said he wanted to get married before he realized I need pain," I say.

"Were you going to accept?"

I shrug. "I guess."

His forehead wrinkles with frustration. "What were you going to do? Fake orgasms for the rest of your life, pretending to be happy with him?"

"Yes."

Tears fill my eyes, not because I miss Dean. I know we're not meant to be together. But the abandonment when Dean finally left still hurts, because it's going to happen again, even with Cash. I finally have someone who understands me, but Cash isn't someone I can have. He's my enemy. I'm not supposed to feel this safe around him. But I do.

And eventually, I'm going to have to leave him.

Cash wipes the tears with his knuckles, then licks them off of his skin. His hand swallows my neck where the bruises are. He squeezes, and the dull ache builds in my spine, reminding me of what he's capable of. His eyes lock on mine, and I know that he's seen everything inside of me. The terrible sides. My shameful sexual urges. The anger I've built up from my stepdad and stepbrother. Rage that I've poured into him.

Still, Cash makes me feel seen. Heard. *Wanted.* Even the ugly parts.

Cash tightens his grip on my neck, but I don't look up. This is stupid. Cash is manipulating me, just like he manipulated Jenna. For fuck's sake, he *assaulted* my best friend.

Whether it's gentle like my stepdad or a physical assault like my stepbrother, no one deserves to be violated like that.

"I'll go on your double date," Cash says.

Those words instantly erase my thoughts. My heart leaps into my throat. I swallow hard.

"With my mom?" I ask.

He nods slowly, his eyes looking down his nose at me, as if he knows that agreeing to this means he can hold it over me. I bite my inner lip, anxious over what he may demand, but it doesn't matter. *He agreed.*

And I remind myself that this is it: my chance to kill him like I promised Jenna. Even if he makes me feel seen, he's too dangerous and too powerful to be free. He *has* to pay for what he's done, or he'll do it again. They always do.

"I've got bad news though," I say hesitantly, running my fingers through my hair. "We're going to an actual restaurant now."

Cash tilts his head. "Another opportunity to expose myself."

"Which means..." I trail off, leaning into him, "we can't have sex in my old bedroom anymore. Sorry."

He chuckles, but that grin only stretches wider across his face. He has another plan waiting for me, one that's much more devious than desecrating my old bedroom.

"You think I'm in it for that?" he asks.

I scrunch my nose. "Isn't that why?"

"Not at all. But I've got to catch up with the contractor now." He winks, then stands between my legs. His hands slip around my throat, holding me without choking me, his fingertips rough and thick. Heat gathers between my legs, knowing that he can crush me in seconds. My breath catches in my throat and I know why he's holding me like this.

Even if he's not choking me, he wants to remind me that he controls me.

"Don't worry," he says. "You'll have other chances to make it up to me."

Chapter 10

Cash

Living in Key West for as long as I have means that I know the properties inside and out, even if I don't own them. From the restored, historic homes to the modern condos, I've worked on them all. And Dean, the ex-boyfriend, lives in a small, two-bedroom cottage developed by the Winstone Company, which means he has the same hatch to his crawl space and the same wide wall cavities as Remedy. It would be amusing, but I'm too impatient. I want to kill him *now*.

By the time the sun sets, I pick the lock at his cottage, letting myself in. The evening is quiet, and though the civilian paranoia means that I have fewer options, I tell myself that I enjoy the change of pace. Everyone is afraid. I'm their boogeyman, and my reign stretches over the city.

In the second bedroom, which he's arranged as his office, I sift through the drawers and filing cabinet. Schoolwork. Essays. Attendance records. Outdated textbooks. It reeks of stale books and ink. There's a large window facing the street on one wall, and on the other, a bookshelf is stacked to the brim with textbooks and binders. But in the desk's top drawer, a red satin thong lies crumbled under some paper clips.

Blood simmers in my veins, my heart rate skyrocketing. He's taunting me. Does he want to suffer? I grab the clump of fabric, paper clips and all, crunching it in my fist, and sniff them deeply. More sour than tangy. I relax. It's not her.

But that means he lied to Remedy. He's not the abstinent ex-boyfriend who deserves a second chance. He's been sleeping around.

But that doesn't matter.

After I investigate the property, I find a space in the master bedroom closet, leaving the door cracked open for the view. If Dean keeps to his typical schedule since I've begun watching him, I won't have to wait long.

And on queue, he drifts into the house reeking of beer and floral perfume, his sweater vest clutched in his hand. He pulls at the collar of his shirt, loosening the buttons, then takes off his clothes, slinging each article onto the bed. A shaved chest. Muscular, like he plays in an adult sports league. Styled hair. He collapses on the bed, and though I can't see much now, I can see his dick in one hand and his phone in the other, like he's jerking off to porn. But no matter how hard he pumps, his dick stays flaccid in his palm. Foster mother number seven was like that. If you got her to drink, she'd pass out, and so I put a tube in her unconscious mouth, funneling as much as her stomach would take. No one blinked an eye when she died of alcohol poisoning.

They're all the same.

He groans and twists in his bed until he finally flops on his back and passes out. It's not even seven o'clock yet, and the bastard is already drunk with whiskey dick. Is this how he treated Remedy? Getting so drunk he can't even fuck himself, expecting her to be okay with that? I creep through the closet door until I'm standing over his unconscious body. I poke my cleaver under his chin, moving his head so I can inspect him. A chiseled jaw. Light eyes. There's a dip in his cheek, like he may have dimples. No wonder Remedy liked him. There's no denying he's attractive, though he'd have more character with his face carved up.

But I'm not here to fix him.

The cleaver pricks his skin. He swats at it like it's a housefly, but the blade slices into his palm and he widens his eyes, focusing on me.

"What the—"

I swing down on his wrist; the hand cuts clean from his body, the bones frozen in the shape of a claw. Dean screams, shaking the nub in the air, too shocked to fight back.

I like to give choices. Options give people hope, and I enjoy watching that hope disintegrate before they die. But as I lift the cleaver, blood shining on the blade, I know Dean doesn't deserve that. He blubbers and whines, but I don't hear him. I hear Remedy: *You don't think I'm crazy?*

I chop the cleaver down again on the other wrist, dismembering it too. Blood squirts around us and I hurl the blade down again and again, each swing filling me with a satisfaction I haven't felt in a long, long time. And I tell myself that this is for my plan. When Remedy's ex-boyfriend shows up dead, Remedy will be one of the first suspects. I can even help the police along, confirming that I saw them in the midst of a heated argument, only days before his death.

But I can't explain the urge overpowering me as I climb on top of him. My cock fills with blood as I drop the cleaver, taking out my pocketknife. He's barely alive—he may even be dead; it's hard to tell—but I fix the blade to his eyes, carving around his eyes until I hit that hard, unmistakable boney socket. I pull out his eye. Stringy red tissue twists around the optic nerve, and with a swift drag of my knife, I cut through the vessels. Then I do the same with the other eye. I hold them up in my leather gloves, admiring them in the shadows, the vessels and nerves hanging from each of them like scraps of seaweed decorating the beach. Even in death, he will never look at my little cure again.

Blood covers me, warm and wet. I hop off of the bed. He's hacked up, his sheets red, his flesh pulped. His face looks more like red clumps of dirt than a human skull. But I want more.

Using the cleaver, I cut off his head. His creamy white spinal cord pokes out of the meaty flesh, but as I hold up his head by his matted, textured hair, I'm pleased with myself. He looks so much better like this. Real. Like the fucked up human he is. I whistle a tune, then place it down on the bed so he can watch me get rid of his body.

I check his phone, curious about his jerk-off material. A picture message fills the screen; a co-ed in red satin lingerie posing on her bed. *See you in class,* the text says. I roll my eyes. It's predictable to a fault. If I hadn't killed him, he would have eventually been fired for the forbidden affair. And he claimed he wanted to commit to Remedy.

Killing him is practically a favor.

With my mask on, I cover the rest of his body in primer, then insulation foam, stuffing him into the crawl space. I even toss the eyeballs on top of it. A trail of blood covers our trek from his bedroom to the closet, but it doesn't matter. I don't care if the police find out. Maybe it's better if they find him sooner. With their protocol, it'll take at least a few days before they even consider doing a wellness check.

I do one last sweep of the cottage, cleaning up hastily, but well enough. Then I grab his head by the hair again, his eyelids closed, bloody, and flat. I let his head drop into a thick black garbage bag. Even though it's only the head, it's heavier than you'd expect, like a bowling ball slung in a duffel bag. I put the garbage bag in the trunk of my sports car, then slam it shut.

Once I've showered, I drive to Remedy's rental house. I fix my sleeves as I stand on her front porch. She opens the door and my jaw drops. A lacey dress clings to her body, a dark thin material underneath barely covering her breasts and pussy. The lace sleeves circle down to her wrists, and the hem of the dress hangs past her thighs. Still, even with the lace coverage, it's revealing as hell. A hint of skin between each piece of lace teases me, making me salivate. Her blood-red lips are different from her usual purple paint, but it works. Black stilettos are strapped to her feet. A wide lace choker covers her neck, and for once, I'm not pissed that she's hiding them. It's for her mother, and damn it, the choker is hot on her. She's a mix of trashy goth and high-class escort, dripping with sex in a black cocktail dress. Ready to kill.

"Hello, gorgeous," I say. She curtsies like she knows how good she looks, and that makes my dick even harder. *Fuck.* She's a pistol, and I'm anxious to tear her apart. I open the passenger door for her and she slides into the seat.

"You know Pirate's Bistro?" she asks, her dark red lips pursed.

I nod, then head toward the shore. I'm dressed in my usual style: the rolled-up sleeves of my button-up shirt, pressed trousers, a leather belt, and a watch—an outfit fairly typical for men of my stature in the Keys. But Remedy? She's completely overdressed for Pirate's Bistro, and that pleases me. She's taking control of her appearance, a last little jab at her mother. Mommy wants a double date, nagging until she gets her way? Remedy's response is to bring her messed up, sadistic, blackmailing boss-with-benefits, while dressing like she belongs in the red-light district. I glance at her and she blushes, tucking hair behind her ear. My shaft strains; it's unlike her to be nervous, and I want to explore that. The urge makes the seconds tick by slower. We need to suffer through the double-date so we can get to the good part, when I can destroy her. I squeeze her thigh, then focus back on the road.

Though the Pirate's Bistro is full of touristy tack on a building designed to look like an old, partially plundered port town, it's on the water with decent food and a fantastic view, which makes it a popular spot for *all* walks of life, even a double-date between four locals. A woman with dyed brown hair and green eyes stops before us, her eyes lighting up as she sees Remedy. Age shows itself in the lines around her eyes, with a golden-brown tint to her skin, a deeper tone than Remedy, but it's obvious that this woman is her mother. As they embrace, their contrast is striking. A cheerful, cream dress with large red hibiscuses, against a skimpy black lace dress.

Her mother pivots to me, her smile wider than before. I hold out my hand and she takes it, beaming up at me. But her eyes hover over mine; the freckles always stop people. Eye freckles are common, but few are as dark as mine. It catches her off guard like there's something off about me. She subtly shakes it away, and I give her my practiced grin.

"You must be Mrs. Basset," I say.

"Please, call me Kim. And you are?"

"Cash." Remedy lifts her shoulders, looking at me. That movement tells me she hasn't actually told her mother that I'm her boss yet. Her mother—Kim—thinks I'm Remedy's boyfriend.

I'm not sure how to feel about that.

"Cash? That's an interesting name," her mother says. She winks at her daughter. "He's handsome too."

I chuckle inwardly. I know what she really means. She's stuck on my eyes and knows she has to say something to distract herself from how strange I look.

A man with shaggy gray hair and bright blue eyes offers his hand to me before Remedy.

"I'm Tom," he says. We shake hands first, *then* he turns to Remedy, as if I'm more important than his girlfriend's daughter. The fucking idiot. "Thanks for meeting us tonight."

Once the hostess guides us to our table, we make small talk through false interactions. No matter how close a family is, these kinds of interactions are always a mask to show how close the unit is to the ideal family. A few of my foster families loved pretending like that when I first arrived, and at first, I thought that family dinners meant quiet, happy evenings. But it's always a fantasy. A way to make someone comfortable enough so they can beat you for those mistakes, like a foster son who refused to talk.

I doubt Kim touched Remedy like that, but I can't shake it from my head. I want to kill Kim to prove that Remedy doesn't *need* this false relationship in her life. But the more her mother babbles about Tom's amazing attributes, the louder and more aggressive Remedy becomes, as if it pisses her off to even be in the same room as Tom. It's entertaining, but the night still blurs together.

A voice cuts through the tremors of conversation.

"Cash?" Remedy asks, touching my thigh under the table. I blink. What are we talking about?

"What do you do again, Cash?" her mother asks.

"I'm a developer," I say.

"Oh! Tom does accounting for Johnson Properties—"

Remedy cuts in: "Cash makes more money than Tom."

"Remmie, sweetie," her mother says, a warning tone in her voice. "Be nice."

Those are the same two words Remedy said to me before I

walked Dean out of her rental house a few nights ago. Even her mother knows that Remedy is ready to kill tonight.

But Tom laughs and knocks his fist into my shoulder. "It's all right, Kimmie. He probably does! Look at that watch." I placate him by showing it off, not because I care, but because I want Remedy to understand how much I'm doing for her. I *hate* this bullshit. "Buddy, is that blood?" Tom asks, aiming a finger at my watch's strap. "You okay? You cut yourself shaving or something?"

I narrow in on it. A drop of blood, smaller than a speck of cement, is dried on the alligator leather strap. I rub it off. I don't even remember wearing this watch during a kill recently. What's it from?

Remedy smiles at me, and then I remember: it's my blood, from when we fucked in her kitchen and she scratched the hell out of my back.

"Something like that," I say to Tom.

Their conversation continues and I stare out at the dark water, but I can't see anything. The lights from the restaurant are too bright. I don't know why I'm at this restaurant. Is it for Remedy? To see her mother and boyfriend, so I can murder them too? I keep telling myself that I'm still here, sinking into this bottomless tourist pit just so that I can make Remedy alone like me, so that I can make *her* take the fall for my crimes. But I know the truth.

I'm curious about her.

We make it through the dinner, and I even chime in once or twice, mostly to tease Remedy into more rebellious action. She can't stop taking jabs at Tom, and it's funny to watch her squirm. But by the end of the evening, her spirit simmers, and I'm relieved that it's time to part ways. The four of us stand in the entrance lobby, an elaborate plastic crow's nest jutting up to the side of us.

"Thanks for convincing her to do this," her mother says, reaching to give me a hug. I stiffen, but follow the gesture. When I finally ran away in my teenage years, I realized that I have to pretend. Have to fit in. Have to play the part of normal.

And normal people give hugs to potential in-laws.

It's not like I'm marrying her. But *that's* what Remedy is pretending.

Why do I put up with this much shit for her?

"It was a pleasure," I say. "I'll be honest: she always wants to stay in. A true homebody. This is the first date she's let me take her on in weeks."

Her mother perks up. "We should do this more often then!"

Remedy smacks my shoulder to get me to shut up, and I give that practiced smile. I love messing with her. I nod my agreement to her mother and Remedy's jaw drops. We exchange one last hug, then her mother and her boyfriend part ways, leaving Remedy and me alone in the lobby.

"I don't want to go home yet. You want to stay here for a while?" she asks, pointing toward the stairs leading to the upper deck. "I'll get us drinks. I'll meet you at the lounge."

I don't question it. I climb the steps to the lounge and find a space along the railing, away from the few people that are still out. It's only a few more minutes until we can focus on my end of the deal. I lean on the railing, peering out into the darkness.

"Hey," a man says from the side. His red nose throbs between his puffy cheeks. "I know you from somewhere."

I face the water. "I have one of those faces," I mutter.

"Is that a scar? Those eyes. I'd remember them anywhere."

I shift away, but the man draws closer, gawking at me like a drunk piece of shit.

"You did the insulation on my house last year, right? On Coastal Way? It's nice, man. We're not dying in the summer anymore."

Insulation from a year ago? *Shit.* Had he seen me during one of the kills?

"I don't know what you're talking about," I warn. "Back off."

"You look nice," he says, patting my arms. "All dressed up. Fancy. Cleaner now. You got a girl tonight or something? Has she seen you in your work clothes? You looked dirty as hell—"

I grab him by the collar of his shirt, lifting his feet off of the ground. My canines gleam in the light, and that makes him gulp; the fear swims in his eyes like a school of fish with no direction. I

113

shouldn't draw more attention to this asshole, but he's pissed me off and he's a drunk son of a bitch that no one will miss anyway.

But there's no place to easily hide a body here. Even if I shove his ass into the ocean, someone will see.

"You don't know me," I growl.

The man swallows. Finally, he nods in silence.

"Cash?" Remedy asks. The drunk man's eyes flicker to her standing behind me, and I drop him, letting him fall to the ground. I swing around to face her as the drunk man scurries away. Remedy raises two drinks: a mojito for her and a scotch for me. I grab it, thanking her, but I don't take a sip yet.

"What happened?" she asks, her voice full of apprehension.

"Drunk asshole," I say. There's nothing more to say about that. "Now, I've met your mother, but what about your father? Where is he?" I can kill her biological father too. Damn it, I *need* to kill someone soon. The pressure is building in my bones. Her eyes rest on the water sloshing below us.

"My real dad died when I was a kid," she says.

I remember that. There's more to that story, but I can tell she doesn't want to share it right now. "And your stepdad?" I ask.

"I haven't spoken to him since the divorce."

She stares out at the water like she can see visions of her past drowning in the blackness. And for some reason, seeing her like that, my heart palpitates, as if I know what it's like. But I don't. Her pain is her own, and mine is mine. You may understand how much it hurts, but you can never know what it feels like.

But I can't stop myself from putting my hand on her lower back. I want her to know that I'm still here for her.

"You can tell me," I say in a quiet voice.

She refuses to look at me. "Will you still want me?" she asks, her voice drifting out to the ocean below.

"Yes."

She slurps down half of her mojito.

"He used to touch me. Under my PJs. After I showered. It was always gentle, you know? He made it feel good. But I knew it was wrong and I felt so guilty. Any time I told him to stop, he reminded me that he wasn't hurting me. He wasn't being rough.

It's like I didn't have any power. And he made me say out loud that it didn't hurt. Then he convinced me to say I liked it too."

My head pounds, flickers of light blurring the edges of my vision.

"No one knew?" I ask.

"I tried to tell my mom once. But she didn't believe me, and when my stepbrother, Brody, overheard, he said that he would kill me if I suggested his dad did anything like that again. And you know, Brody still hurt me, but I could handle the pain. It was easier to process. Easier to make sense of it. But my stepdad? He never stopped until *he* was done. And I felt like I couldn't tell anyone, you know? Why try to get someone in trouble when they've technically never hurt you?"

Rage boils inside of me, a tingling sensation that makes my scalp itch. I'll be the first to admit that I abuse my power over others, including Remedy, all the time. I hurt Remedy, just like her stepbrother did. And honestly, I don't care that her stepdad warped her sense of healthy affection, because that happened to me too. It gives us an understanding of each other. I'm not a stranger to that kind of fucked up 'love.'

What pisses me off the most is that her stepdad used a connection like *family,* forcing her to believe that it was okay. He used it to silence the passion inside of her.

And that kills me.

You don't get to choose your family. They desert or destroy you. And Remedy's family?

They ruined her.

The water sloshes along the rock barrier lining the edge of the restaurant, and the moonlight illuminates the choppy waves. A tear runs down Remedy's cheek, disappearing into the darkness. I wrap my arm around her, pulling her closer to me. She smells sweet, mixed with the salt from the ocean. I'm supposed to frame or kill her, but all I want is to destroy anyone who ever hurt her.

I'm the only one who hurts my little cure.

"What happened?" I ask.

"I told Jenna. And even though my mom didn't believe me at first, Jenna did, and she helped convince my mom. It was so stupid. How could my mother believe my best friend, but not me? It's like she didn't trust me. Damn it." She clutches an arm around her stomach. "It still makes me sick to even think about it."

I grip the glass of scotch so tight it almost breaks in my hand. I would have let the glass slice through my veins, but I need to hear Remedy's story. I need her to trust me, and that includes listening to her. That way, I can destroy her too.

But it's not only that. I want to absorb every gory detail so that I can kill them all.

"Someone like that deserves to die," I say, the anger leaking through each word. Remedy turns to me, her eyes wide. I guess it's strange; people rarely talk about who they want to die. Or perhaps she's confused that I would care, when I abuse my power, just like her stepdad and brother. But I don't hide behind false claims like 'family.' Remedy knows exactly what she is to me: a victim of blackmail.

"What do you mean?" Remedy whispers.

"Your stepdad hid behind these false ideas of respect. Family. Kinship. You'd think people like that would put up a fight, but they don't." I shake my head. "They're pathetic. Fucking cowards. They'll do anything to survive."

She fidgets for a second, running her fingers along the sides of her glass, wetting her fingertips with the condensation.

"But didn't you do the same thing to Jenna?" she asks, her words quiet.

I lock eyes with her. I want her to understand every word I'm about to say.

"I use people, Remedy," I say. "I'm not going to lie about that. But I'm always upfront. When it comes to *using* people, I give everyone choices, just like I did with you."

"What choice did you give Jenna?"

"You can ask her."

She furrows her brows, suddenly frustrated. "But you spanked her. And she's not like me. She can't deal with that kind of stuff."

"I've done much worse than spank you."

She lets out a haggard breath, the guilt filling her up with tension. This is why she hates *wanting* me, because of what it means when it comes to her best friend.

"Don't you wish you could kill him?" I ask.

Her eyelids flutter, surprised by my blunt honesty. Though she doesn't agree with me verbally, I can see the desire shimmering in her eyes.

I press the highball glass to my lips.

"Hey," she says, reaching for the glass. "Don't drink that. I saw the bartender lick the rim of it or something." She takes the glass from me, dumping it out over the railing, the contents splashing down below, muted by the waves. With a gleam in her eyes, she tilts her head at me. "I can make you a better drink at my house anyway."

I know the truth. She put something in my drink. And now, she's second-guessing that decision.

Finally.

"I have a better idea," I say.

I lead her back to my car, opening the passenger door for her once again. I circle the car and pat on the trunk as I get into the driver's seat. Dean's eyeless head is still back there. Even in his death, he can't see or touch Remedy, and that gives me pleasure.

We drive along the coast past the main section of the island until we reach a dirt road between the trees. After a short distance, the road changes from dirt to pavement, opening up into what looks like a secluded parking lot without any lines to mark the spaces. It's an abandoned project from the Winstone Company, forgotten after a hurricane.

No one will find us here.

CHAPTER 11

REMEDY

As I close the car door and step onto the asphalt, I suck in a breath. It's fishy and slightly musky, like decaying algae, and honestly smells like the rest of Key West. But there are no lamp-posts. No parking spaces. Just asphalt in a huge rectangular shape: trees on three sides, and the sea splashing onto the rocks and jagged bushes on the fourth. The sprawling fanned leaves of the thatch palms spring out, mixed with grayish-green, eye-shaped leaves. I've lived in Key West for my entire life, and I've never been here.

Cash stares out at the water like he's waiting for a storm to come in. If I have to run, it will be hard to escape here. I can hide, but Cash will find me. His words swirl inside of my head.

Don't you wish you could kill him?

Emotions rage inside of me, fighting for control. I believe my best friend. I know Jenna told me the truth. So why do I feel like Cash is *also* telling me the truth?

What actually happened?

"If you didn't hurt Jenna, then who did?" I ask. "Did you hire someone to pretend to be you? Are you Winstone's secret son? I don't understand why you can't tell me the truth."

"I give everyone a choice, Remedy. Even you," he says, lifting his upper lip. "If it bothers you that much—" he points at the road leading back to the main streets of Key West, "—then leave."

And though he doesn't say it, I can hear it in his voice. If I leave, he won't stop me. Somehow, I don't think he'll give that video to the police either.

So why am I still here?

My eyes fall to the ground. The asphalt is dark like it's recently been paved, or like no one has ever used it. There are large cracks on the edges, but no other visible signs of use.

I'm not sure what this place is, but I know I'm not going anywhere. Not now.

Cash wraps his arms around me from behind, then pulls up my dress and forces me to face the water.

"You've been teasing me all night," he breathes down my neck. Chills erupt on my skin as he thumbs the edge of my panties. He creeps inside, skimming my skin with his rugged hands. I melt down, ready to surrender, pressing into his firm, chiseled chest. He arranges my dress until it's bunched under my breasts, then he cups my pussy, playing with my folds, like his fingers are another leash guiding my soul. I don't know who Cash is or why he's doing this to me, but he presses my clit and I don't care. His nails dig into my sensitive tissue with a sharp, stinging pain until I give him what he wants: I moan. Then he bites my neck through the lace collar, the tension spiraling up to my head and down to my toes in waves of pain and pleasure.

I hate him, I remind myself. *I hate him. He's the worst. He's the enemy.*

"You," I stammer. "You are—"

"In control," he says. "I know what you want, Remedy, and I'm going to give it to you. All you have to do is crawl for me."

My brows furrow together, but he shushes into my ear, the sound calming, like the ocean waves bashing against the rocks.

"I'm going to make you come so hard that you don't know who you are anymore, like you asked," he says. "Trust me."

I force myself to close my eyes and shake my head, but it's just for show. I want everything he can give to me so damn bad, and I believe him. With all of my heart and soul. But I *can't* let him take me like this. He hurt Jenna, and she won't be free until he's in jail or in the ground. And since she can't take him on, then I *have* to fight him for her.

But what if he hasn't done anything to her? What if there's another part of the story, one I don't know yet?

Someone like that deserves to die, he said. And he said it like he was completely serious. Like he wants to kill people like my stepdad.

They're pathetic, he said. *They'll do anything to survive.*

What is Cash capable of?

I blink at him, trying to reconcile everything Jenna told me about Mr. Winstone, matching that up to Cash.

He wants me to call him Cash, but insisted that Dean and Jenna call him Mr. Winstone.

He spanked, slapped, and hit Jenna for tiny mistakes. But me? He gave me a choice: jail, or him.

Then he made me beg for it.

He made me *like* it.

He smacks my bare thighs and I yelp, the pain zapping through me.

"There you are," he says, growling in my ear. "Don't you dare leave me like that again. Your brain goes somewhere else, and I swear that if pain keeps you chained to me, then that's what you'll get." My body tingles with anxiety and lust and I unconsciously bring myself closer to him, his cock twitching against my back. "I own you, Remedy. From the day I first saw you until your very last breath. You. Are. Mine."

My insides twist as he massages my pussy and breasts with a hard grip like he's wringing the life out of me, the pressure building inside of me like a pot of water boiling over the edge. He shoves my panties to the side while he milks every sensation from me until I can barely stand on my feet.

"Cash," I whisper.

A hard, waxy substance tickles my ear and I flinch out of the way, but Cash squeezes my throat, holding me still as he stuffs it into my ear. All noise vanishes from that side.

"What are you doing?" I ask, my voice louder in my head, now that I only have one ear.

"Taking away your ability to hear and see," he says.

What the hell is going on? I'm not okay with this. My lips tremble.

"But I thought you just wanted me to crawl?"

"And you will." An evil grin spreads across his lips. His eyes flick down to my breasts, streaked red from his powerful hands, then his eyes slide back up to me. "Did you think you'd get off that easily, little cure?"

He fills my other ear with wax and suddenly, everything is muffled, like I'm buried underground. The ocean violently crashes against the rocks, but I can't hear a single thing. Without any sound, my heart races and anxiety devours me. I'm supposed to love and trust my family. I'm supposed to marry someone like Dean. I'm supposed to hate Cash. I'm not supposed to let him take away my hearing and vision. I *need* my senses. I need to lock every door, to shut everything out. To always know what's going on. That is how you stay safe.

And for some reason, I keep letting Cash inside of me.

My heart vibrates in my chest, each beat increasing in speed, and my breath comes out in staggered pants, intensely loud in my ears now that everything is muted. Cash's words melt into deep tones, cascading through me. He motions for me to lift my hands, then he takes the sides of my dress until it's off of me. The dress falls to the asphalt, then the lace choker, and my bra.

He hooks his thumbs in my panties, pulling them down until he's on his knees. His tongue swirls around my clit, making my insides burn with desire, and every so often, he gnaws at my tender skin, reminding me of the pain he can give me. Fire burns in his eyes, daring me to stop him. To pretend like I don't want this. But I didn't let him drink the poison, and I know now, with each swirl of his tongue, that I'll never be able to kill him like this. My knees buckle under the pressure and he grabs me, holding me up. His lips peel back, revealing his teeth, but it's not a smile. It's a show of dominance that he has complete control over me.

Once I'm steady, he stands and removes a blindfold from his pocket, twisting it over my head and onto my eyes. Everything goes dark. He grabs me—his hands hot and heavy, like an iron resting in the fire—and pushes me down to my knees. I fall on my palms, the loose chunks of rock biting my skin. The pebbles pry into my flesh and I hiss at the pain. His words vibrate through me, low and melodic, like music playing in the back of a bar.

A necklace circles my neck, almost like the choke chain, but this time, instead of metal, it's coarse, like rope. He pulls it like a leash and it cinches around my neck. I crawl, following him around the empty lot. Each time I move my knees, they ache like knives are hacking little divots into my skin. It stings like hell. There's a noose around my neck and my knees spike with pain, and I'm so sure that my knees are bleeding. No matter how slow or fast he goes, I'm bleeding for him but I can't feel him; I can only feel his rope. I'm so alone like this. Crawling. Not knowing where he is. Why isn't he touching me?

Why am I letting him do this to me?

He's capable of destroying my life.

The noose cinches around my neck, cutting off my air, and the pressure builds in my face, the skin stretched and puffy. But Cash pulls the noose, loosening the rope, then props me up on a cold, metal surface. I touch the edges, trying to figure out what it is; it's a folding chair. Liquid races down my knees to my calves and I know I'm right; my knees are bleeding. Does he want me to bleed?

He secures the rope to something—is it his car?—then he spreads my legs, forcing them apart. A few seconds later, he brings my hips forward, his hands swallowing my thighs, lifting me up just enough so that I straddle him, and he lowers me down, straight onto his cock. I gulp, holding back a scream. His hips gyrate, his cock circling inside of me, stretching me out. He removes one of the earplugs.

"Be as loud as you want," he says. "No one can hear you scream. Show me what a fucking animal you are. Show me that you're my depraved little fuck doll. That you're nothing but a hot little cunt for me to use. And fuck, Remedy, I'm going to use you until there's nothing left to fuck." His nails dig into my hips as he pushes the chair backward, the noose tightening around my neck.

"What are you doing?" I scream.

"Are you willing to die to fuck me?" he asks. I whimper, not sure what he's talking about, but the rope slinks tighter around my neck, and I keep shifting my hips forward, trying to impale myself with his cock. "Damn it, Remedy. Do you feel how hard my dick is for you? It's so thick it hurts and I still can't get enough of you." He growls, though his grin is clear in that primal hunger. "When you're like this, you can't do anything. You can't see or hear. And if you make a sound, no one will hear you. You're nothing but my little fuck doll."

He smashes the earplug in again and he fucks me harder, my body bouncing up and down on his cock, every piece of flesh jiggling like he can't screw me hard enough, and I'm not a person anymore; I'm an object. A toy. A doll. His little piece of ass. And I hate it so much but I want it all. His cock rips me apart, thrust by thrust, and tears roll down my cheeks, mixing with sweat, and all I hear is my own rapid heartbeat, his words repeating in my mind: *You can't do anything. No one can hear you scream. You're nothing but my little fuck doll.*

His hands wrap around me as his mouth consumes my neck. His ragged breaths heave onto my skin. I skim his chest with my fingertips. The unruly chest hair. His muscles tense as he fucks me. His pulse races against mine until we're in sync and there's no difference between me and what *he* wants.

Suddenly, he pulls us both back and my breath sucks out of me as the noose tightens, the pressure building, blood clawing at the surface of my skin, but his dick pumps me harder, his cock stretching me so damn wide. One day, he's going to tear me apart, and that thought alone pushes me over the edge—because at that moment, I'm not anyone to him. I'm not a person. I'm not a woman.

I'm his.

He yanks the noose free from my neck and the orgasm thunders through me until I feel myself coming apart. Cash holds me close, binding his arms around my body as if he doesn't want me to disappear. His come pumps inside of me, filling me up, and I don't question it because I want every hot pulse of his cock. It makes me realize something: I'm not afraid of being powerless around him.

Once the final twitch of his cock subsides, he yanks the blind-fold, earplugs, and noose from my body, letting them fall to the ground. His arms scoop me up, carrying me to his car. For a moment, I sink into him. But then he puts me down. My clothes are already on the front seat. I stumble to put them on, the exhaustion weighing down my shoulders, and Cash watches me, the look of amusement gone.

And then everything is empty, and I'm lost. Like nothing happened. And I only want reassurance that we're fine. That I haven't done anything wrong. That we're okay.

I know this is a remnant of the past. Where I felt like it was my fault for what my stepdad did to me. But I can't stop myself from needing reassurance.

"How come you've never kissed me?" I ask. He scoffs as he goes to the driver's side.

"Have you ever been turned on by a kiss?" he asks.

Cash is right; I've never enjoyed a kiss like that.

He pushes the start button and the engine roars to life.

We drive in silence, but inside, I'm furious. He made me come, and it was by far the craziest, most fucked up and pleasurable experience of my life. But I feel so used. I honestly won't be surprised if he drops me off on the side of the road to make me hitch a ride home with tourists. Everything is a facade with Cash.

So what part of him is real?

"What was that?" I ask, pointing in the direction of the secluded parking lot.

"Sex," he says.

I clench my fists. Is he mocking me?

"You only met my mom so you could *use* me like that," I say, raising my voice. "What? So you could dump me off like a lousy secretary? What the hell is your problem?"

He keeps his eyes on the road, a coolness settling between us. Everything about Cash is relaxed. No matter how loudly I speak, or how pissed off I am, every muscle in his body is always loose, like he truly doesn't care what I say.

And it drives me insane.

"We're even, now," he says. "I went to dinner. You let me use you." Finally, he looks at me, a hint of amusement crossing his lips. "You tried to poison me again, didn't you?"

Anger rushes through me in a hot burst of light. I cross my arms and stare out the window. How does he know everything?

"Why didn't you?" he asks.

The crappy part is that I don't know. I should have done it. It would have been the best thing for Jenna, and maybe it would have been the best for me too.

My face is hot but I can't stop the words from coming out of my mouth: "You agreed to go to dinner with my mom *because* you feel something for me. I don't care what you tell yourself, but deep down, you know it. You have feelings for me, Cash."

He slams on the brakes in the middle of the empty road. The seatbelt tightens across my chest and I gasp, not because of the sudden stop, but because of the expression on Cash's face. His temples are strained, the vein throbbing in his forehead like he's ready to rip me apart.

He grabs the back of my neck, forcing me to look at him.

"I will do anything for you," he says. "Meet your mother. Cover your crimes. I'll even kill for you, Remedy."

The words still my heart, my breath catching in my throat.

He'll kill for me?

Those words seem real. But he's an abuser. A manipulator. And above all else, a liar. But I can't shake the instinct that he's telling the truth. That he truly will do anything for me.

"But you won't kiss me," I say, my gaze flicking back and forth across his dark eyes. He sucks in a deep breath, then grabs a small item from a locked compartment in the center console: an anchor grey flash drive. He drops it in my lap.

"This is the video of you trying to kill me that first night."

I blink. Is he serious?

"Is it the only copy?" I ask.

"Yes."

I stare at him, but he doesn't say anything else. What is he trying to prove?

Neither of us says another word, not even when he drops me off at my rental house. I stay on the porch, watching his dark grey imported sports car until I can't see it anymore. My throat dries, and it's hard to swallow, but I don't know what I'm supposed to do about him anymore.

Maybe I need to go about this in a different way. Maybe killing him isn't the exact right thing to do. Maybe I'm not even supposed to blackmail him.

But there are cameras everywhere in his estate. I can get those recordings of our sexual encounters and use *them* to destroy his reputation. It won't even be that bad since it'll be the truth. I just have to do it before I change my mind, like I did with his drink.

But inside, I don't know if I will do anything. Maybe I don't want to ruin him anymore.

———

The next day, Cash leaves me alone in the estate. He's running errands, which is good for him; he's getting out of the estate more and more each day. But I can't stop the sinking feeling in my stomach that screams that this is a test. He knows I have the flash drive now. It's almost like he's giving me a chance to go to the police.

But I don't go. Instead, I make sure my personal camera is still working in his office, then I check to see if I can access his computers yet, but none of my password attempts work. After that, I do my tasks for the day: double-checking one of his proposals, invoicing a contractor for some insulation work, and taking Bones to the vet for a checkup. When I find a few free seconds, I check the bedroom upstairs on the left, but the door is still locked. I bend my bobby pins until I've got a pick and a lever, but I can't figure out the locking pins. I'm not sure if I can't do it, or if Cash has proofed this lock somehow, *or* if I'm giving up too soon because I respect him. Instead, I kneel, inhaling sharply at the pain from my scabbed knees, then I lie on the ground with my nose against the small gap under the door. But I can't see, smell, or hear anything. There's nothing there, like Cash's expressionless face.

Right before lunch, Jenna asks to meet a deli shop halfway between our assignments, and I'm so excited I send her a string of emojis to say *yes!* When I see her, she looks better than she has in a long time, maybe *months*. Her skin glows with a fresh tan, and her lips are bright and glossy. There's a bounce in her step. She's smiling too.

"I've missed you," I say.

"I've missed you!" she says. "I've missed the world." She waves to the man in an apron behind the counter. He nods at us. "Do you think he missed us?" she whispers.

I laugh. After we get our usual sandwiches and seat ourselves at the only rickety metal table outside, I adjust my pants. The fabric keeps brushing my knees, irritating the scabs. I try to get comfortable, but it's difficult. I take a bite of my panini, then wipe my mouth.

"You like the new assignment, then?" I ask.

"She's a queen," Jenna says. "It's so different working for a woman. I can't stand working for a man."

"Me too," I say automatically. And maybe with everyone else, it's true.

But it's different with Cash.

"How's it going?" she asks, tilting her head.

I stuff a melty string of mozzarella back into my sandwich. "It's fine," I say, trying to play it off like it's nothing. "Cash is just another male boss. You know how they are."

"Cash?" she gasps. "He lets you call him 'Cash'?"

I lift my shoulders. "So?"

"He *made* me call him 'Mr. Winstone.'"

I press my lips together, peering down at my food. I wouldn't be surprised if he uses his name and title to manipulate people. He's like that.

"He acted weird when I tried to call him 'Mr. Winstone,'" I say.

"Has he done anything to you?"

I shake my head. I almost blurt out, 'of course not,' but I stop

127

myself. Then I adjust the black scarf around my neck, covering the bruises. It looks ridiculous, and from the way Jenna's eyes flickered when we first arrived, I know she noticed it too.

She lets out a sigh. "Thank goodness," she says. "I'd die of guilt if he did."

I suck in a breath. The wilted arugula springs out my panini like little arms stretching for a lifeline. What am I supposed to do? Do I tell Jenna that I'm fucking him *willingly?* Do I tell her I'm fucking him *only* for the blackmail potential? Or do I wait until everything is done and he's finally ruined, in jail, or dead?

What if it never happens?

"I was thinking," Jenna says carefully, wiping her mouth with a paper napkin, her lipstick blotting the edges, "Maybe I could go back to his estate. Talk to him. For closure, or whatever."

A weight crashes down on my shoulders. She's back to her normal self. Why does she want to torment herself like that again?

"Why?" I ask.

She shrugs. "I talked to my mom about it. She thought it might be a good idea."

"You talked to your mom about him?"

My heart rate increases. How many people are involved now? And what will happen when I tell Jenna the truth?

"I don't have to go there when you're working," she offers. "I can go after hours. Or on your day off. Whatever works for you."

"Is that a good idea?" I ask, a sharpness to my tone that I immediately regret. Jenna's jaw drops.

"Really?" she asks, leaning forward. "You're the one who chose to work for him. I can make decisions for myself too."

"You're right," I mumble. The simultaneous urge to protect Jenna and Cash *from* each other burns inside of me. But none of this is right. Even when we part ways, both of us going back to work, I can't make any sense of it.

I'm supposed to avenge her.

I promised myself that I would kill him.

At the very least, I'm supposed to ruin him.

So why can't I stop thinking about crawling to him?

CHAPTER 12

CASH

THE NEXT DAY IN MY OFFICE, I CLICK THROUGH THE SURVEILLANCE footage on the wide computer monitor, finding the front porch. A red-headed man with blue eyes stands there casually, like he's stopping by to see a friend. He's dressed in a sweat-wicking golf shirt and shorts, but he *looks* like a cop. This is the man Remedy's mother keeps suggesting as a potential boyfriend. Peter Samuels. He's a rival. I don't tolerate rivals.

But killing a cop always gains more attention than necessary. Sadly, I can't get rid of him like the ex-boyfriend. There has to be another way to deal with him. He knocks again, and the sound travels through the open windows. I quickly text an old associate to get a file on him. When you have shady obsessions, you find equally shady people, and with an associate like him, he can find enough information to bury even the best cop in hell.

I jog down the stairs. Luckily, I tossed Dean's head in the woods by the college after the double date.

"Detective Peter Samuels," I say as I open the door, offering my hand. He smiles, surprised that I know his name.

"Nice to meet you, Mr. Winstone. May I come in?"

"Of course."

I motion him inside, and we both sit across the long dining table. His eyes study the open windows, the breeze rustling the curtains. A diluted light shines through the space. It's like a slice of paradise.

"You know there are rumors that you keep every window boarded shut," the detective says.

I raise my brow. Rumors float so damn freely in the Keys. "Times change," I say. "I didn't take you to be a gossiper."

"It's my job to know what people are saying, even if it's not true," he says. He presses his lips together, pointing at the open windows. "You're not concerned about the murders happening across Key West?"

Funny. He thinks I'm *that* kind of recluse.

"An open window—even a boarded one—isn't going to keep a killer out, Detective. You know that."

He nods to himself, thinking over my words, and I take the chance to study him. He may be a year or two older than Remedy, in his late twenties, but still young, especially for a detective. Perhaps it's easier to get a title like that in a small town where nothing happens.

Honestly, he should thank me for giving him something to do. It must make him feel important.

"You'll find the criminal soon," I say. "It's too small of an island for the culprit to run wild forever."

"That's the idea."

I straighten in my seat, then spread my arms across the back of the table, claiming my space. "So what can I help you with, Detective?"

"I came to ask you about the murders, actually." He ruffles his hair, then pulls out a notepad. "Mind if I take notes?"

"Not at all."

He brings out a small rectangular device. "Is recording okay too?"

He's not going to catch me in a trap with a recording device. "Go for it."

He clicks the button, and once the red light flashes on the screen, he nods at me. "So you're aware of the circumstances of the murders?"

I nod. "How many is it now?"

"Five that we know of," he says. Darkness spreads across his face. "We're not sure of how long this has been happening. We think there may be other Key West murders connected to this killer from past years. Montana and Northern Nevada too."

"Shit." I rub my forehead, feigning distress. "Who does something like that?"

"Who knows? But this asshole needs to end up in jail."

I stare off into space, playing my part. But he's so sure of himself, it's *hilarious.*

"What happens now?" I ask.

"You're aware that a few of these murders have occurred on or near your properties?"

"You'll have to be more specific, Detective. I own a lot of property in Key West."

"I agree. It's hardly a coincidence. But perhaps you've heard something? A suspicious worker? A passerby? Anything you might remember?"

This is my chance to frame Remedy as my suspicious personal assistant. She tried to steal my hard drives and tried to kill me multiple times. But as I lock eyes with the detective, I can't say her name. I imagine ripping the detective's head from his body. He's not a practical option for Remedy without a head.

"What are you saying?" I ask.

"You have access to all the general contractors and subcontractors that work on your projects. Even the renters. All the staff. You even have access to LPA."

LPA is Lavish Personal Assistants, the agency which directly employs Remedy. But it seems strange. Out of all the businesses he can mention, why is he bringing up LPA?

"You're as much of a suspect as, say, your personal assistant is a suspect," he says. There's a gleam in his eye like he sees something there.

My blood pressure rises, my chest constricting. We both know it has nothing to do with Remedy. So why is he bringing her up?

He's baiting me. He knows about our relationship. He knows *something.*

I thought he was her childhood friend. But he's outing her like this?

I glance at the stairs. Remedy is in one of the extra bedrooms, working on her laptop with her earbuds on. It's easy; I shift the blame to her, then walk away. The detective won't blink an eye.

Instead, I do the unthinkable.

"If you're suggesting someone specific, then please be clear, Detective," I say, unable to hide the agitation in my voice. Am I actually defending her?

"Not at all. But we are checking every outlet. And the only common thread between the victims is the connection to your work."

My throat tightens. I don't care about what he thinks. All I have to do is leave Key West and never look back.

But I keep thinking about what he said: *Your personal assistant may be a suspect.*

It's coming together, and for some stupid reason, I want to protect her.

No. I don't want to take *responsibility* for my actions. So why can't I shift the blame?

"We'd like to get in touch with your workforce," the detective says, interrupting my thoughts. "Could you direct the contractors to the station?"

I grit my teeth but force the words out: "Absolutely. Someone has to have seen something."

"That's the hope," he says.

We shake hands, our eye contact level. I'm not ready to let this go.

"There's a lot of pressure to crack this case, isn't there, Detective?" I ask.

"Of course," he says. "Murder frightens everyone."

"It would be a shame if this case changed the department's belief in your abilities."

His eyes scan me, wary for a moment. That's it, then. He *needs* this case, or he's risking his job.

"I have faith in our department, Mr. Winstone," he says, his jaw straining. "But thank you for your time today."

"Of course."

I escort him out of the estate, then check on Remedy. Standing in the hallway, she doesn't see me. Rock music blasts from her earbuds as she types rapidly on her laptop. The sun shines from the bedroom windows, her deep orange cheeks tinted into a reddish hue, like a sunset washing over her skin. She's so damn beautiful, and yet I know that this moment is brief. Once the sun shifts, that light will be gone. Nothing is permanent. Time is always moving.

Staying in Key West means Remedy. Seeing her come apart. The way she turns into a beast when she comes. The passion and rage in her eyes when she lets herself go.

But staying also means my death in so many ways. Not just getting arrested.

Bones's new collar dings down the hallway, her random reappearance breaking me from my inner struggle. The cat survived on her own before. I can find her a new home, or let her roam freely again, and either way, she'll be all right.

But Remedy? If I don't frame her, if I don't do anything *to* or *for* her again, will she ever be truly free?

I stomp down the hallway, then descend to the ground level, finding my office. The urge to close my door so she can't come inside grows within me, but I force myself to stay at my desk, to work on the spreadsheets, to return phone calls, to send the emails notifying the contractors of what they're supposed to do. I can't let Remedy affect me like this, and if I shut her out now, that means she's getting to me.

By the time my blood cools, Remedy appears in the doorway.

"I'm off now," she says.

Her purple lips fill my vision and I don't think about what I'm about to do or say.

"Come sit with me," I demand.

A hesitant, nervous smile crosses her face, but she perches herself on the sofa to the side of the desk. Piles of newspaper lay in heaps on the floor underneath each open window. The sun shines into the room, making it brighter. And for once, Remedy doesn't wrap her arms around her body, protecting herself. She relaxes her shoulders, sinking into the comfort of the light. And that expression *stays* with her as she focuses on *me*.

I don't make her nervous anymore. Not like that.

I clench my jaw. This is wrong. All of it.

"Can I ask you something?" she asks. Instead of answering, I wait, letting her stew. Silence is one of the last forms of power I have over her, and I intend to make it painful. Finally, the discomfort gets to her, and she continues: "Would it be okay if I brought Jenna here?" She tilts her head and laughs. "Maybe closure will be good for her. I don't know. I'm just trying to help her. I've been such an awful friend lately. And this is what she wants, so…"

With that, Remedy's shoulders slump and she looks away from me. She feels guilty. Sleeping with me. Her sworn enemy. And enjoying it. Logically, I understand what she's feeling and why. But instinctually, the guilt makes little sense. She can't help that she has feelings for me. Why hold back when you know what you want?

I narrow my eyes on her. I know what I'm supposed to want. And yet, I can't seem to make myself do anything about it.

"Whatever you need," I say calmly. Relief flickers through her body, her shoulders sagging with those words even more.

"It's her birthday soon," she explains.

"What about your birthday?"

She pauses, pulling inside of herself. And there it is—her arms clutching her chest like she'll never be warm or safe again. But then her hands find her sides, and she stretches her fingers open, one by one, forcing herself to be brave. To confront those memories. I know what that's like. Shoving it down. Feeling like you can't control your life. Not until they're in the ground.

"It's been a while since I've celebrated it," she says.

"Why's that?"

Her eyes flicker around the room. "When I was nine, my stepdad had this custom dress made for me. It was gorgeous. All these different shades of pink. Frills and ruffles. Shiny. Sequins. Sparkles everywhere. They got on everything too. I used to love the color pink." She laughs to herself, and I smile. Seeing as how she only wears black or white or gray, it's amusing to think of her in pink. And sad. The color must have a lot of memories attached to it.

"Anyway, I loved the dress," she continues, "but he wanted to see me in it, and he said I had to put it on in front of him. Said that he needed to help me zip it up in the back. That kind of thing." She glances away. If she was nine, why did she need him to help put on her dress? Why couldn't she ask her mother for help? "He was always so nice. Bought me nice things. Had these reasons he did everything, even when he touched me." She presses her lips together, holding back her shivering chin, and her eyes flutter to the floor. "He never hurt me, you know?"

She says those words like she's not sure if he's done anything wrong. Everything shifts inside of me. She might believe it, but I *don't*. Not for a second. He may not have physically hurt her, but he broke her emotionally. And now, she doesn't trust men. The only reason she trusts me is that I'm so damn brutal and warped that she has no choice *but* to trust me. She always knows *exactly* where she stands with me. It's a curse, but it also comforts her.

And at least I can give her that.

"After that, we celebrated, but it was never the same," she says. He must have abused her for years, then. "I always felt trapped. Because no matter what I said, he always got what he wanted. And I swear, he even had my stepbrother in on it. Brody hurt me if I even *suggested* his dad did anything. And so I hid. Locked my doors. Kept my blinds shut. Because at least then, I'd know when he was coming, you know? And I didn't really date until I met Dean. And even then, it was short-lived. He didn't know me, because how could he? I couldn't put that on his shoulders." I ball my fists, ready to make her stepdad and stepbrother into roadkill. "For a while, I thought it was my fault that he touched me."

I can't stop myself anymore.

"It was never your fault," I say. "Your stepdad and stepbrother were supposed to protect you."

"But I didn't fight it. I didn't tell my stepdad to stop."

And then it surfaces—years of silence when I was growing up. Using those lack of words as a way to protect myself. Only speaking up when I knew I could win.

"You were a child, Remedy," I growl. "A fucking child. He was the adult. Why would you have told him to stop?"

"I don't know. But I didn't do anything."

She quivers like she's close to tears, and I want to tell her everything. That my parents abandoned me when I was an infant. That two addicts left their baby in a garbage can on the beach. That I had been beaten and abused and neglected on and off for years, being shoved from one house to another. I want to tell her that in the beginning, I tried to be good, but no matter what method I used, the results were always the same. I want to tell her I understand where she's coming from. I know what it's like to be completely powerless underneath the fucked up pieces of shit who are supposed to take care of you. That I know exactly how to restore her power.

But I don't say any of that. This isn't about me. She needs to believe that it isn't her fault.

"You did nothing wrong," I say again, my voice stern.

She grins to herself like she's already made up her mind. As if nothing is wrong.

"I've been thinking about what you said the other night," she says carefully. "I do wish I could kill him. I've imagined his death for years now. Sometimes it's creative," she forces a nervous chuckle, probably ashamed that she's actually admitting this out loud, "but mostly, it's just a knife. I can always get one in the kitchen."

And for that, I smile. I remember my first kill with a kitchen knife, and I remember when Remedy tried to attack me with one.

"Do you know how hard it is for me to be alone with a man?" she continues. "Or how I wish I could have normal sex and enjoy it? I've tried. I've tried so many times, but I'm just numb." Her jaw tenses and her fingernails dig into her sides. "I can't enjoy softness anymore. It makes me feel like I'm trapped, even though he's hundreds of miles away. Even though I know I'll probably never see him again." She lets out a long breath, then stares down at her feet. "Maybe if I killed him, I wouldn't feel so trapped." She laughs, her tone skittering and anxious, like a butterfly trapped in a net. "I sound terrible."

How do I tell her that I've killed more people than I've loved? That watching someone's life leave their body is more familiar to me than believing in a person's smile? That seeing her mouth twist in delicious agony for the first time is when I realized that she may actually understand everything?

"You don't sound terrible," I say. She perks up, confused and intrigued. "Humans are animals. We have primal instincts. And sometimes, that means murder. It doesn't make you any less human. In fact," I press my teeth together, baring my canines, "it makes you *real.*"

She nods, but my words aren't enough for me. I have to do something. I want her to be free to live her life. To do what she wants. To never think twice about what's right or wrong again.

"How would you do it?" I ask.

"With a knife," she says immediately.

"You want the mess, then?"

"Of course."

I wink. "Dirty girl."

She laughs again, still hesitant, but fuller, like she's beginning to accept herself. Her hands rub at her sides, then her eyes flicker to the cameras on the ceiling and the one on the mantel above the fireplace. It dawns on me: she knows she's being recorded; she's worried I'll use this conversation against her too.

But right then, I have no interest in that.

"What about you?" she asks, her voice light and airy. "Birthday celebrations? Childhood trauma? Desired murders?"

"I don't remember my birthday," I say. She blinks at me, questioning if I'm serious. There are holes in my memory, and the parts that I do remember are enough to eat a person alive. But once I started killing them, it gave me peace. Hit and runs. Muggings. Planned 'accidents.' Poison in their drinks. Bullets. Knives.

And that's what I want to give to her: *freedom from her past.*

"You don't remember anything?" she asks. "Why?"

My chest tightens. I don't want to lie to her like I do to everyone else. I want to tell her the truth, or at least part of it.

"I never prioritize it. There's no point." And in some ways, it's the truth. No one cared about my birthday when I was younger, and there's no reason for me to care now. "It's a date."

The silence stretches between us, but Remedy quickly changes that. "Let's pick a date then," she says, straightening her shoulders. "We can celebrate our honorary birthdays. Or our unbirthdays. Whatever you want to call it. Screw those past years. This unbirthday will be *ours* to celebrate."

I press my lips together to feign amusement. She wants to make everything seem okay. Like our trauma is nothing compared to who we are now.

I also know that she needs this birthday celebration more than I do, and that makes me want to give it to her. But I want to do something even more for her like she's trying to do for me. I want to wrap her stepdad's head in a box and present it to her as a gift.

"All right," I say, agreeing to the unbirthday. I don't know what I'm getting myself into, but as long as Remedy is satisfied, I don't care.

And with that thought, I realize that I don't want to kill her stepdad because I want to frame her. No—my reason is purely selfish.

I want to kill him because he hurt her.

She squeals in happiness, giving me a side hug, and I pull her into my chest, holding her close, not letting her get away with a half-assed hug. I sniff her hair, sucking in a breath, squeezing every damn part of her closer to me. Then I let her go.

"Okay. I'm going to go prepare for our party," she says. "Have a good night."

"Get home quick," I say. "There's a killer out there."

She smiles at me like she's not afraid. Though she doesn't know that I'm the Key West Killer, she knows that I'll do anything to protect her.

Once she's gone, I do a quick search and learn that her stepdad is living in Tampa.

I could kill him. But that seems off.

No. I want to give him to her. Like a sacrificial offering before an angry goddess.

She has to kill him herself.

CHAPTER 13

REMEDY

THE WOODEN STAIRS CREAK AS I TAKE EACH STEP. IT THUDS IN MY chest like a hammer, and my lips tingle with nerves. I hold Jenna's hand. Her hair is freshly bleached, her red lipstick bright as maraschino cherries, and it makes me think of war paint. I cross my fingers, hoping that this tells me what I'm supposed to do. If this destroys Jenna, then I *have* to get revenge for her. And I'm not sure that I want to do that anymore.

I unlock the front door and step inside, guiding the way, even though Jenna knows this place better than I do. She motions at the open windows.

"It's so weird," she says, her voice quiet. "It smells good. It was always so stale, like everything was rotting."

I haven't noticed anything like that at all. The fresh air must have cleared it up.

"Wait here," I say, directing her to the kitchen. "If you need anything, you know where it is. I'll be right back."

I creep up the stairs as quietly as I can, then sneak down the hallway. Cash is sitting behind his desk, his nose deep in a report on his computer. His phone flashes beside him in silence. He always ignores phone calls. Maybe it's a part of his reclusive nature, though I'm not quite sure.

"She's here," I say. He keeps his eyes on his work, like he's not concerned with the meeting at all. Cash is like that; he rarely cares about things. But this is different. He knows Jenna hates him. She's the reason I pursued him in the first place. Why doesn't he care?

Downstairs, Jenna holds a cup of water, peering out the windows. My heart vibrates, my body tense. I don't want her to be in pain any more than she already is, but she needs this.

Still, I have to make sure she's ready.

"Are you sure you want to do this?" I ask.

She forces a smile. "Let's go."

I stand in front of her, leading the way up the stairs, as if I can protect her. Outside of his office, I raise my hand, blocking her from entering. Then I check first: Cash is in the large leather recliner at the far end of the room, with his back to us.

I step to the side, letting Jenna in. She enters, lifting her chin. I stand behind her.

"Mr. Winstone," she says.

Cash doesn't move. It's almost like he's a statue decorating the chair.

"Do you remember me?" she asks.

She touches her lips, staring at the back of Cash's head.

"You made it so that I couldn't defend myself," she says, tears shaking through her voice. "I worked hard for you. And you hit me? Like you could beat my mistakes into me?"

Jenna clutches her hands to her chest. Nerves swim inside of me, and I gnaw on my bottom lip until a bitter taste fills my mouth. This is what Jenna needs, but I also know that this is why Cash hates being around people. These kinds of interactions don't make him sympathetic; they irritate him. But he stays silent.

Is he ignoring her?

Why does this seem worse than if he retaliates?

"Can't you at least pretend you're sorry?" Jenna asks, frustration growing inside of her.

I hold my breath as my heart pounds. A tear rolls down her cheek.

"Stop being a coward," she shouts. "Look at me, damn it."

At those words, Cash finally stirs. He stands up, then slowly turns to face her. Their eyes meet and Jenna's jaw drops, her lips shuddering to make words, but nothing comes out. Cash's eyes are vacant, like he can see past her, and it gives me chills. Jenna presses her fingers to her lips, her eyes wide.

Then she quietly leaves the room. I follow her. She flattens herself against the outside wall, but she keeps her eyes on the open office door.

"What happened to him?" she asks, her words trembling out.

I search her, trying to understand what she means. "What do you mean?"

"He looks different now."

"Different? How?"

"I rarely got to see him," she says. Her eyes keep shifting over to the open door like she's afraid he'll hear us. "He always had his back to me. Made me keep my eyes on the floor. But even if he dyed his hair, it doesn't explain his face."

"He got plastic surgery," I say. That's what he told Dean. Getting work done isn't that uncommon, especially being this close to Miami. But the more I think about it, the less it makes sense. Why would Cash get plastic surgery, unless he's hiding something? And what is he hiding?

"Does Winstone have an heir?" she asks.

I shrug. I honestly don't know. The idea that Cash is just covering for his father fills my mind, and part of me is relieved. If it's not the real Mr. Winstone, then my feelings don't matter. I can set my vengeance on his father.

But Cash never talks about his family. And when he does, I get the feeling that he doesn't get along with them. He never even celebrated his birthday. How can he cover for a father he hates?

"Who is that?" she whispers. But I don't know. He's always been Cash to me. And if he's not Winstone, then I'm not sure who he is either. "Why are his eyes like that?" she adds.

I shake myself out of the trance. "Like what?"

"Like his pupils are broken."

At the right angle, his eye freckles look like his pupils are leaking into the whites of his eyes from ocular trauma, but I know his face so well that it doesn't faze me anymore.

They aren't the kind of eyes you can forget. And the fact that Jenna doesn't recognize his eyes, confuses me.

Who am I working for?

"They're so sunken in. Like his eyes will be completely black soon. He looks—" she pauses, glancing around, then settles her eyes on the open office door again. "He looks evil."

My heart rattles in my chest, thinking of his words: *Someone like that deserves to die.*

At the time, I tried to tell myself that those words were full of justice. All he wants is to make things right for people like me. And yet, now, I'm not sure if it's that. There's something else behind his words, something I can't explain.

But if he's not Winstone, then I'm not sure I care about his evil actions. If he hasn't done anything to Jenna, then I can shift my blame onto someone else.

But I have to make sure.

"You don't think it's the same person?" I ask her.

"If it's not him, then who is that?" she asks, pointing toward the door. "And why is he here?"

The two of us stare at the open doorway. Relief rushes through me, heating my cheeks. Cash isn't the same man who hurt my best friend. I don't have to try and kill him anymore.

But who is he?

———

After that, Cash leaves for a business trip. At first, it seems strange, as if Jenna's visit spooked him so much that he forced himself to go on his first business trip in years, but that would mean that he *is* connected to Jenna, and I don't think that's possible anymore.

Still, our interactions over the phone are short. He gives me directions: a few meetings with people on job sites, emails to send in his name, how to take care of Bones. But for those few days, it's only Bones and me in the estate. I can probably close and lock the windows if I want, but I don't feel the need to. I consider staying overnight in the estate, but I don't. I want to wait for him instead.

Then, out of nowhere, I find Cash sitting in the downstairs

office with a smile so wide his jaw strains and it scares me. He's cast in shadows. The windows are actually closed and the curtains are drawn. It's dark. Like he's back to his old self. The one who may have known Jenna. The hairs on the back of my neck stand up. He seems oddly entertained, right then, like he knows something that I don't, and it unnerves me.

"What's going on?" I ask.

"You wanted a birthday celebration?" he asks. "I got you a present."

I tilt my head, then a bang startles me. The closet door rattles, like a large animal is fumbling around inside.

"What the hell is that?" I whisper.

Cash's shirt is unbuttoned at the top, revealing his chest hair, and though his sleeves are rolled to the elbow, they're more scrunched than usual. His hair is matted with styling wax, but it's flat, like he hasn't had the chance to wash it. I sniff hard; his sweat lingers in the air, infused with a coppery aroma, like blood.

"Do you trust me?" he asks.

My stomach tightens. Something big is about to happen, and I have no idea what to expect.

Even though I'm not sure who he is, I do trust him.

"Yes," I say.

He wraps a blindfold around my eyes, tying the black sash at the back of my head, then leads me to the sofa. He sits me down, then walks away, each step calculated and even. The closet door creaks open, and a heavy object crashes into a person's body. The person—a man—whimpers, the sound hollow. Chills erupt all over me. I know that whimper. I know *him*.

The person is dragged across the office, then stops in front of me. Cash circles the sofa, standing behind me, his hands on my shoulders.

"I told you I'll do anything for you," he says. He pulls the loose end of the sash, and the fabric flutters to the floor. I blink, letting my eyes focus.

Light brown hair covers the person's head, some patches thin, others thick. Bloodshot blue eyes. The man's face is still tan, but it's weathered with age now, like leather. Fish and ginger waft from his pores.

My stepdad.

Everything inside of me strains with fury. "What is this?" I hiss.

Cash chuckles, patting my shoulder. "You said this is what you wanted."

My stepdad's lip is bloody and puffy and a crust of blood circles his nose. Frustration rumbles in my chest. Did Cash punch him? Why is he doing this?

But then something else trickles in, mucking up my thoughts: flattery.

Or is it pride?

I don't know who Cash is, but I know he did this *for me.*

But I'm not supposed to be pleased like this. I'm supposed to be repulsed.

"Why are you doing this?" I stammer, my heart beating rapidly. "You hurt him, Cash."

"I don't know what you need," he says with an edge to his voice, frustration building inside of him. "But I'm offering your freedom." He squeezes my shoulders harder than before, but then lets go. "Kill him, Remedy."

My stepdad's chin quivers, his hands tied behind his back. His head hangs down, and for some reason, that irritates me. He can't even look at me; he can't face what he's done. For so long, I've hidden myself from the world, from true love and affection, because I know that anything can hurt me. Even gentle people can hold power over you.

Maybe that's why I like Cash. I may not know who he is, but I know what he wants and is capable of. And he listens to me.

Like when I told him I want to kill my stepdad. He brought him to me.

But can I actually do it?

"You know what he did once he left?" Cash asks. He stretches his fingers into the shape of a gun and taps it on his temple. "He found another family. Another teenage daughter to abuse. You and I both know a piece of shit like him never changes. But you want to be mad at me for punching him in the face?"

My throat constricts. I can barely swallow. It's what I've always been afraid of. If a man like him gets away with it once, he'll do it again, and again, and *again*. I hold my abdomen, the pain swirling inside of me. Sweat beads on my forehead. A faceless young girl clouds my vision. I should have done something. I should have protected her somehow.

How can he do this to us?

"Is that true?" I whisper.

My stepdad's mouth hangs open, but his lips don't move. He won't answer me.

"Answer me, Alan. Is it fucking true?"

He flinches at my words, like I'm being too harsh. But he stays silent.

And to me? That's enough.

Cash holds up a knife, smooth and unblemished, the metal gleaming in the dim light. The handle is a deep maroon, the color of wine and deoxygenated blood. He offers me the handle, and my fingertips tingle as I clench the grip. It's lightweight, like it may not do any damage. Like this is all a dream.

But it's not. Nausea bubbles inside of me, thinking of the times I've had to fake an orgasm. Every time I leave my body so that I'm not reminded of him. I think of the guilt. I think of being a failure. I think of letting my mom down. How even a hug or a touch on my shoulder can make my skin crawl.

I didn't know it then, but I know now that I will never be normal. He stole that life from me.

Cash rubs my shoulders, his musky, metallic scent swallowing me whole.

"If you don't do it, I will," Cash says, a chill in his words.

A numbness washes over my body. I watch myself go through each action, like a memory that keeps replaying in my mind. I'm not myself anymore. But I know I have to do it. I have to save girls like me.

But inside, I know I'm not that pure or righteous. I *want* to kill him.

My stepdad's pale blue eyes, murky with guilt, look up at me. "I'm so sorry, Remmie," he says.

My blood pressure spikes, my vision blurry. *Sorry?* He wants to say he's sorry? He has no right to say that. He isn't sorry. He's sorry he finally got caught.

I stand behind my stepdad, but I quake with nerves, shock coursing through me. I fall to my knees, then I hold the knife in both hands, raising it up like a dagger.

"You fucking monster," I howl.

The knife slips into the flesh of his back easily, like cutting through butter. My stepdad twists in pain, his desperate cries filling the room. But that doesn't stop me. I do it again and again and again, for each of the times he'll never be able to hurt another young girl like that. Blood splashes on me, but I don't stop. *I can't.* Not until I know for sure that he's dead.

His body collapses. My hands tremble so hard that the knife rattles to the floor. I stare at my palms, completely soaked in blood. There's blood on my cheeks, on my neck, drenching my clothes, and I'm cold and hot at the same time. My skin is burning, but I can't stop myself from shivering. I look around, trying to find my breath, to determine if this is real or another dream. Bones perches in the doorway, licking her paws. She glances at me, then goes back to grooming herself. As if this is a normal occurrence. As if it's not surprising that I would kill my stepdad.

Cash kneels beside me, then holds my hands.

"You are so brave. So fucking brave," he says. "I'm so proud of you."

My eyes flicker back and forth across his face, but his raw, hungry gaze scrutinizes me. Has he always seen this inside me? He brought my stepdad to me, but he gave me the knife and let me take care of the rest. He believes in me.

Cash holds my face, blood wetting his fingertips. I open my mouth, trying to force him to kiss me, to make the horror of my actions disappear, but he spins me around, holding me from behind, making me look at the corpse. His hands slide into my pants and underwear, his thumb circling my clit.

"Look at what you did," his voice rumbles through me. "You

killed a man. A man who hurt you. A man who hurt so many people. And he will never hurt you again."

I shake my head, pressing my lips together, trying not to panic. This isn't real. It can't be. It's a daydream.

But I know it's real.

"I'm going to jail," I whisper. Then a sudden giddiness sweeps over me. Someone is going to find out. My life is over. "I'm going to go to jail. Jail. Jail. Jail," I laugh. My whole life will be gone soon. I'll be taken away from Key West. From my mom. From Jenna. *From Cash.* These thoughts scare the hell out of me, but I laugh like a maniac, my body shivering, my hands icy cold.

Cash moves in front of me, blocking my view of the corpse, then he squeezes my throat until I stop laughing.

"Listen to me closely," he says. "No one is going to jail. This isn't the end for anyone, *except* this piece of garbage." He kicks the corpse, then wipes his fingers across my chin, the wet liquid, part blood, part come, smearing my face. "I'm not going to let anything happen to you, Remedy. I promise."

A calmness, like a heavy, warm blanket, weighs down on me, because I believe him. I fucking believe everything Cash says. Cash told me he'll do anything for me and he proved himself with his actions.

"No matter what happens," Cash says, "We're in this together."

He yanks me to my feet, his thick, bumpy hands engulfing me. My weak knees shudder from the shock. But he holds me close, my stepdad's blood staining his body.

"Come fuck me, Remedy," he says. He strips, then sits on the sofa, his legs spread. Coarse hair darkens his thighs and those puffy pink scars decorate his chest like the sprouted eyes of a potato, but I want all of him. He fists his shaft, the head brutal and red, but his eyes never leave mine. "You are so damn hot."

I touch my cheek. I'm covered in my stepdad's blood.

Cash thinks I look good like this?

With each step forward, the numbness waves over me, but I go through the motions, taking off my clothes, blood smearing my body.

"Why don't I feel bad?" I ask, my voice barely audible. I kneel on the sofa, straddling Cash, my calves pressed against his thick, hairy thighs. He's warm where I'm cold and dead, and I want to dive inside of him until I can't see or hear anything anymore. "All I want is to fuck you right now," I say.

Cash growls, his primal words vibrating through me: "Next time you do it, it'll feel good."

A chill runs through my stomach, up to my throat. He's so sure of himself, like he knows there *will* be a next time.

And if I'm honest with myself, maybe I want it too.

He lifts my hips then rams me down, fucking me so hard his cock smashes into my cervix, the pain annihilating my nerves. It's like he *wants* to make this hurt. Like he wants me to remember this. Every little thing I can't take emotionally, he wants me to take physically instead. He pulls the hair at the back of my neck until I'm looking straight up at the ceiling like a woman possessed. He licks my neck, tasting the blood and sweat on my skin, and I know that I *am* possessed. I'm possessed by him. He slaps my face and the shock ripples through me.

"That's right, slut," Cash says in a low voice. "Look at what you did. I'm so proud of you."

My stomach tightens at those words. I hold Cash's face in my hands and his eyes burn holes into me. It's true. Every word. He *is* proud of me. He believes in me just as much as I believe in him.

Maybe this has been inside of me all along. Maybe I'm meant to be here, right now, like this, with Cash.

"You know what this makes you?" he growls.

"What?"

"Mine."

Adrenaline sweeps through me and I can barely breathe. Each swell of my lungs stutters with pressure. But I keep fucking Cash, digging my nails into his skin, exploring the fresh scars on his back. Scars from me. His body is stained with blood, just like mine, and it feels like a dream. Like nothing in the world can be *this* perfect. But my stepdad is there, right behind us. He's a man who used to control me, who will never have power over me again. He's a lump of flesh and bones now.

Cash gave that to me.

The sweat drenches our bodies as Cash stands, hoisting me up, using my stepdad's head as a brace to steady himself. But I reach down with my feet, dismantling from Cash, then I guide him until he's lying on the ground, next to the corpse. Cash bares his teeth, his face somewhere between a predatory warning and a grin. But this time, *I fuck him*. I show him who I am. I raise my hips up, then slam down, making his dick impale me until it hurts, until I cry. I'm alive and more powerful than ever.

I grip Cash's chin between my fingers. He said he'll do anything for me, and he's kept to his word. And I realize that *this* is it. This is what I wanted. Why I wanted to kill Cash in the first place. It was never about what Cash did or didn't do to Jenna. It was about my stepdad. And now that he's gone, with every fiber of my being, I believe Cash. He didn't hurt Jenna, and he will never hurt me.

I dig my nails into his skin and he growls, his jaw clenched, but his cock twitches like he can't control himself, no matter how hard he tries, and that sensation sends us both over the edge. His eyes roll into the back of his head as he lets out a primal howl, and I keep my eyes on him even as the uncontrollable spasms crash through me. We're invincible. We can do anything together.

Once our breathing settles, I lean down, putting my tongue against his ear. He's exhausted, his breathing rapid, and I love it all. *I* did this to him.

With teeth pressed against his earlobe, I whisper, "And you're mine."

CHAPTER 14

REMEDY

THE NEXT DAY, ENERGY HUMS THROUGH ME, BOASTING CONFIDENCE in each step. I look up at the empty blue sky, the sun shining down on my chilled, wintery skin. Maybe this is freedom.

But I still feel off somehow. Like there's something rattling inside of me. I'm not sure what to do with myself. It's not like before; my stepdad will never bother me or anyone else again. And yet, I still have this urge to do *something*.

But I don't know what.

The door chimes as I enter the bakery. The cakes are illuminated in the display case like little pieces of art. Baby blues. Pale pinks. Light greens. It seems stupid. Cash gave me the opportunity to take back my life, and I get him a damn cake.

In the back corner of the case, I spot a white cake with red streams of frosting dripping over the ribboned edges, and I see flashes of my stepdad's blood splattering Cash's scarred chest. A warmth tingles in my lower belly at the thought. It was so hot.

My stomach turns. *He used you,* my logical brain argues. *Manipulated you. Got you to kill your stepdad so he could have even more blackmail over you. How can you be so stupid?*

I clutch my abdomen, trying to force myself to stop questioning him. But there are video cameras. Everything is caught on his surveillance and my personal camera, which is still sitting on the mantel in the office. Even if Cash is charged with abduction, I will be charged with murder.

But I can't let that fear immobilize me. Cash had set me free.

He hurt your best friend, that nagging voice says.

Not the same man, I argue back.

The baker clears her throat, her eyes signaling that I need to choose a cake already. I peer around each row of treats, trying to think. My phone buzzes.

"Remedy Basset," I answer.

"Remedy Basset? This is the Key West Police Department calling. Is there any chance you'd be able to come down to the station? Detective Samuels would like to speak with you."

My shoulders tense. Peter? Why does he want to talk now? Does he know about my stepdad?

No. There's no way he knows. I watched Cash paint the body in primer last night. *This way, it won't stink as bad,* he said. *But I promise you, Remedy. We're in this together.*

I have to stay calm. Anxiety is getting the best of me, and I can't let it control me. I straighten my fingers, rubbing my palms against my pants. Why would Peter suspect me of anything?

"Yes," I say. "I'll be right over."

A low dull pain grows in my stomach. I pay for the cake and take it home before heading to the police station. The department is in a salmon building with sea foam green diamonds patterned across the edges. I haven't been here in years, not since my mom first told them about my stepdad.

But they didn't do anything back then. This won't be the exception.

Cash promised me that we're in this together. We're safe.

I walk slowly to the front desk, my feet sticking to the ground with each step. It's hard to move forward. The clerk looks up from the computer, smiling at me.

"I was told to come in for questioning?" I mumble.

"And you are?"

"Remedy Basset."

"Ah! Yes. Follow me."

She takes me to a room to the side of the building. There's a mirror on one wall and a window on the other, showing the main lobby. A water cooler hums in the corner, and a metal table splits the room in half.

"Coffee?" she asks. I shake my head. I'm too nervous to drink anything, even water.

A few minutes later, Peter bursts through the doors, a casual hand running through his reddish-blond hair. He gives me a side hug.

"How are you doing, Remmie?" he asks, taking the chair in front of me. "Have you been here long?"

"Not at all," I say. "I've heard horror stories about how long they'll make you wait."

"I'm not going to go through those games with you. You're too smart for that." He tilts his head, giving me a quick smile. Then his face shifts, dropping the playfulness; he's ready for business. "You're working for Mr. Winstone these days, yes?" he asks. I nod. "Are you his only personal assistant?"

"Yes."

"Does he have any other house staff?"

I lift my shoulders. "He fired them before he hired Jenna."

"Huh. Why'd he fire them?"

My cheeks flush red. "I guess he thought they weren't very good."

"And why did Jenna leave the job?"

I sink down into my chair. Have I already said something I'm not supposed to say?

"You'll have to ask Jenna," I say.

"Or you can save me the trouble."

I keep my head down. I want to protect Jenna *and* Cash. How can I get through this next part without lying?

But Jenna doesn't need to be protected. She hasn't done anything wrong.

But Cash and me? We murdered my stepdad.

That isn't right either. Cash hasn't done anything. *I have.* I'm the true criminal here.

As long as Jenna and Cash don't go down with me, everything will be fine.

"Remmie?" Peter asks. "Why did Jenna transfer from the Winstone Estate?"

"They had an argument," I say, touching the back of my neck.

"That happens. Know anything about the specifics?"

I shrug. "I just know they didn't get along."

"And what about you?" He sits up in his seat, leaning forward like he knows I've got something juicy I'm holding back. "What's it like to work for him?"

Where am I supposed to go with this? I don't want to put Cash out there, but I have to say something realistic.

"Why?" I ask. "Is he a suspect?"

"With a small town like this? Almost everyone is a suspect. Even you!" Peter laughs. My stomach twists, but I force a smile. The grin drops from his face and he lowers his voice: "Off the record, we've been interviewing his contractors to see where it points. We know the killer is connected to the Winstone Company. We haven't figured out how, but we have a few leads."

I bob my head in agreement. After all, in a way, he's right. I killed someone and I'm technically supposed to be Winstone's personal assistant. Does Peter know I'm a killer?

"Can you describe the way Winstone looks?" Peter asks.

My nose squeaks and Peter cocks a brow at me, his jaw stern and unamused.

I clear my throat. "Sorry. Did you ask me to describe how he looks?" I ask.

"Seems he's gone through some plastic surgery recently. I wanted to confirm it with you."

"Sorry," I say. That's right. "He's—" I pause, trying to think. What did Jenna say about his appearance? "He's older, you know? He's got one of those faces, like he could be anybody," I say, but I know I'm rambling. I need to mesh up the two images I have—the one Jenna described to me, and the one of the real Cash, so I can protect him. "Dark eyes. They've got these spots in the whites of his eyes." I cross my arms around myself. "Seriously, what's this about?"

"You have access to his files, correct?"

I sink down in my seat. "Yes and no?"

"How old is he? Would you say he's in his fifties or sixties?"

He looks a lot younger than that, but does that really matter? "I'm not sure. What's going on?"

"There's something that doesn't add up with Winstone, and I don't like it. I met him the other day." He shakes his head. "I'm worried for you, Remedy." He reaches over the table and holds my hand. Every hair on my body raises at the touch, but I stay still. "You're backing yourself into a corner. I can help you get out of Winstone's grip, but you've got to work *with* me."

I pull my hand back, keeping it in my lap. "What do you mean?"

"He's a powerful man. Even if he's not committing the crimes himself, I'm sure he can make someone else do it for him."

I grit my teeth. Why does this sound so familiar?

"He hasn't done anything like that to me," I say.

"Good."

But that's a lie. He *has* done something like that. Cash gave me my stepdad as a gift. And I killed him.

If you don't do it, I will, he said. But I didn't let him.

Had he tricked me into doing it for him?

A sinking feeling swarms inside of me, fighting to take over. Even if killing my stepdad is somehow justified, even if I'm honestly *glad* that my stepdad will never be able to hurt another girl again, I'm not sure what I'm supposed to do when it comes to Cash. If he's capable of abducting my stepdad from Tampa and bringing him to me, what else is he capable of?

If I know he's committing crimes, is it my duty to stop him?

"Remedy?" Peter asks.

I startle, jumping in my seat. "Yes?"

"Do you want me to take you back to work?" he asks. "These kinds of questionings can be shocking. I completely understand that. I can escort you back to the estate and make sure Winstone doesn't try anything."

Peter is sweet, and in a way, I'm grateful that he's offering. But no one can be trusted. Especially not someone like him.

So why do I trust Cash?

"I'm fine. But thank you," I say. "I just want to get back to work."

Peter nods. "Please call me if you think of anything."

As I walk out of the room toward the front of the station, I try to mentally block out the noise. The copy machines whirring. The chatter between employees. The phones ringing. I need to think straight, and none of this is helping. A man in a police uniform looks up from his desk and stares at me. Another officer gawks, and it's like every pair of eyes in the entire building is staring at me, but I don't know why. I rush toward the door, but the clerk at the front desk increases the volume on the television and I hear: *More on the Key West Killer.*

I stop in my tracks. Then I face the screen, flattening my fingers on my sides.

The reporter sits with her feet inside of a hatch to a crawl space, her expression neutral. Her platinum blond hair is perfectly styled, and it seems like she's the kind of person who will never be touched by these crimes. *Investigators now believe that the Key West Killer, now dubbed 'the Crawler,' is linked to over thirty known murders across the US. We spoke with Veronica Long, a professor of criminology and a long-time profiler in Miami, who believes the Crawler to be in his late thirties, early forties, with a knowledge of construction—*

A ringing fills my ears. On the screen, the investigators clear out each crime scene while the profiler dissects the Crawler. Chunks of white insulation foam. A broken painting. White paint and dried red blood. I swallow a dry breath. None of the victims are my stepdad. There's no reason to be upset. But I can feel police officers' eyes burning into me. I'm going to explode.

I swing around to give the officers a dirty look, but everyone is busy. No one seems to notice me.

Am I being paranoid?

I stagger toward my car, bile bubbling in my throat. The reporter's words flash in my mind: *thirty known murders.*

Thirty people are dead.

That's what they know. There may be more.

If I know something—if I know *anything*, is it my job to tell the police? To make sure that no one else dies?

I slip into my car, tapping my fingers nervously against the steering wheel. What do I know? I know Cash abducted my stepdad. I know *I* killed my stepdad. Cash, according to my knowledge, hasn't killed anyone.

But as I drive back to the estate, that sinking feeling threatens to take over. Right now, Cash is at the hardware store, picking up and dropping off an item for one of his newer developments. I have time to process this before he returns. But that stops me.

He knows about construction. He fixed my door. He even knows the people at the hardware store.

But he *should* know them. He's a real estate developer. It's his job to build things.

And yet I can't shake that he's connected to these murders somehow. I drive back to the estate, chills running through me. No matter what I tell myself, I can't get rid of these feelings.

So I force myself into his downstairs office, where I killed my stepdad the night before. I pick through his desk drawers. Pens. Paperclips. A pair of reading glasses. But I can't stop searching. I try his computer again, but no matter what password I try, nothing works.

Bones jumps in my lap, circling until she finds a comfortable position. My breath catches in my throat, and I try her name. It doesn't work. But for the hell of it, I try my own password: *Bones1934*, a reference to the tattoo on my back and the year Bonnie and Clyde were killed. The password prompt disappears, and video files fill the screen. I recognize myself in the thumbnails, so I double-click one.

In the video, I'm sitting on a computer chair. From the expression on my face, I'm intrigued by whatever I'm watching. I almost exit the video—there are surveillance cameras everywhere in the estate—but then I see my unmade bed in the background.

This video isn't from the Winstone Estate. It's from my bedroom.

Did Cash hack into my laptop?

I quickly log out of the computer. It frightens me, but it doesn't mean anything. It means he's a voyeur, or even a stalker. But it doesn't mean he's the Crawler.

I shift my focus to the back of the room, in the closet, where he keeps his safe. I try a few different combinations on the lock, but each time, red letters blink back at me: *Access Denied!* Finally, I try my own birthdate, and it opens. My stomach does a belly flop. It's like he *wants* me to find what's inside. And that scares me.

There's an old birth certificate. *Cassius Winstone.* The mother and father are listed in the middle, but the birthdate seems off. I do some quick math in my head, and if I'm right, Cash should be sixty years old right now. But he can't be more than forty, if he's even *that* old.

An idea pops into my mind: maybe he doesn't remember his birthday because he can't tell me the truth without revealing himself as an imposter.

This is my proof. Cash isn't Cassius Winstone.

But I don't feel relieved anymore.

I pace back and forth in that closet. What am I supposed to do? I know he isn't the real Cassius Winstone. What if I'm okay with that? What if I'm relieved? What if I don't care if he's somehow linked to these deaths across the country, because at least he's not my best friend's abuser?

I stumble, tripping over the lip of a maroon rug tucked underneath the shoe bench and the safe, falling on my hands and knees.

"Damn it," I mutter. I push myself up, admiring the brightness of the rug, and that stops me. It's *new*, and it covers almost the entire closet. Like it's been added recently. Like it's hiding something.

With some grunting, I move the shoe bench and the safe, then lift the rug.

There, on the ground, is a cutout in the wood with a single metal handle, almost exactly like the one from the news report. It's a small door, just big enough for someone like Cash to fit inside.

It's a closed door. Cash told me *not* to open any closed doors.

But this isn't a door to a room. It's a crawl space. Like the news mentioned.

Many houses have them. It's a coincidence.

But my heart thuds in my chest. I hold my breath, my body buzzing with energy as I pull the metal handle, opening the door.

It's dark and empty; there's nothing there. The stench of sour alcohol and rotting bouquets surrounds me. It's stale, but not alarm-worthy yet. I exhale slowly, but I freeze in place. I need to know for sure.

I turn on the flashlight on my phone, then aim it at one side of the crawl space. My stepdad's body shines in the light, his face painted white like a plastic doll. I check the other side: an older man with gray hair and shriveling skin is frozen in place. The white paint peels in places, exposing his yellow, purple, and black skin. The real Mr. Winstone.

The stench of the bodies grows around me. I breathe through my mouth, trying to think straight, but I can't. I close the small door.

Who is Cash? Is that even his real name?

And why did he kill Mr. Winstone?

Sweat drips down my body as I move the rug back into place, then put the shoe bench and the safe back to make it seem like I didn't disturb anything. Because this isn't real. If I hadn't gone snooping, then Cash would be the practically harmless Substitute Mr. Winstone.

But I can't let it go. I have to get out of here.

At the front door to the estate, I weigh my options. Going through with this—confronting Cash—may not actually get me anywhere. If he's been playing me for this long, then he's always known that I'll eventually find out. Maybe he *wants* me to know everything.

I follow my instincts. In my car, I rip through the streets, barely avoiding collisions. It's like my body is racing with my mind, and I have to get home. Have to do something. Have to make sure I'm safe. I race into my rental house, then lean against the wall, completely out of breath.

The closet door catches my eye. There's a hatch in the ground. One that hadn't been there before.

My temples throb, but I force myself to look. I open the closet door, then gaze down at the hatch. I remember the times Cash silently got into my house. What if he was already in the house, hiding in my crawl space?

It's insane, but I can't let it go. I stand up. All I want is the truth. Trying to manipulate a serial killer into telling the truth is stupid. He has endless opportunities to kill me. And he can kill me right now if he wants.

Except he hasn't. The choke chain. The noose in the parking lot. Taking my eyes and ears. With the knife that killed my stepdad. There are so many times he could have killed me, but I'm still here. And I have this instinct that he *wants* me to know the truth. Like he left this puzzle for me.

I open the hatch. Pine trees and faint chemicals waft from the crawl space. As if he's been here recently.

Who the hell is Cash?

CHAPTER 15

CASH

When I bound down the stairs, ready to start the day, I find a cake on the counter with candles poking out of the top. Remedy stands in the kitchen, a black dress clinging to her frame, her lips painted red like the frosting on the cake. Her thick thighs press together and I imagine my face crushed in between them. Anything I want to get done seems pointless. I want to have her first.

"I can sing to you," she says. "Or we can just eat cake."

It's a nice thought, but I'm not interested in the cake.

I run a hand up her side, the curve of her hips making me salivate. The bruises on her neck are mostly healed now, with only a few greenish-yellow spots from the noose, but I want more. I want to see my marks all the time, to proclaim to the world that she's mine. But the more I work her skin, the harder it's going to be to bruise her, no matter how hard I try. It's an omen, a reason we can't get more attached, but Remedy grins, and I lose that train of thought. The more intertwined our lives become, the stronger she gets. One of us is going to break, and it's looking like there's a chance it may be me.

Why am I still with Remedy?

I cup her ass, squeezing that juicy bubble that connects with her thighs. My cock stirs awake, eager to slide into her warmth again. I can never get enough of her.

"If it's my birthday, do I get to spank you?" I ask. A shiver runs down her spine and she bends over the counter, pushing her ass into me, grinding on my dick. Blood floods to my cock, but something stops me. She glances over her shoulders at me, and there's hesitation there. She's not only my lover treating me to a fake birthday celebration, but a woman who thinks I owe her. Hunger simmers in her movements, too calculated to be genuine. She's hiding something from me.

And maybe I *do* owe Remedy. She's been through physical and mental torment for me.

But she grabs my hands, smirking, dragging me toward the bedrooms. I yank her back, twisting her from her clothes until she's naked with her chest flat against the countertop. As I press into her upper back, her breasts smash on the surface, and her cheek lays against the marble, a hazy reflection of her face in the smooth material. I rub her ass, teasing her supple curves. She wiggles her hips. She wants this as much as I do.

I smack her ass so hard, the palm of my hand stings like hell. My hand is red, and her ass too, and she lifts her foot, the pain shooting through her body. I don't care for spankings, but when it comes to Remedy, I like physical contact. It hurts me almost as much as it hurts her. The recipient and the aggressor *both* feel the sting. Everything is connected. I lick my fingers, getting them ready to tease her, then I press my hips into her back.

"How old do you think I am?" I ask, teasing her dark hole with my fingertip.

"I-I—" she stammers, "I don't know."

"Don't move."

I wait for a moment, making sure she stays still, and though the bottom of her spine curves, like she wants so badly to press into me again, her feet stay flat on the ground, her ass in the air. I check the kitchen drawers: wooden spoons, plastic utensils, knives, and other tools. But I want something that will hurt. A weapon that can cause damage, to remind her that I own her. Just like she owns me.

I find it: a large metal spoon with straining holes on the end. This will count as my fake birthday spanking.

The air whistles through the holes and the spoon bounces off her skin. She screams, curling her toes, the hairs on the back of my neck raising at the high-pitched squeal, and *that* makes it worth it. A swollen, purple oval darkens her ass, taunting me for more. It's a bruise that will last for a long time. She'll feel my touch whenever she sits down.

But I want *more.*

I hit her with the spoon again and again until she's panting like a dog, twisting to get off of the counter. But I hold her down, making sure that she endures every blow. I want her to know what it feels like every time she barges into my mind, every time she fucks up my world until it doesn't make sense. Why am I still here? I hit her again. Why haven't I saved myself yet? The spoon claps on her ass again, and I wonder how I'm so wrapped up in Remedy that I'm willing to risk everything, even my life.

She's destroying me.

"How does that feel?" I ask, my pulse elevated, the veins throbbing in my temple. She writhes against the counter like a snake, and I pin her down with my weight, then play with her pussy, her wet lips making my eyes roll into the back of my head. "You want to come, little cure?"

"Yes," she moans.

"Then show me how desperate you are."

She bucks her hips on my hand and I pull back her hair, watching her face contort as she moves. Her body crashes through each motion, but her eyes stay fixed in place. I've seen that look before. The vacancy that occupies her mind. This isn't a fake birthday celebration. She's toying with me.

I remove my hand and her jaw drops in surprise.

"Tell me what it is," I demand.

"Tell you what?"

"Why did you fake that orgasm?" I breathe through my teeth. "I'm not your ex. I know when you come. And that was a spectac- ular performance, but it's not enough for me."

Her tongue runs across her lips. She's trying to think of the right answer. She rubs her hands against her sides as the panic sets in, but then she lifts her chin, looking down her nose at me.

"I saw the body," she says.

"What body?"

"You're not Cassius Winstone."

I instantly straighten myself, giving us distance. "I never said I was Cassius Winstone. I said to call me 'Cash.' *You didn't listen.*"

"Then who are you?"

I stare at her, willing her to pretend like she truly wants me to be the same Mr. Winstone who abused her best friend.

"Face it," I say. "You're glad that I'm not him."

"Tell me who you are."

There's tension in her eyes, like she's angry and doesn't know who or what to believe. But I've told her the same line before, and I'll say it again. Nothing is going to change that.

"Call me 'Cash,'" I say.

She lunges at me, her nostrils flaring, fire in her eyes. She howls like a wild animal and her nails pry at my skin, trying to hurt me. Like she's trying to scrape out my heart with her tiny fists. But I've been through worse.

"Why are you upset?" I laugh, letting her do her worst. Her nails sear into me, but I don't care. I know how to channel it out. "You were going to kill him anyway."

"You stole that from me."

Her fists hit my chest like a dull drum, but I stand still. Each blow hammers into me, and I don't give a damn. After a minute, she huffs out a breath, then screams as she rakes her nails down my chest again. I hiss through my teeth, little beads of blood sprouting on the swollen skin, but she does it again, her fingertips damp with my blood. She paints my body red like she did with her stepdad's blood.

But it's my blood now.

She grabs my face, forcing herself forward to kiss me, but I pull the gun from my holster, using the long barrel against her throat, cutting off her air just enough to make her stop. She squeaks in surprise, and I bare my teeth.

"You should have known better, little cure," my voice reverberates. "You thought I only keep knives? I keep guns too."

But still, she doesn't run away. She holds my face again, cupping me like a child, and for a moment, it's like she's holding me up. I want to let go of everything and vanish inside of her.

But I can't. No matter what I do, I have to dominate her. I press the gun's muzzle into her temple, and this time, she bites her lip so hard that her skin turns purple. I'm getting close. She'll break soon, and then it'll be over. The only thing left to do will be to frame her.

Or else she'll destroy me.

"On your knees," I say. She falls instantly. I knock the gun lightly into her chin until she opens her mouth. "Suck it," I order. She closes her eyes, tears forming at the edges. But once her lips press into the metal, she pushes that fear away and pleasures it like a cock. My dick swells at the sight. Her purple lips press into the metal, her cheeks suctioned, drool wetting the sides of her mouth. She looks so good like that. On her knees. Her life in my literal fingers.

And yet she has no idea how much she controls me.

"You want the real me?" I ask. "I've been more real with you than anyone in this world. And that's what pisses you off. That you still want me for it."

She pulls off of the gun and snaps her teeth together, her eyes full of fury. I pull her up to her feet, ripping off my pants and spinning her around, pressing her into the countertop again. I use the arousal from her pussy lips to wet my dick, then I force myself into her ass. Her lungs empty in a sharp, breathtaking gasp, and I slam inside of her, holding the gun to her back. She may be the first person I haven't killed, but that doesn't mean she's safe. In a second, she can join the rest of them, trapped in the insulation of their own homes, rotting with the foundation.

And yet, inside, I know that's no longer true. I will never hurt Remedy like that. I refuse.

But I can still control her.

"You think you can see everything if you're always on the attack," I growl. The muzzle digs into the skin between her shoulder blades, right in the middle of the tattoo of those two skeletal bodies. She arches her spine again. Her breaths come out in rapid succession; she's scared. "But I always had you first, Remedy. You always were, and you will always be *mine.*"

I wrap my hands around her hips as I push my dick deeper into her ass. Her clit is wet and swollen, and I circle it with my fingertips, my hand frantic. I need her to come. I need her body to convulse in a way that's completely mine, and not the performance she gives to everyone else. Each time my full length fills her up, she gasps. Her ass is so damn smooth, it's intoxicating. I can barely hold on to my goal. She's so close to orgasm that I suck in her tangy musk like it's the last breath I'll ever have. And when her muscles start to constrict, I pull out, letting her suffer through the lack of fulfillment. Her jaw drops, anger flashing in her eyes. And I study her.

Her green eyes flicker like she's trying to find the missing clues. But I'm here. It doesn't matter who she thinks I am anymore.

"You killed Cassius Winstone," she says confidently. "I owe you for that."

"And you killed your stepdad."

She nods and keeps our eye contact. "Which means, whether or not you like it, we're in this together."

I laugh. *Together?* "All it means is that we're both killers," I say.

"You said it yourself, Cash. 'No matter what happens, we're in this together.'"

I said that right after she killed her stepdad. She was hyperventilating about the murder. I had to do something to help her accept it, since she couldn't take it back. I instantly regretted those words, knowing that I was marking myself as someone she can leave behind.

I refuse to depend on anyone, including her.

I put a finger under her chin, narrowing my eyes at her. She knows I can erase her; it's as easy as pulling the trigger.

But she also trusts me not to, and that infuriates me.

"You're going to get hurt, little cure," I say. "Just because we're wrapped up in each other, doesn't mean you're free."

She bites her inner lip but steadies herself. "But you set me free, Cash. You did this to me."

"And I will never leave you alone until we're both dead."

Our heavy breaths mix in the air, both of us covered in sweat. She's naked, and I'm disheveled, but this is our truest selves.

As much as I hate it, I know I'll do anything to protect her, and at the same time, I want nothing to do with her.

If anyone destroys me, it will be Remedy.

And now, I want her to leave before I do something I regret.

"Go check on Jenna," I order. Remedy gawks at me in surprise, but it's the quickest way to get her out of the estate. "Now," I say with a low threat in my voice. "Make sure she doesn't suspect anything." Remedy blinks, then quickly dresses and disappears through the front door.

I sigh, running my hands through my damp hair. My feet are rooted, but I want to be free. Just like Remedy does. And the only way to live a free life is to do what I want, ignoring the moral and legal repercussions, and *never* let anyone hold me back.

My phone buzzes. I groan, then check it: *Some detective has been asking about you,* one of the general contractors texts. *Where the hell have you been? Get back to work! Let me pay you, damn it!*

I had backed out of more projects than I could count recently, only taking a few small ones to cover my ass and pretend to be the same subcontractor that's been around the Keys for years. A man no one notices. And most of the time, it works.

But the longer I stay with Remedy, the more I unravel. I need to leave now to throw that detective off of my scent. I need to leave everything behind.

I should kill Remedy. Or if I'm that weak already, I *should* just frame her. But I don't want to focus on those options anymore. I want something else.

I remove a manilla folder from my desk, the file my old associate from Montana prepared on Peter Samuels. The detective's picture is on the front, and he's smiling like he hasn't got a care in the world. I've been through the file more times than I can count, trying to figure out a way to shift the blame on him instead of Remedy. But the bastard is clean. A regular town hero. He's never even smoked weed. The only indulgence he has is a white car with shiny black rims. He was even pulled over by a coworker for speeding when he first started, but he took the ticket because he knew he deserved it. The private investigator found that he had a reputation for being a druggy in high school, but what he actually did was make sure that people didn't choke on their own vomit. When a classmate almost drank herself to death, he brought her to a separate room with a bucket and water. He asked her not to tell anyone so that he could keep his reputation. He's a damn fake!

So the rumor Remedy knows from high school isn't true. Peter wasn't the one to drug the girl. Instead, he watched over her. Like a guardian angel.

And right now, he's probably looking out for Remedy. Trying to warn her to stay away from me.

Killing a cop is risky. It's easier to stay away from their kind. But the idea of finishing him off and somehow making the deaths fall on him fills me with serenity.

But I don't have to kill him or Remedy. I can leave. Start a new life, like I always do.

But I can't make myself do it yet. Instead, I text Remedy like a pansy: *Let's do a make-up unbirthday. Tomorrow night.*

I have a favor to ask, she immediately replies. She doesn't even acknowledge my text.

I groan deeply. A favor disturbs me. It means that she knows she can ask me for things. Like she can rely on me. But I'm ready for it. And the worst part is that no matter what that favor may be, I know I'll do anything for her.

What is she going to ask of me?

CHAPTER 16

REMEDY

THE NEXT DAY PASSES IN A BLUR. I WATCH THE CLOCK DURING work, completing each task Cash assigns me. It's like nothing's changed, and yet now I know that we're both pretending that Winstone is alive. My mind buzzes with energy, the pressure growing with each passing minute. Cash has a date planned for us tonight, and it makes my thoughts race. He never plans anything. I should be afraid.

But one idea keeps me grounded in that internal chaos: if I show Jenna Winstone's body, then everything will be all right. Because if Cash gives me permission to let another person in on our secret life, then it'll prove that he trusts me and that I can trust him. And tonight, I'm going to ask him for that permission.

In the evening, the doorbell rings, and I suck in a breath. Anxiety grows inside of me. What is he going to say when I ask him? Is he finally going to kill me?

The doorbell rings incessantly, like someone is panicking, which tells me that it's not Cash. But I open the door anyway, my chest sinking when I see who it is.

My stepbrother, Brody, stands on my front porch, a baseball cap on his head, just like he used to wear when we were kids. I haven't seen him in years. He looks down at me.

Finally, I stammer, "How did you—"

He cuts me off: "Your mom told me I could find you here."

"Damn it," I mutter under my breath. Of course, she told him. She always liked him. I'll have to remind her *not* to give out my information without my consent the next time I see her.

"Mind if I come in?" he asks. Then he steps around me. The question is a formality, not a courtesy, to him. I close the front door.

"What are you doing here?" I ask, crossing my arms.

"Do you know where Dad is?" he says. I scratch my side, thinking of my stepdad's body in the crawl space of the Winstone Estate. A tension burns through me, but I shake my head. "He disappeared," Brody continues. "Ghosted his new family completely."

I shrug. "I haven't spoken to him since the divorce."

"I figured you'd say that." He lifts his baseball cap to run a hand through his light brown hair, then caps it again and tilts his head, scrutinizing me, like he can tell I'm lying. The fluorescent lights shimmer on his tanned skin and my stomach flips; he looks more and more like his dad every day. But they're different kinds of evil; my stepdad pretended to be nice, while Brody doesn't care if the world knows he's cruel. "You want to get dinner somewhere?" he asks.

He wants to get dinner? We're both adults now, but that doesn't mean we can sit through an entire meal together without ripping off each other's heads. Besides, I have a date with Cash.

"I've got plans," I say.

"Then I guess I'll stay until you're available to talk."

I furrow my brows. "Stay *where?*"

"I know he disappeared because of you." Brody peers into each room, checking for his dad behind the toilet and under the desk. "Did you finally kill him like you swore you would?"

My stomach lurches and my cheeks flush red, but I force myself to scoff. "Shut up, Brody."

"I remember that. You swore up and down that you'd kill him one day," he chuckles. I forgot I told Brody that right before they moved away. I wanted him to know that I wasn't going to forgive and forget as easily as Mom always does. And I kept my word, thanks to Cash.

"Maybe Dad came back for that pussy," he says.

I step back, my skin tingling with knives. Brody has always been convinced that *I* asked for it. As if I seduced my stepdad by wearing skimpy clothes and prancing around, when I was a normal girl, doing normal things, wearing normal outfits. I didn't *ask* him for anything. I didn't understand what sex was until he touched me.

And yet, for a long time, Brody convinced me that it was my fault.

But not anymore. I suck in a breath. "You are disgusting."

"Have you seen him lately?"

Why does he keep asking? My heart races; there's no way he knows what Cash and I did. *What I did.* Brody is only acting on a hunch.

I raise my voice: "I told you: I haven't seen him."

"Then why do I get this feeling like you're lying?"

He shoves me against the wall, lifting his fist. I kick my legs out, trying to knee him like I used to when we were younger, but he's bigger now, smarter too, and pins me so that I can't touch him.

"You were always big about justice being served, right, lil' sis? Should I 'rape' you like you *claim* he did?" he asks. "I bet you're wet right now."

"Fuck you," I hiss.

"No. A girl like you wants it in the ass. Dad told me how wet you got when he fucked you there."

I grit my teeth. Anger swells inside of me, threatening to boil over, to show *him* what it's like to be powerless, like his dad made me. But Brody is mostly bluster; one punch, one blow, one kick, then his conscience kicks into gear and he lets me go. I should endure it like I always do.

But the taste of revenge is thick in my throat like the sour taste of alcohol. I *want* to kill him. He thinks I'm the same little girl I was years ago, but I'm not. I killed his father, and I am *not* afraid of him.

But I can't overpower him. All I have is my voice.

"You never learned how to get a girl wet, did you?" I snap. "Maybe you'll end up like your daddy. Raping little girls since no one wants to fuck you."

He huffs through his teeth and I brace myself for his blow, but his eyes widen as he clenches my shirt, and we're both pulled back, knocked off balance. He lets go of me and swings around to see who tore him off of me.

Cash glares down at him, his eyes full of fire. The dark spots in his eyes are like black clouds of smoke and ash, threatening to consume everything. I glance behind him; the hatch is open in the hall closet. My heart beats rapidly, and suddenly, the moral issues of the situation get to me. I can't kill Brody, but Cash can and *will*, and I don't know if I'm actually okay with that. Brody and I fight like step-siblings who hate each other, but I don't know if he deserves to die, when I fight him just as much as he fights me.

I whisper: "Cash—"

"Get up," Cash says, his eyes locked on Brody.

Brody stumbles. "The hell do you want?" he asks. "Who are you?"

Cash shoves him so hard the wall cracks with his body, and when Brody goes to punch him, Cash grabs his throat until Brody chokes, his mouth sputtering with spit.

"You will never touch Remedy again," Cash says, his voice eerily low and controlled. His knuckles are white, but there's a calmness in his expression, like he knows exactly how he's going to break every bone in Brody's body. Brody paws at Cash's hands, trying to break free, and his face transforms from bright red into a dark purple.

Brody's lips mouth: *I won't. I won't—*

Cash drops his grip and Brody falls to the floor, coughing and clawing at his neck. He doesn't even look at us as he races to his car. I hold my breath. Cash pulls me to my feet and I cross my arms, my mouth gaping.

I don't know how to feel. Am I disappointed Cash didn't kill him? Or am I relieved? Will Brody tell the police about Cash?

Cash's eyes flicker, but the smoke and ash consume him, a

dullness simmering behind his gaze like this is a matter of fact. As I search him, I realize why he didn't kill Brody yet: he doesn't want the evidence contaminating my rental house.

He's protecting me.

Still, I know what I'm *supposed* to say. "Don't kill him."

"Do I need to keep you in the estate?" he asks, like he's telling me to order more food for Bones. Like there's nothing wrong here.

"I'm fine. But don't do anything to him, okay?"

He nods toward the front door where a truck is parked. "I have to cancel tonight's date," he says. "We'll make up for it tomorrow. I'll see you at work."

"Cash—"

He stops with his hand on the front doorknob.

"Don't do anything to him," I say. "My stepdad is the one who hurt me. Brody is just an asshole. We always hit each other. It's what we do."

Cash sniffs, then lifts his nose in the air. I realize my error: *we always hit each other.* It doesn't matter who it is, if it's rape or consensual or a stupid fight between ex-step-siblings. Any touch from someone else won't be tolerated. Cash isn't okay with sharing that part of me.

"I'll see you later," he says.

My gut crawls, but I follow him to the doorway. "He only hits me once, then it's over—"

But Cash slides into his truck, then drives away, and I know there's nothing I can do. Brody didn't hurt me, but he did touch me, and there's no way that Cash is going to let that go. Even if I know how to handle myself—even if I know how to handle Brody —I will never be free of Cash.

Because Cash won't let me go.

———

Cash

I stare at the brown door of room one-zero-two, waiting for the stepbrother to be brave enough to leave his motel room. It's dark now, but I'm willing to wait. Tonight was supposed to be fun. I was going to surprise Remedy with a cage big enough to lock her up forever. It's a solution that may fit us. Find a cage. Make her want it. If she's not going to let me go, then I may as well capture her like she's caged me.

But instead, I'm hunting her stepbrother.

I'm in my truck, parked across the street, but Key West is compact and I can see clearly. His silhouette shifts across the curtains, and he moves like he's dancing to music. Like he doesn't care that he just assaulted his ex-stepsister and threatened to rape her. Like he hasn't got a care in the world. They're all the same.

From what Remedy said, it sounds like he's too much of a bitch to actually go through with anything, but I don't care. You don't fuck with what's mine.

Finally, an hour later, he leaves, talking on the phone as he gets in his car. He used to be a local, so he's probably going to meet some old friends on Duval Street.

I put on an old baseball cap. It's leftover from a victim and it's dirty, marked with dust and dirt, but there's no blood on it. In the motel's front lobby, I angle my head to the side so the receptionist can't see me directly.

"Lost my card," I say.

She doesn't look up from her game of solitaire. "It's twenty dollars for a replacement."

I slap a twenty on the desk. "That's fine."

"Room number?"

"One-zero-two."

She quickly swipes the new card, then hands it to me. I'm out of the lobby fast.

His room is humid from a hot shower, his cheap, spicy cologne stinking up the room. A duffel bag sprawls open on the bathroom counter. A pair of boxers lies to the side of the zipper opening. Deodorant and tweezers on the floor. One large window looks out to the parking lot, covered by thin curtains. It's a standard room: a bed, a bathroom and shower, a coat closet, a dresser, and a small desk. To be honest, everything I see here is average. Remedy is probably right. He wouldn't have done anything.

But I don't care.

I hide in the narrow coat closet and wait. I've used this tactic on one of my foster parents before: find their motel, wait till they come back drunk, and kill them, making it look like suicide. It took patience to wait in a cramped space all night, but in the end, it was worth it.

Several hours later, when the window to the parking lot is completely dark and his motel neighbors are quiet, the front door opens. There's a crack in the closet doors, but I can't see anything. All I can do is listen. A feminine giggle. Staggered footsteps. Wet lips slobbering against each other.

"Let me do it," he says. "You always liked it before."

"How many times do I have to tell you, Brody? Not tonight." She grunts, then the bed squeaks with her body weight on top of it. "But if you can be good, you can have me there tomorrow."

His pants unzip, then fall to the ground. A few seconds go by. They slobber again.

"Baby," he says in a hoarse voice. "Please don't make me wait. Doesn't it feel good?"

"If you use me for anal again, I swear to god I will beat your ass," she says.

"Fuck. Fine."

I adjust my gloves and wait for them to finish. Her stepbrother may not be into underage women, but he *is* into pressuring them, just like his father.

But that doesn't bother me. Why should I care about rape when I kill for amusement? Both actions are a way to control someone. They're forms of power.

But you don't touch Remedy Basset and get away with it.

The bed squeaks and the woman's moans are dramatic, like she belongs on a soap opera. The stepbrother lets out a wail, and it's over. They rest in silence for a few minutes. Then the stepbrother clears his throat.

"You should get going," he says. "Don't you have school tomorrow?"

"So that's it? Really?"

"I'm just looking out for you."

"I'm not driving home. You can deal with me until the morning," she scoffs. "Asshole."

The lights switch off, and about twenty minutes later, their wheezy breaths fill the motel room. To be safe, I wait another hour, then let myself out of the closet, creeping across the floor until my shadow hits their forms. I go to his side of the bed. He's a mess of light brown hair, his cheeks puffy with sleep, and I wonder if Remedy is right. Is he not *that* bad? Does he *deserve* to die?

Perhaps it's better to fuck him in the ass and beat the shit out of him like he threatened to do to Remedy.

But I'm not here for that. And I don't care if he doesn't deserve to die. *I want to kill him.*

I put the gun to his temple and pull the trigger. The silencer muffles the sound, but the woman still stirs and blood sprays on the pillow, a drop wetting her face. She smacks her hand across the stepbrother's chest.

"What was that?" she groans. "Brody?"

Her hands hit the wet spots on his pillow and she finally opens her eyes, seeing me. She opens her mouth, ready to scream.

Too late.

I shoot her in the throat. Her eyes are dull and empty; she reminds me of foster mother number seven. I put the gun in the stepbrother's hand. The serial number has been erased before I purchased it, so it won't be traced back to me. And with his track record—he's been kept overnight for disorderly conduct a handful of times—it won't be that surprising to find a gun on him like that. A hasty murder-suicide with his old fling. The evidence may not hold up for long, but I don't tolerate rivals. No one touches or hits Remedy, but me.

After I change into a fresh pair of clothing, I head back to Remedy's rental house. It's late—almost three a.m.—but she's sitting on the bed, and her eyes are dark. She hasn't gotten any sleep.

She's been waiting for me.

She turns to me slowly, but her mouth is closed, and it stays that way. I know what she's asking, even if she doesn't say it. I switch off the light, then sit next to her, the mattress dipping with my weight.

"He won't bother you anymore," I say. "I'm the only person who can hurt you." I press her shoulders back until we're both lying on the bed. Wrapping my arms around her, I suck in the sweet, fruity scent of her hair. Then I squeeze her so tight, she lets out a slight wheeze.

When I let go of the tension, she whispers, "You didn't have to do that."

"Close your eyes," I say. "You're safe."

She sighs. I stay there until her breathing calms and she falls asleep in my arms.

CHAPTER 17

REMEDY

BY THE TIME I WAKE UP, CASH IS GONE AND I HAVEN'T ASKED HIM about Jenna. If she's anything like me, seeing Winstone's body will comfort her, but it's more than that. Cash held blackmail over me and watched me kill my stepdad; why can't I hold this over him?

Maybe I want to see how far Cash is willing to go for me. Maybe I feel like I have to do *something* to take control of my life.

I need to know that I have power too.

A yellow light flashes in my mind, telling me to slow down, but I can't. Brody is gone. I don't need to hear the news or see his body to know that Cash killed him. Cash is the Crawler, and his crimes aren't limited to Key West. They span years.

And he's obsessed with me.

I go through the motions at work, thinking over how I'll ask Cash for the favor with Jenna. Once Bones is fed and the rest of the tasks for the morning are done, I search the estate for Cash, but can't find him. The downstairs office is closed and I remember his rule about closed doors. But that rule applied when I thought he was only a billionaire real estate developer. Now I *know* he's a killer, and I'm one too. Opening a closed door doesn't seem that bad.

I hold my breath and my clammy hands slip on the door handle, but it opens. At first glance, the office is empty. The windows are still closed, and the light shines through the panes, lighting the dust particles floating in the light. I hurry to the closet, moving aside the safe and shoe bench, then I open the hatch. Rotten fruit, sweet and foul, drifts up, mixed with a hint of strong paint. The bodies don't stink as much as you'd expect, but now that I know, it's obviously the stench of decay.

I use the flashlight on my phone to spot the general direction of the bodies, then I switch to the camera and turn on the flash. The light washes out some of the features on Winstone's face—Jenna is right; his mouth, even shriveled in decay, hangs like a bulldog's jowls—but you can't tell in the pictures. Pins and needles spike in me each time the flash illuminates the bodies. They look fake in the pictures, too plastic to be real, and for that, I'm sort of glad. It's a good excuse. If things go wrong, I can tell Jenna they're Halloween decorations.

Happy Birthday, I text Jenna. *Drinks later? Ready for your present?* I'm about to attach the picture when a shadow hovers over me. I quickly send the text without the photo.

"What are you doing?" Cash asks. Chills run down my spine and I hide my phone.

"Nothing," I say.

He cracks his neck, and the flicker in his eyes tells me that he knows I'm lying.

I may as well ask now. "I was just going to send Jenna a picture of Winstone," I say.

He shuffles a hand over his mouth. "Why?" he asks. I ball my fists; his tone patronizing, like he thinks I'm stupid. And that pisses me off.

"I know what I'm doing too," I say.

"Did you send it yet?"

I'm tempted to lie. "What if I did?" I ask.

"You want to risk my life and freedom, just so you can comfort your friend?"

I want to scream at him for those words. His cloudy eyes glare at me. "This isn't about you, Cash."

"Winstone is dead. Mission accomplished. Whether or not your friend knows is irrelevant."

"If she doesn't know, then what's the point?" I ask, raising my voice. "I want to give her the comfort that I always needed."

He nods, and for a second, it seems like he might understand. But it's never that easy with Cash.

"Come with me," he says.

I follow him up the stairs to the bedroom on the left, and my heart pounds. It's the only room in the house that has been locked since I opened it on my first day. Impulsively, I run my fingers over the smooth metal of the bobby pins. The last time I tried to open the door, the lock pick didn't work. It seems strange that he's letting me in now.

The door creaks open, and it's dark inside. Each wall has been covered by a thick layer of concrete now. I turn on my phone's flashlight again, but Cash goes to the back corner of the room, finding a single standing lamp. It barely lights the room. And that's when I see it: a metal cage, big enough for an adult to stand inside. He unlocks the padlock, stowing the key in his pocket, then goes inside, waiting for me to follow.

"What the hell?" I whisper.

"Come here."

My skin tingles and his face is covered in darkness, but I'm drawn toward him. I go deeper into the cage. A scent similar to wet asphalt surrounds us, and I clench my sides. Cash keeps his head bent, but his cavernous eyes are focused on me.

"What is this?" I ask.

"It's yours," he says. As he smiles, the light from the open door catches his teeth, and they gleam like knives. "Your new home, if you choose it."

"What?"

"Give me your phone."

His eyes are cold and heavy, like he's not giving me a choice. I pat my pocket, then stuff a hand inside, holding the device. "No."

"Give me your phone, Remedy."

"If you want my phone, you're going to have to take it from me."

He steps forward and I rush to the back of the cage, flattening myself against the metal. It rattles like thunder and I quickly open the messaging app, opening a new message to Jenna.

Thanks, lady, she sent earlier. *Birthday present? When?*

I attach the picture but Cash knocks the phone out of my hand. The screen cracks on the ground, but it stays lit. As I reach for it, Cash pulls the gun from his holster and steadies it on my temple.

"I should have gotten rid of you months ago," he says.

Tears fill my eyes, but I'm not sure why. Is it anger or frustration or lust? Because I know I'm not afraid.

"You're right," I snap. "So why don't you just do it?"

Light reflects in his dark pupils as he stares at me. Then he pulls back the hammer. The pine cologne on his skin drowns me. Each breath skips through my lungs, so I hold my breath, closing my eyes.

"Did you send the picture?" he asks.

"No."

"Are you lying to me, Remedy?"

And that's what hurts the most. He doesn't believe me.

The gun leaves my temple and the shot goes off. I gasp, but when I open my eyes, the gun is aimed at the back of the room, and there's a new, small crater in the concrete wall. He didn't kill me. And that knowledge makes me laugh. This is crazy. He's crazy. And I'm just as crazy for following him into a giant cage. It's hilarious.

Once I stop laughing, I squeeze my arms around myself. "You don't trust me," I breathe. He releases his hold on me for a moment and I shove his shoulders. "This is ridiculous."

His eyelids flutter as he thinks it over. "You're right. I don't trust you."

Suddenly, he's gone, leaving me inside of the metal cage.

"Where are you going?" I ask.

He puts the padlock on the hitch.

"What? What are you doing, Cash?"

The lock clicks into place, and he pockets the key. His eyes hold me, and he shifts back and forth like he's curious. And that pisses me off even more.

"You're insane," I yell. I run my hands across the ground, trying to find my phone. "Locking me in a cage because I won't give you my phone?"

He leans against the doorframe. "You have a choice," he says.

I want to stay in this cage to prove that I'm not going to give in. But Cash isn't the kind of person to bluff, and if he threatens to leave me here, he'll do exactly that. I find my phone and briefly consider calling Jenna for help, but there's no service. Is that what the concrete walls are for? To block the signal?

I stomp to the door of the cage, then shove the device under the gate. "Screw you," I yell. "Have my phone. I don't care."

He picks it up, then taps through the different screens. Recognition lights his eyes. He knows I'm telling the truth now. I didn't send her anything. But it took *proof* for him to accept that.

And it's like I'm back in middle school again, trying to tell my mom about my stepdad as she brushes me off. She didn't believe me.

And now Cash doesn't believe me either.

Maybe Peter is right. Maybe Cash is using me to kill *for* him. That's why he doesn't trust me. I'm just a puppet.

"Let me go," I shout. He turns off the phone and tilts his head. My pulse races. I gave him my phone; how long will he keep me here? "Please," I whisper.

"Pick the lock," he says, gesturing at the padlock. "That's what you tried to do before."

I touch the bobby pins. My heart stops.

It's not about locking me in here, then. He knows I can get out.

He wants me to choose his cage.

He unlocks the door of the cage but I go to the back corner, sinking down to the floor, wrapping my arms around myself in the fetal position.

"Stand up," he demands.

I don't move. "You don't trust me," I whisper harshly. "Why should I do anything you say?"

He drops to his knees in front of me. Still, I refuse to move. He drapes his arms around me and I shove his shoulders, using my legs and fists to get him off of me. But still, Cash comes back, pulling me into him. He fights me to the ground until his body pins me against the cold, hard concrete.

"Jenna won't say anything," I say, tears in my eyes. "She needs to know. I can tell her it's a joke. A Halloween prop."

"This has nothing to do with Jenna," he says.

"She's the reason I pursued you!" I scream. "She's the reason I'm fucking you in the first place."

But I know he's right. This pain isn't about telling Jenna. This hurts because I want to know that Cash and I can trust each other, but by denying me the permission to tell her, he's saying that we don't have that kind of foundation.

"She'll protect you, Remedy. Not me."

My eyes widen, but he stays on top of me, holding me still. In the darkness, I can't see the clouds and ash in his eyes, and it's like he's hiding his real self from me. But once again, he's right. Jenna doesn't care about Cash, and if it comes down to it, she won't hesitate to rat him out. But she will protect me, like I've protected her. And the fact that Cash is right makes me so upset.

And it hurts to know that he doesn't care if we trust each other.

Gripping my chin, Cash forces me to look into his eyes. He pulls down his pants and boxers, then rips me out of mine. He thrusts his cock inside of me and I grunt, spreading my legs to let him in. But then the mood shifts. He relaxes, moving slowly, an overwhelming softness in his movements. His lips press to my neck. And he kisses my skin like he wants me to feel good. Like he wants me to enjoy it. Anxiety rises inside me like a bubbling pot. I slap his face so hard my palm stings, but he keeps his rhythm, circling his hips, his lips on my skin, like nothing happened. His body presses against my clit, rubbing me back and forth, and those memories of my stepdad surface. I shake them away. I don't want them here. I bite Cash's shoulder, digging my canines in as deep as they'll go, and though a low growl vibrates through Cash, he stays at the same, easy speed. Like he knows that I'm breakable. Like he knows that this softness is torture to me.

"Are you punishing me?" I whisper.

He doesn't answer. His eyes narrow slightly, daring me to stop him, but then he subdues his actions again, like he wants me to understand that he knows *exactly* what he's doing. He knows me better than I know myself. He's right; this is about testing Cash, to see if he trusts me or not.

And it's clear that he doesn't trust me.

He closes his eyes, tenderly pressing his lips to my shoulder. I rip at his hair, trying to yank as much as I can out of his head to make him stop, but he pins me down, just hard enough that I can't move. Wiping the tears from my eyes like he's afraid for me, he puts his lips on my collarbone, forcing me to endure that false kindness. His lips on the underside of my chin. On my ear. On my chest. His fingertips skim the back of my neck, sending shivers down my spine, and my insides crawl. I'm helpless. I can't do anything. I have no power. My body will react and nothing I say or do will make a difference.

But this *is* different. I do have power, and that's why Cash is screwing with me. The concrete scrapes across my back, rubbing my skin raw, and his tongue reaches for my lips, searching for my open mouth, but I close it shut. I can't take it. I bash him in the back of the head with my fist until his nose knocks into mine. My face is heavy and for the first time since he started this, his eyes flicker open, but he stays still, pinning me down. Showing me that while I have regained some power, he's still in control, the one who will decide whether we make love or fuck. Whether Jenna knows or not. Whether I live or die. Whether he'll aim the gun at me.

His hips press into me, and my body relents, letting the passion take hold of me. A burning heat sweeps through me, and I let the tears go, my body finally relaxing. And for once, I enjoy it. This—our love, our fucked up sense of connection and control— is a fire I'll never be able to put out. Cash killed Cassius Winstone. He abducted my stepdad so that he could watch me kill him. Then he killed my stepbrother for threatening me. Nothing will undo any of that. We're melded together like the foundation protecting a home, and no matter what happens, nothing can break us apart.

But the most messed up part is that Cash *knows* how much this gentleness hurts me, and the fact that he's purposefully doing it, is what fuels me. He tickles my neck with his tongue and makes every nerve ending come alive. And I like it. I hate that he can read me like this.

My body drums, nearing that brink, and though his eyes flare with fury, he keeps his hips moving in a steady rhythm. I wrap my arms around and legs around him like a cocoon, never wanting him to stop, until finally, those twitches run through me and I come undone. The pleasure rides through me, but Cash doesn't stop. He fucks me in that same steady rhythm like he needs to come too, but his eyes burn with frustration. It's too hard when it's this easy.

Finally, he pulls the gun from his holster again, pressing the barrel against my throat, making it hard to breathe, my pussy tightening around him once again. I strain, coughing, my eyes watering, and *that's* when he comes inside of me.

He pulls out, then stares down at me. There's no emotion on his face, not even a hint of amusement. He's completely detached, knowing that he can't be fully present at this moment, or this will break him too.

"You remember the parking lot?" he asks.

The noose. My bleeding knees. The blindfold and earplugs. Of course, I remember.

I nod.

"Tomorrow night," he says. He fixes his clothes, but I stay naked on the concrete floor. "We'll figure it out then. But you have to meet me there."

I cross my arms, sitting upright. "What about Jenna?"

"Tomorrow night."

He hands me my phone. The screen is shattered and some pixels are dead, but the touch screen still works. I check the gallery, expecting to see the photos deleted, but they're still there. I don't know how I'm supposed to take that. Does Cash trust me to know what I'm doing now? Or is it a test to see if he can trust me? Just like I want to test him.

"Tomorrow night," he repeats. He leaves the door to the cage unlocked. "Seven o'clock."

As his footsteps filter down the hallway, my stomach flips. He's putting so much pressure on tomorrow night. What will happen if I don't go? Will he kill me?

And what will happen if I go?

CHAPTER 18

REMEDY

THE NEXT NIGHT, I STARE OUT AT THE WIND BLOWING THROUGH the palm trees. Even now, Cash keeps the windows open, and I know why. He's not afraid. It's long past my shift, but I can't move. I have no idea where Cash is. But Jenna is with her mom, which in my mind, means she's safe. But I know another person won't stop Cash from doing what he wants. If he thinks Jenna needs to die, she'll die.

Maybe I'm stupid, but I *trust* him not to do anything. Besides, I haven't sent her the picture messages yet. I'm not sure if it's because I don't trust Cash, or if I don't want to test him anymore. But I have to let it go for now.

I'm supposed to be with him in that parking lot. But I'm not.

The doorbell rings, startling me out of my daze. The black lace dress that I wore on the double date clings to my skin, and now, I can't remember why I chose it. Maybe I thought that if I pretended like nothing happened, like we were still that couple from the double date, that we would be okay. Sometimes love is volatile, and you can't explain why you do the things you do, even if you kill everyone in your path. You accept each other for every wrong and fucked up thing inside of your souls, and you hold on tight, knowing you may kill each other too.

The doorbell rings again, and this time, I check the security hub; it's Peter, his hands tapping his sides in impatience. He knocks hard on the door. Each thud lands in my chest like a hammer.

I open the front door. "He's not here," I say.

"Good. I was hoping it was just you," Peter says, his shoulders relaxing. He tilts his head, his eyes glimpsing at my dress, then gives a small smile. "Can I come in this time? I promise I won't take long."

I hold my breath, but I automatically nod. I have to let him in, don't I? I pour us glasses of sweet tea and bring him to the long dining table to the side of the kitchen. The more accommodating I seem, the better Cash and I will look. Like we're normal people. Even if I'm pissed at him, I have to protect both of us.

Peter gazes through the windows to the pebbled side yard. Though there's a small white fence around the property line, the trees create a natural barrier, giving the estate privacy as if it's *not* inside one of the biggest tourist destinations in the state. But Peter's eyes are ruminating. Something is eating away at him. Dread fills my stomach. What can he possibly say now to make everything worse? His eyes skim the room, searching for something.

"You have a laptop?" he asks, pointing to my computer. "Can I check something? My service has been down and I've gotta check my next appointment."

I shrug, waving him forward; whatever gets him out of here quicker, right? I sip my tea as he slides around the table, settling into the seat across from me. He types for a few minutes. His eyes race across the screen, but at this angle, I can't see what he's doing. He must be trying to keep his appointment private. It must be a cop thing. I clear my throat and he finally closes the laptop.

"Thanks," he says. "Got it."

"What's going on?" I ask, gnawing the inside of my lip. "What are you doing here?"

He sighs deeply, then straightens his chest and locks eyes with me.

"Dean is dead."

Those words rock through me. My fingertips scale the sides of the glass of sweet tea, the condensation rushing to the bottom of the glass like tears. I just saw Dean. Dean is young. Too young to die.

How did he die?

Guilt presses into my shoulders. I *know* how he died, but I have to ask. I have to make sure.

"What happened?" I whisper, my voice trembling.

"We found his body in the crawl space of his house, same as the other Crawler victims. His head was found in the woods behind the college. We think the killer is someone who knew him." He rubs his brows. "When was the last time you spoke to Dean?"

My mind buzzes as I try to make sense of it. "A few weeks ago. I don't know."

"Did he say anything odd?"

I shake my head. "He was fine."

"You may have been one the last people to speak to him."

I lean back, away from the table, then touch my clammy cheek. "I don't understand," I say.

"I spoke with your neighbor. She said that Dean visited your rental house right before he died. Said you two were arguing. Also mentioned that another man in a button-up shirt with dark eyes visited too." Peter posts his elbow on the table. "Any idea if Winstone and Dean have any altercations? A reason to consider each other enemies?"

My mind flashes to that day, when Cash showed up unannounced, his eyes burning like he could push Dean six feet underground with his sheer force of will.

Had Cash killed Dean because of me?

For me?

What am I even thinking? Dean doesn't deserve this.

"Found your stepbrother and his ex dead in the motel off of King Street."

I can't stop myself from panting. I know how this looks: everyone around me keeps dying, and I'm the only one still alive.

Did Cash plan this too? Did he *want* me to be a suspect?

"Murder-suicide," Peter says. "But Brody never struck me as

the killer type. Maybe that's why he offed himself. Or maybe something else happened."

I blink my eyes. Is Peter suggesting that it *wasn't* murder-suicide? Is he implying that *I* have something to do with his death?

And I do have something to do with it. Cash killed my step-brother to protect me. But I have to cover this up.

"But you saw him hurt me," I stammer.

Peter stifles a laugh. "I saw you kick his ass too. But that whole thing may be a coincidence. Not sure." He pushes himself forward. "But Winstone is involved in this. I can feel it."

On the street, a car honks, and laughter floats into the room like crashing waves, making the real world seem far away. Winstone *is* connected. He's connected because he's dead, underneath the floorboards right now. He's not the killer, but the person who killed Dean is the same person who killed Winstone.

"We're going to have to check everyone's crawl spaces in Key West," he says. "Even here. We're just waiting on the authorization."

I gulp. "Do you think you're going to find something?"

"People will fake drama for their fifteen minutes of fame. But when we find something real, we'll know." He slaps the table hard. "Don't worry, Remedy. We'll catch the killer."

"But what if he disappears before then?"

"He won't."

My heart races. Where will Cash go? What will he do?

"But Winstone doesn't have any motive," I argue. *Besides me.* And that doesn't even make sense. "Why would he do anything like that?"

"You don't need a reason," he says. "People are messed up. They do things because they enjoy it. Ask yourself this, Remmie. When a person doesn't have a soul, what's really stopping them from destroying everything in their path?"

I snicker, running my hands through my hair, but inside, I know he's onto something. Because if Cash actually killed *all* of those people, he probably doesn't have any reason. He killed them because he wanted to. Because he always does what he wants. It almost makes what I did with my stepdad seem morally righteous, and Cash's delivery of my stepdad, a gift.

But everyone else? Killing Dean? Killing Winstone? How am I supposed to moralize their deaths?

"You say that like murder is a regular thing in Key West," I scowl.

"Are you trying to downplay these deaths?" he asks, narrowing his eyes. "Murder *is* a regular thing now, Remmie. Don't you get it?"

My skin prickles with heat, my body hair lifting at that implied accusation in his words. What can I say to put him off of our scent? And why do I *want* to protect Cash?

"I can help you," Peter says. He draws closer to me, holding my hand like he wants to comfort me, but my stomach churns, making me weak. "Winstone isn't as powerful as he thinks he is. Even men like him have weaknesses."

I flinch out of his grip. I'm not sure why we're still talking about this.

"I think you should go," I say.

He rubs his hands together. "There's only so much I can do to help you," he warns. "But if you help me *right now*, I'll do whatever I can to make sure you're safe."

Safe.

All I've ever wanted is safety. But Peter hasn't given that to me. Nor the police. Nor Dean.

The only person who has given me that safety, is Cash.

I follow Peter to the front door. "You take care," he says. "I'm here for you, all right?"

I nod, unable to make myself say another word. I close the front door, then let out a breath, but I'm not relieved. Yet I still have this instinct that Peter will protect me now.

But if that means protection from the Crawler, will I ever feel like myself without Cash?

My phone buzzes with a text from Cash: *Tonight.*

I close the message without answering. I can barely breathe, so I call Jenna, even though I know Cash is probably tapping my phone calls somehow. I just won't say any details.

"Hey lady," she says.

"You have a minute?"

"Of course." The noise in the background dulls; she's moving to another room. "What's up?"

"Say you've done something bad," I say.

"How bad are we talking?"

"Murder bad?"

She laughs. "Gotcha. Keep going."

"And you're—" I smack my chest; I hate saying this, but it's true, "—and you're in love with someone who does way more bad things than you do. And now you've got the chance to turn that person in to the police."

"Is your question whether you should do what's right or protect your love interest?"

I cup my face. She always knows me. "What do I do? I feel like I'm going crazy."

"What do you think you should do?"

I scoff: "The right thing."

"And what do you *want* to do?"

I suck in a deep breath. "The wrong thing."

She sighs, a wistful sound to her voice, and I wish I could tell her everything. How is it that being with Cash makes me feel safe, comforted, and more isolated than I have ever been in my life? Why am I drawn to his constant danger?

If he takes Jenna from me, I'll never forgive him.

"You know I don't judge," she says. "Messed up things happen. But it's up to you to do what you think is right. Life isn't fair, and we don't get second chances, you know?"

All of that rings true; there's nothing fair about any of this. My mother constantly trusted the wrong men. Winstone assaulted Jenna, treating her like she didn't deserve common decency. My stepbrother punched me into silence. And my stepdad, a man I was supposed to trust, raped me for years. These murders? In the end, they don't seem *that* different. They're another crime. Another choice.

And I've killed too. I'm the same as Cash.

But Dean didn't hurt me like my stepbrother or stepdad.

Dean's only fault was being too nice for us to be compatible. And now, he's dead.

Cash, on the other hand? Cash has more faults than almost anyone I know, and yet I *trust* him. I know he'd do anything for me. Even if it means locking me in a cage or killing everyone I know.

"He hasn't killed me yet," I say quietly.

"Your lover? Who is this guy?" she laughs. "That shouldn't be a factor, Remmie. You're just joking, right?"

I wish I was joking, but Cash is real. My phone dings and I check the notification: *Cash* flashes on the screen, with an alert on the top bar for six missed calls. The hairs on the back of my neck stand up again. The last time I missed his calls, he showed up at my rental house while I was talking to my ex-boyfriend. It's like a single missed call can make him homicidal.

He's dangerous. And he wants me.

"I gotta go," I say.

"Keep me posted. And later, you *have* to fill me in."

"Deal."

As soon as I hang up, a text message from Cash lights up the screen: *WHERE ARE YOU?*

When we were at that parking lot, I crawled until my knees bled, and everything seemed perfect. Like we could take on the world and no one will stop us. But now, my knees are healing, and the scabs are red and pink, the edges bruised. The scars they'll leave will be deep and dark, and they'll be with me for a long time.

We'll never be able to take any of this back.

CHAPTER 19

CASH

WHERE ARE YOU?

I send the text and pocket my phone. Taking the point of my knife, I cut a pit into the top of my hand, like I'm trying to remove a splinter. Blood oozes out like a bubbling fountain, but it doesn't calm me. I've spent hours waiting, and I'm still here. What's more pathetic? A man who calls repeatedly until he finally realizes she isn't going to answer, or a stupid son of a bitch who thinks their relationship has any value in the first place?

Every moment leading up to this empty parking lot flashes before me. Watching through the wall cavity for a glimpse of her bare arm. Killing her new boss, because why the hell not? Blackmailing her. Going on a stupid double date with her mom. Delivering her stepdad. Giving her *freedom*. I should have killed her best friend since she's a threat too, but I spared her. And now I'm sparing Remedy.

I didn't kill her. I let her out of the cage. I even let her keep those incriminating photos on her phone. I want to give her the chance to prove that I can trust her like she keeps saying I can. But she's standing me up.

Headlights graze the parking lot, and her matte red car comes into focus. Like the frosting on my cake. Like her lips on our double date. The same night I brought her here to fuck her in a noose. I can see the outline of her in the car window and I ball my fists. A million thoughts rush into my head.

Where the fuck were you?

If you let another man touch you, I will cut off his dick and choke you with it.

What made you finally show up?

Don't you understand that I've done everything for you?

The car door opens, and it's like she's mocking me. She's in that same dress from the last time we were here, like she wants to recreate our memories. When I was just her fucked up black-mailing boss, and she was just my personal assistant and muse.

Times were simple then, weren't they, little cure?

Her movements are staggered and hesitant; she's afraid of what will come next. And I'm glad. She should be afraid of me.

But I should be running too. Instead, I'm digging my own grave.

"What are we doing here?" she asks.

We. The two of us. A damned unit.

I'm supposed to tell her how to escape this mess. To find her true freedom. A practical step-by-step guide on how to avoid the cops. I even considered telling her that I'll meet her again when it's finally safe.

But with the missed calls and the rejection on my mind, I want to destroy her.

That unit. A relationship. *We.*

I force myself to grin and act like this is nothing out of the ordinary. I hold my knife in one hand, the sharpening stone in the other, then flick the metal back and forth across the stone, the chilling scrape cutting through the dull ocean waves. She gazes at my calloused hands. Her musky body odor drifts over the breeze and her skin prickles with goosebumps. The air is cool, but it's the knife that makes those bumps rise, like little fingers reaching up to crawl out of her skin.

"You remember what we did here?" I ask. Her eyes flicker up to mine, but she keeps her tongue still. That night, she was on her hands and knees like an animal. I had my knife then. I could have gutted her like a pig.

"I could have killed you that night," I say.

She wraps her arms around herself, but she lifts her chin like she knows this is a mind game. I clench my jaw.

"Why didn't you?" she asks.

She knows the reason as well as I do, and that's what kills me the most. She knows the power she has over me. I'm not going to admit that my weaknesses belong to her.

Instead, I tell her about my past.

"When I was twelve, my foster father couldn't stand that I didn't talk. Please." I slide the knife to the right. "Thank you." The knife slides back to the left. "You're welcome." I stop the blade, then stare up at her. "What did I have to be grateful for? Being fed half of the time? Being put in another home where I'd get the shit kicked out of me too?"

The ocean waves crash like a pendulum, and in the distance, a black cloud hangs over the sea, threatening to storm. Soon, it'll be so easy to swim. To go as far as I can. To drown. To take Remedy with me.

"All I had to do was say a word. But I refused to," I continue. "And he beat me, promising that he would kill me unless I said something. Anything." A deep chuckle erupts from my chest as I let that memory wash over me. I was so used to the pain by then that I didn't feel a thing when he hit me. None of his words held any weight. I didn't care about dying, but I wanted to see how far I could push him, even if that meant speaking for once. "You know what I finally said to him?"

She blinks her eyes, holding her hands to her stomach.

"I called him a coward."

She sucks in a breath. I stow the sharpening stone, but keep the blade in my hand. As I step forward, she angles back on her car, trying to give us more distance. I hiss through my teeth, letting her know that I can read every micro-movement.

"Eventually, he stopped. But I couldn't go to school for weeks, because then, they'd know. So you know what I did instead?" My fingers brush over the pistol, the metal smooth like Remedy's skin. I want to crush her with my bare hands, but I keep stroking the pistol and adjusting my grip on the knife. "I stole his gun. And ten years later, I shot him with it."

I put away my knife, then lean each palm down on either side of her, caging her against her car. The moonlight reflects on her glowing skin, giving her a dark-gold hue, and it reminds me of ancient stones, like she's burying me alive.

"He wasn't the only one," I say, "but you know that."

She bites her inner lip, then presses her empty palms on her thighs, trying to find the strength to face me. I want to rip her from her protective shell, to make her see exactly what she's done to me.

I can kill her, and then she won't have power over me anymore. She'll be another victim. And I'll move on. Like I always do.

But I can't fucking do that to her.

"What about your parents?" she whispers. "The biological ones. Is Winstone your father?"

I laugh so hard, my chest hurts.

"You think we're connected like that?" I ask.

"That's why you killed him, isn't it?" she stammers. "Because he left you in the foster care system as a child."

She's putting meaning where there is none. I grit my teeth. "I didn't kill Winstone because I have a family revenge fantasy to fulfill. I didn't kill him because I was avenging your best friend. I killed Winstone because I wanted you, Remedy."

A small gasp escapes her lips. She flinches, trying to get away, but I have her cornered; there's no way out. Even if she breaks through my arms, there are trees, bushes, and the ocean surrounding us. She can only run so far before I'll find her.

Physically, I'm with her in that empty lot, but in my mind, I'm back in those broken homes where I was left in a trash can. Pushed around to each house where I had nothing. Life used to be simple; I knew what to expect. It's always been me.

But now, there's Remedy. She stole that life from me.

"Those fucking breeders, the ones that actually had me?" I sneer, then toss my head to the side. "They left me to die. So I killed them too." I put a hand around her throat. "I don't give a shit about anyone. Not even you."

Fear shivers through her. She knows that this is it: the moment I'll finally kill her. But then her lips spread into a smile, and she *laughs*. She cackles like a hyena. The sound echoes through the lot, mixing with the waves. It's her nerves, not true amusement, but it disturbs me. My insides twist and I clutch my grip on her throat, compressing her windpipe.

"What's so damn funny?" I ask. Her mouth moves, the smile still there even as her face turns red. I let her go and she holds her chest, laughing again.

"You're the coward, Cash," she says, smirking. "You're afraid of me because you know this is something. That I mean something to you. And that terrifies you." She straightens her shoulders, standing on her two feet. "If you're going to kill me, then stop being a coward and just fucking do it."

My vision goes red as I clutch my knife, aiming at her face, but at the last second, I swing and hit her car instead. The blade slices through the metal. Leaving it stuck in the door, I grab her face with both hands, digging my nails into her skin, and fuck it all, I want to kiss her. I want to rip her tongue out and show her that I need her and I hate it, but I can't. I force her to her knees, then whip out my dick and shove it in her mouth until she gags, the tears welling up in her eyes. I push myself down, down, down, until her throat encases me like a second skin and she can't breathe. She tries to gasp, pushing me off, but I hold her down until I feel her nose flatten against my abdomen. I can kill her like this. Suffocate her on my dick while I stick two fingers into her tight little cunt until she constricts around me, reaching her sweet little death.

But I pull out. She coughs at the sudden air. I rip the knife from the car, adrenaline surging through me, the breath in my chest expanding like I'm a fucking god. I'm invincible, and not even Remedy can stop me. I put the knife to her throat, keeping her steady, to show her that I'm in control.

But Remedy isn't afraid. Even as she tries to find her breath, she licks the knife up and down like she's teasing a man's cock. My dick twitches and that rage drifts away. She's so hot I forget to breathe. Her tongue tickles the tip of the knife, a drop of blood budding on that wet muscle, and I can't imagine another person in this world understanding me like this. I have no idea if she's doing this to mess with me or if she's just as depraved as I am. But I take a fistful of her hair and move her back to my cock. I keep the blade against her neck and she moans.

"We're alike, Remedy," I say. Her tongue laps around me and my dick pulses, swelling up. *Damn it,* I want to choke her with my girth, but I want to make this clear to her so that she never forgets it. "We're alike in ways that will never let us go. We see the world for what it is. We know who we are. The only person who will accept every messed-up part of you is *me.* Because I understand you, Remedy. And I will make sure that you always do exactly what you want."

I slide the knife across her cheek, letting a superficial cut break her skin, blood pooling in beads across the red seam. I hope it leaves a scar, just like she marked my back. I want her to see that scar in the mirror every day for the rest of her life and know that I'm there, written in her skin. I'll never let her go. Even if I'm dead, I'll always be there.

She puts pressure on her lips, her tongue flicking over the sensitive skin on the head of my cock. Her eyes gaze up, holding me. And at that moment, I know I'm never going to kill her. I want to let her *live.* Fuck everything—I want to see how much of a fiery pistol she is in her eighties. I want to see her skin get saggy with those blotchy tattoos. I want to kill some spritely twenty-something and fuck her over his dead body, like we did with her stepdad, even when it's too hard for us to fuck like animals. And I'll do anything to make sure that she lives to be that age, even if it kills me.

I push her shoulders, moving her off of my dick, and she leans back on her palms. The lace tattoos mixed with the hair on her pussy make me salivate. Fucking hell, she's not wearing panties, and her pussy is already soaking the pavement. And that pisses me off even more. She knows what she does to me, and every damned day, she uses that power against me.

And like a man on a leash, I fall to my knees and crawl to her. I'm a fucking slave to my queen.

"Spread your legs," I order. She moves her thighs wider, and I reach between her legs. Her arousal pools under her like an insatiable slut, the liquid silvery-blue in the moonlight. A drop of blood runs down her cheek, then her neck, and I wipe it with my finger, licking it up. It's metallic and salty, her sweat and blood.

I use her arousal to lube up the knife's handle, then I jab her pussy, not caring if it hurts or feels good, but she writhes her hips like she's in heat, getting so damned into it that her pussy grip takes over, making it hard to control the blade. I adjust my hand, getting a better hold on the knife, but the blade cuts into my palm. I'm the one fucking her with the knife, and somehow, I'm the one who's hurt. She's dragging me down with her.

"You love me, Cash," she pants through each word. "You love me so much that it terrifies you."

My skin spikes with needles, but I keep fucking her with the blade, deeper and deeper until I hit her cervix and the blade gashes my palm. But I don't stop.

"If this is love," I growl, "then it's going to kill us."

And I can't take it anymore.

I rip the handle from her cunt and throw it to the side, pulling her into my lap, squeezing her as if I'll never have her again. The grit from the asphalt smeared with our come and blood washes over both of us, and my hands skim her body, knowing that this is it. There will never be another time for us. If this is love, then this is the end, because neither of us is going to survive the night.

So I don't care about holding back anymore. I hold her body, entwining my legs and arms around her, and I press my mouth to hers, my tongue so deep in her mouth that she surrenders, giving everything to me. Letting go. And it feels so fucking good. Her mouth on mine. Her teeth, her velvet tongue. I want to remember this. Her mouth tastes sweet, like a honeyed wine she drank with dinner, the mellowness of her saliva rinsing it out. The huff of her nostrils tickles my skin. Her heart pounds into mine. She takes my breath away with that kiss, and I hold her, wanting to hurt her and fuck her and love her, to do everything and anything that I can to show her that she's right. I don't know how or where I went wrong, but just as much as she's mine, *I'm hers.*

Then she freezes. Her tongue goes placid in my mouth, like a dead fish floating in the water. Energy builds in my veins.

She's shutting down *now?*

I break the kiss, then examine her. Her face is blank. Empty. Like she's not here anymore. And I know what it is: her stepdad must have kissed her like this. And that makes her a shell of herself.

I've never been in control when it comes to Remedy.

I push her off of my lap and stand up. I wipe my mouth with the back of my hand, blood from my palm smearing my skin. She sits there, her eyes blank.

"Get up," I demand.

Her eyelids hang low, but she doesn't move. What is she doing?

"Stop messing around. Get up."

I stare at her, but she's still petrified. Have I done this to her? My chest tightens, pain churning in my stomach. I pull her to her feet. Her dress is still bunched around her hips, but her eyes are glassy and vacant. She's gone.

I don't know if it's the kiss or the fact that I threw away the knife. But I've finally broken her. And I hate it. Every single second of it.

And I hate that I feel this way. Because I shouldn't care. I should just leave her here.

But I can't. And that enrages me. Because this isn't enough. I have to let her go.

"Leave," I say. "Run away from here. Never think of me again."

Finally, her pupils shift, focusing on me. A tear falls from her eyes, and that tear, that single drop—not from face-fucking or passion, but from the fear of the softness, fear of what it means for a psychopath to actually love you, fear of *me*—that tear breaks me.

"Why me?" she asks.

I close my eyes, then turn away. Every person wants to believe they're the chosen one, but I can't do this to her anymore.

"You were never more than a person for me to frame," I say. Her lips tremble, and I know it hurts her. It's ripping me in half, but she needs to go and forget about me. "I got you to kill your stepdad so I'd have your prints on the weapon. You're a tool. Nothing more."

She shakes her head, not believing me at first. I laugh, hoping that it twists the knife.

"Why do you think I let you kill him?" I ask.

"Fuck you," she growls.

"You think I'm afraid that you mean something to me?" My tone is cold, every word delivered with perfect precision. I want to hurt her. I want her to feel everything. "I was using you, Remedy. Just like everyone else in your life. You mean nothing to me."

It kills me to say those words, but I *need* to lie. I need her to leave me.

She huffs through her teeth, still reading through me. "You're lying."

"Why would I lie about this?" I toss my head to the side. "You passed the time. You were a decent fuck. And you almost got me off the hook for some murders." I snicker and she bares her teeth. "If you don't want to end up in jail, then leave. Go to your detective. Tell him everything and see what happens. I'm sure he'll protect you from me." I press my lips together. "Or maybe I'll kill him too."

With that, she pulls down the hem of her dress until she's covered again.

"Get your things from the estate. Tell the agency," I say. "Consider yourself officially fired."

She refuses to look at me. The blood speckles her face like fingerpaints, her eyes angled up at the empty sky, holding back angry tears.

"Run fast now," I say.

And she does. Soon, her car peels out of the parking lot, the tires screeching. I watch her leave. That emptiness fills me again like I'm nothing but a half-eaten carcass, not even good enough for a vulture. I'm trying to prove to myself that she means nothing to me. That I don't deserve her.

Except this time, Remedy isn't a foster parent or a breeder who doesn't give a shit about me. She's someone who's screwed up like me. A person who sees inside of me, even when she doesn't want to. And somehow, she isn't afraid of me. She didn't even leave until I forced her to.

And letting her leave like this isn't good enough.

In my truck, I shift the gear into drive, then head to the estate. I don't know what I'm doing, but I can't let her leave yet. I have to tell her how to survive without getting caught.

If I drive fast enough, she'll still be there.

CHAPTER 20

REMEDY

THE ESTATE LOOMS LIKE A DARK SHADOW SWALLOWING UP KEY West. I slam on the brakes and my chest crashes into the seatbelt. I'm the only one out. No one goes outside anymore, not when the Crawler is stalking Key West. I unlock the white gate, then drag myself to the front door.

The door creaks open, and I glance around, making sure that I'm the only one here. Without Cash, it's cavernous. Cash acted like he would have been okay with killing me off when he knows that I've stayed by his side, even after he told me his secrets. And that *hurts*. If he doesn't want to accept that we have something real, then I'm done. I'm not going to wait for him to figure it out.

I grab my surveillance camera from the downstairs office. Everything is straight and orderly, as if Cash is always like this, but that's a lie too. He's not this kind of man, and I want to destroy that image.

I tear everything out of his desk. Rip the coats and jackets from the hangers in the back closet. Throw the paperweight and globe at the closed windows until they break. I want him to know that I see the real him and that I know what he's doing. I do the same in the upstairs office. I want him to see me there, no matter where he looks.

Suddenly, Cash is behind me, leaning against the wall across the hallway. There are swollen cuts on his hands and strikes of blood across his face. But his face is smooth, uninterrupted by emotion. There's something fascinating about a dangerous man with blood marking his body. I suck in a breath. If I didn't hate him so much, I would want him.

But I want nothing to do with him now.

"Having fun?" he asks.

I hiss through my teeth. None of this means anything to him, but damn it, it feels good to destroy it, like it's giving me strength over my memories.

"You followed me," I say. "Surprise, surprise."

I go past him, marching down the stairs, and he bounds down after me, our steps in sync, rocking through the house.

"Are you ever going to stop following me?" I ask.

"There's a guy in the Panhandle. Manny Littleton. He owns a car wash. Manny's Sparkling Cars, or something like that."

I scoff. Why is he telling me this? "So?"

"He can get you a new identity."

He's trying to help me, isn't he? My heart stops, completely confused. I swing around; Cash's eyes are full of hunger and greed, but it's not real. He can admit that he wants me, that he's obsessed with me, that he *used* me. But even when he's trying to help me find a stable future without him, he'll never admit that he has *feelings* for me.

If he's telling the truth about this person and their car wash, then he's trying to help me run away. It's probably hard for Cash to do something like that. But if he can't acknowledge his own feelings, then I'm not going to put up with him anymore. I'll find my way without him.

I reach the front door and pull the strap of my purse higher on my shoulder. The camera is in there. I don't think I'll do anything with it, but I like having it as security against him.

But my last thought is Jenna. I still haven't texted her with the pictures of Winstone's corpse, but if I know Cash, he sees her as a loose end. Even if he doesn't kill me, he won't hesitate with her.

"If you touch Jenna," I say, my voice quivering, "If you so much as lay a hand on her, *I will kill you*, Cash."

His eyes stay unmoved. Those dark brown spots dot his vision. All he sees is me.

"I have no interest in your friend," he says. "I never touched her, and I never will."

"But you've thought about killing her." I ball my fists, then raise them up. I want to punch him in the face, but it won't make a difference. "You thought about killing *me*."

He blinks. "That honestly surprises you?"

I flatten my hands against my sides. "I thought I could trust you," I hiss. "I thought you were the only person I could be real with."

"Funny, isn't it?" he sighs.

And in a way, it is funny. It's pathetic and sad and I want to scream. By giving me this information about getting a new identity, he's throwing me a lifeline. And yet he's still denying his feelings for me.

I don't want his help anymore.

"I didn't need this," I cry. I point to the downstairs office. "Winstone. Brody. Dean. My stepdad. I wanted you, Cash, because I thought you saw me. But all you see is yourself."

He huffs through his nose like I'm a housefly that he's finally going to squash.

"Good luck turning in those videos," he says, tilting his head at my purse. "You're incriminating yourself just as much as me."

Cash knows me better than anyone else, and yet, he still thinks I'm going to turn him into the police. He truly can't trust me, and that *hurts*.

"I left the rest of the cameras for you," I say, motioning at the little black devices littering the ceiling. I open the front door. "Don't follow me."

I stomp down the steps to my car. I drop into the front seat and immediately start the engine, getting the hell off of that street. Cash might follow me, but right now, he's too proud to do anything.

I stop the car in front of my rental house. It's empty and dark, and I can't imagine going inside anymore. Cash used to wait for me in the crawl space, but for some reason, I can't shake the idea that it's really done this time.

The tears surprise me, like a trickle, then suddenly, the sobs take my breath away. I hit the steering wheel until my palms hurt. My shoulders heave, and I find myself looking over my shoulder, hoping that I'll find him there. But I'm alone. I can't breathe. Cash killed Winstone, and I killed my stepdad. We don't need each other anymore.

But I know the truth. Cash never needed me. I'm the one who needed him.

Exhaustion fills me. The walk to the front door seems like a trek through the mountains, and I consider sleeping in my car. But if someone finds me in the morning, I'll have to explain or lie about what happened, and I don't want to deal with that.

Once I'm inside the house, I plug in the security camera to my computer. I need to erase the footage, but as I scan through the recordings, I watch the night I killed my stepdad. I should be mystified by seeing myself do something so horrific, but in those frames, I fixate on Cash. He looks at me with glowing eyes, like he's truly proud of me.

I wish we still had that.

I collapse on my bed, then find a dark spot on the wall above me. It's got a hole in it—small, like the width of a pen cap, maybe bigger—and it's always been there. It makes me think of Cash.

I zone out on that little hole. As I shift into murky dreams, I imagine Cash on the other side of the wall, peering into my life, seeing everything I kept hidden. It's infuriating, but somehow, it's comforting too.

"Please come back," I whisper. I lift a hand in the air, swatting at the hole. I sniff deeply, searching for his piney scent, but I can't smell anything. My nose is stuffed, but even if it wasn't, I know he's not there. "Stay with me."

Soon, sleep finds me, swallowing me whole.

———

A fist pounds the front door, followed by multiple doorbell rings. My heart stops in my chest. Is it Cash?

But it's not him. He'd never knock like that; he'd invite himself in. I glance at the clock; it's midday. How did I sleep for that long? I click out of the security footage program on my laptop, then straighten my clothes. I find Peter in jeans and a shirt on the front porch. His eyes widen.

"Remedy," he whispers. "What happened to your—"

"Cat scratch," I lie. The cut on my cheek from Cash looks worse than that, but it doesn't hurt. "What's up?"

"I've got a favor to ask." He wipes his nose. "Mind if I come inside?"

I don't like being alone with men, besides Cash, but after what I did to my stepdad, I'm not as scared. I step to the side and let Peter in. The door closes behind us, and Peter's shoulders sink. His eyes hold me like he regrets what he's about to do. Have I made a mistake?

"What's wrong?" I ask. "Why are you looking at me like that?"

"Do you trust me, Remedy?" he asks.

In my mind, I scream: *No, no, no.* But I stare back at him and keep my facial expression straight. "What is this about?" I ask.

"I saw the footage."

I roll my eyes. "What footage?"

He gestures to my bedroom. "That's where your laptop is, right? The footage from Cash's office."

My chest tightens and my throat runs dry. He saw *the* footage? If Peter saw the footage of me killing my stepdad, and Cash *helping*, then what are we going to do?

Is there even a 'we' anymore?

My head pounds, each heartbeat suffocates me with pain. I want to shake him and ask what the hell is going on.

But I can barely move.

"What?" I whisper.

"I'm going to have to arrest you," Peter says slowly. "I'm willing to help work out a plea bargain for you, but the thing is that I *need* Winstone. And the only way I'm going to get him is through you."

I don't realize I'm moving backward until I stumble into the wall. I slide against the surface, trying to find another way out. This is the perfect time for Cash to pop up like he always does, but there are no footsteps or piney cologne.

Peter and I are alone.

"I don't want to hurt you," Peter says, stepping closer. He pulls the handcuffs from his back pocket. "I'm just trying to do the right thing."

"Is this even legal?" I pant. "How'd you get the footage? You don't have a warrant for that."

"Sometimes, you have to do what's illegal to do what's right," he steps closer, and I'm backed into a corner. My heart rate increases and I start to hyperventilate. "I knew you weren't going to help me, so I resorted to other measures. Like hacking your computer."

The image of Peter using my computer at the estate flashes in my mind. Did he only pretend to need my laptop?

He lied, and I'm trapped. I want to scream for Cash, but I can't rely on him to save me every time. With all of my strength, I shove Peter back and that shock stuns him long enough for me to stumble out from under him. I race for the front door, but he lunges, latching onto me, and I kick my feet, but he pulls my shoulders, maneuvering until I'm pinned inside of his arms. He reeks of soap and chocolate and I want to rip his tongue out for eating a damn candy bar before coming to arrest me. But I whimper in defeat. This is so messed up. After everything we've been through, I'm still being used to capture Cash.

Screw this.

I spit and scream at Peter. "Fuck you," I hiss. But he holds my wrists tighter until he locks them in the handcuffs in front of me. I twist against the bindings, the metal scraping my skin, but it's no use. I'm already locked in. I try to take a deep breath, but I can't. He presses my arms, steadying me on my own two feet. Chills erupt all over my body; I hate it when he touches me.

"I want to help you," he says. "You've done some bad things, but you're not the criminal here."

"You don't want to help anyone," I scowl.

"Of course, I do."

"You're just going to use this as an excuse to drug and rape me too, just like that girl from high school!"

Peter furrows his brows, but otherwise, he ignores my retort. "Cash was manipulating you. Psychopaths are good at that," he says. My heart rams into the sides of my rib cage, threatening to break loose. "If you come with me, Cash will come on his own. But if you don't come willingly..." He shakes his head, but I can see right through his false reluctance. "He needs to die in prison, Remmie. I don't want to kill him."

Those words stop me. Finally, I meet Peter's eyes. There's a hint of pride inside of him. He knows he has me trapped under his thumb now.

"But I will kill him if I have to," he says.

I can't let Cash die.

My phone vibrates, knocking us both out of the trance. Peter's eyes light up. He grabs my purse, then pulls out my phone and glances at the screen, reading the text message preview.

"The parking lot, huh?" he says. "Ten o'clock."

"I'm not going to tell you where it is," I snap.

"I know where it is. I put a tracker in your car. You went there the other night, right?" He clicks the touchscreen. "Now, what's the passcode? I want to text him saying you'll be there soon."

"No fucking way. I'm not helping you."

He opens the front door. "Then we'll meet him there anyway."

His white car with black rims sits out front. I'm surprised that it's not his police car, but then this whole thing must be under the radar. Whatever this is, it's personal to Peter, like he *needs* to capture Cash to prove himself. He helps me into the backseat, buckling me in, and I glare at the rearview mirror.

"We've got some time to kill. And I can help you as much as you help me," he says. "Is there anything else you want to tell me about your relationship with Winstone?"

I clench my jaw, my body heavy with anger. Even if I'm pissed at Cash—even if I know I'm going to jail anyway—I'm *not* going to pretend to be sorry for what I've done, nor am I going to help

Peter. I'll take the blame for my stepdad's death, and Cash will have to answer for his own crimes.

But they're my crimes too. My stepdad. My stepbrother. My ex.

My wishes. *His fulfillment.*

Cash had killed people. And I had killed my stepdad.

When no one else had, Cash saw me. He understood me. He listened to me.

Cash is fucking crazy.

But so am I.

Peter turns the key in the ignition. "I didn't think so," he says. He drives back to his house, and we wait for the night.

CHAPTER 21

CASH

I LAY IN THE BED OF MY TRUCK, STARING UP AT THE BRIGHT BLUE sky. I should go. Drive fast. Buy a new fake passport. Get out of here while I still can. Forget that Remedy exists. Murder anyone who touches a dark-haired woman like her until those feelings are obliterated from my system for good. And never, ever touch another woman, because I'm not going to deal with this shit again.

But none of that feels right.

Instead, I text her to meet me at the parking lot one last time. An urge swells inside of me to tell her how to avoid getting arrested, and I can't tell her any of that through a text or call. But she doesn't answer. I think about opening the surveillance app on my phone to see if she has her laptop open, but I don't. I shouldn't be helping her anyway. This is pointless.

A visiting snowbird passes the truck, peeking her nose inside the bed, then moves on with her chin held high. The blood is gone, but I still look like another drunk tourist who got locked out of their vacation rental. And no one cares. If I leave now, I'll be invincible again.

Remedy is smart. Even if she gets arrested, she'll survive on her own.

I have to go.

I climb into the front of the cab and start the engine. The truck rumbles awake like an old man waking up from a long nap, and that's what it feels like; I'm finally thinking straight. The truck has more personality than Winstone's push-to-start cars, but it's comfortable. Familiar with its undesirable traits. I slap the steering wheel, then sigh. I'll have to get a new one soon.

The Seven Mile Bridge zips by, but as I near the Southern Glades, a dull sensation sinks in my stomach. It's a foreign feeling, a physical manifestation of my emotions, and it's awkward and unpleasant, like I've got indigestion. And no matter how hard I try to distract myself, that emotional pain keeps growing, getting worse.

I don't want to leave Remedy behind, but I have to.

If she's not careful, she'll probably take the blame for my actions. Just like I always planned.

I imagine her inside of a prison, bordered by concrete walls and metal bars. I built her a cage, but I gave her a way out. In a correctional facility, she'll wither away until she's completely numb. Worse than before.

Fuck it. I'm not going to let that happen.

As soon as I'm able, I flip the car's direction and head back to Key West. I don't have any remorse for what I've done to those people, but I'm not going to let Remedy take the fall for me like that.

It's dark by the time I make it back to the Keys, but I still have a little time before our ten o'clock meeting. I see a loner on the side of the road and I pull over.

"You got a cell phone?" I ask. "I don't have any service. Can't seem to find directions to this place." I force a nervous laugh. "Meeting this chick. This chick is banging."

"Yeah, yeah," he says, nodding his head. "I get you, man." He looks down, grabbing his phone from his pocket. "Sure thing—"

I yank him into me, punching him in the gut until he wheezes, using that brief second of struggle to put him into a headlock. I push on the back of his neck until he loses consciousness. Throwing him in the back of the truck, I gag him with a dirty rag and bind him in rope. I add the cover and lock him inside.

Farther in town, a man turns the corner, going to the back of an ice cream parlor. His eyes shift like he's waiting for someone, but I'm too impatient to find someone else. I park nearby, then walk to the back of the shop, pulling out an empty box of cigarettes.

"You got a light?" I ask.

The man reaches into his pocket without a word, but when I lunge to pull him into a headlock, he socks my jaw so hard that my lip bleeds. I punch his nose until he's drenched in blood and finally, he relents, knocked unconscious from the final blow. I toss him in the back of the truck too, locking the bed cover into place.

Before I drive, I text Remedy: *Don't come. Tell your cop friend to meet me instead.*

I'll even use the insulation gun to be safe. There'll be too much evidence for the police to consider any other options. Remedy can move on. It'll just be me.

It's better this way.

We leave the main road, and the lights dim as we get closer to that abandoned parking lot. I pull both of the hostages out of the truck's bed. The second hostage fights me again. I grab the maroon-handled blade from my back pocket and stab him repeatedly in the neck until he crumples to the ground. The first hostage starts to cry, and I pull him to his feet.

"Y-y-you killed him. You killed him, man."

Even if Remedy never shows up, as long as the maroon-handled blade and the foamed bodies are in the police report, Remedy will know that it's me. That I'm doing this for her protection. So she can be free.

"I'm s-s-sorry, man," the hostage stutters. "P-please, don't—"

My skin crawls. This is irritating. I rub my nose, then adjust my grip on the maroon-handled blade. The hostage's eyes blink, but as headlights flash over the lot, the idiot falls to his knees, piss covering his pants. He looks at the car like it's his last shot at life.

But then I see it: the white car with black rims. The detective.

I grab the knife from the ground. This is it.

I squeeze the marron handle like I'm holding Remedy's hand, helping her stab her stepdad to death. But Remedy never needed my help to do that, and I love that about her. And now, the detective is going to arrest me.

"Please——" the hostage says. I stab him in the neck, making sure the detective can see me.

The car stops, and the door opens.

"Hands up," the detective says, holding his gun. Playing along, I lift my hands, keeping the knife in my palm. "Drop your weapon."

The detective pulls back the hammer, and I tighten my grip on the handle.

"Go for it, Detective," I say. "You saw what I did. I'm the one you want."

"Remedy's here too."

I hold my breath. Did he say Remedy?

"Now," the detective says slowly, "If you care about Remedy, drop the knife."

The blade clatters to the asphalt. I can't do anything until I know she's safe. I tilt my head, keeping both hands up.

"And what did Remedy tell you?" I ask.

"I saw the surveillance footage. What you did with her stepdad was almost sweet." He steps closer, keeping his gun aimed at me, and the silhouette of Remedy's face glows in the back seat. The window is cracked for air, but she's just watching us. Is she in on this? Did she bring the detective like I told her to? The detective cracks his neck. "Making sure that her stepdad died? That's more than anyone could have done for her. But it's my job. I would have taken care of him the right way."

He's so damn proud; it's laughable.

"So what? You put her stepdad in jail? Then he gets out and does it again to someone else's daughter?" I laugh. "We did you a favor."

"We?" the detective asks, his brows raised. "*We?*"

A warmth surges in my chest, full of strength and passion, burning all over me. *We are a unit.* I'm here, making sure that she lives, even if that means that I don't. Remedy is my ride-or-die, and I'm never going to give her up.

I have to make sure the detective doesn't question Remedy.

"You're right. Let me take credit," I say. I waggle my fingers. "Remedy was a pawn. She doesn't mean shit to your investigation." I narrow in on that truth. I have to make it seem like it's entirely mine. I hate myself for saying this, but I have to show him that she means nothing, so that she can be free. "The dumb slut probably didn't even realize that I was manipulating her."

"Nice try, but I saw her kill her stepdad," the detective says. "Even if you manipulated her, she held the knife. She's not innocent by any means. The judge and jury may have mercy on her, considering she was abused by her stepdad and manipulated by a psychopath." He narrows his eyes, straightening his stance, ready to take me down. "But you are the worst piece of garbage that could've crossed her path."

The detective is right. Remedy is better off without me. But I gave her freedom, a chance to be her true self, and I don't regret that. I'll do it again if it means that she's at peace with herself. And if that means going to jail or dying for her, then I'm going to fucking do it.

You have to do anything to protect someone you love.

"Kill me," I demand. "You and I both know it. I'm like her stepdad. I'll keep killing. And trust me, Detective, you'll be next."

He inches forward with his gun still aimed at me, then kicks the maroon knife out of the way. It skitters toward the bushes and rocks.

"I'm not going to kill you. I'm going to put you in a cage, you insufferable bastard."

I laugh. The son of a bitch thinks he's doing the right thing.

"You're so honorable," I mock.

"What's it going to be?" He points his gun toward the car, then focuses it back on me. "Are you going to let me arrest you or are you going to fight me?"

I can't kill the detective without putting more eyes on us, especially Remedy. If she's in the back of his car, then there's a good chance that someone knows they're together. He shows up dead, and she'll be the first person they check.

"Let her go, and I'll let you arrest me," I say.

"You know I can't do that, but I'll make sure she gets a good judge. She's still a good girl."

A good girl. My nails dig into my palms at those condescending words. The detective has the nerve to belittle her after everything she's been through? Treating her like a victim and not a fucking survivor? Not even acknowledging the fact that she's a killer like me.

And that irritates me.

She's not a good girl. She's a damned nightmare.

And she's all fucking mine.

I swing my fists forward and he attacks me with the back of his gun. I swirl around, dodging his blows. But he kicks my feet out from under me and I lay back, pretending to be stunned, then knee him in the chest, knocking the wind from his lungs. I tumble onto my hands and knees, searching for the knife. By the time I find it, he's back on his feet. I grab the knife with one hand and throw a handful of dirt and rocks with the other. The pebbles hit his eyes and he howls. Pride flames in my chest. It's a cheap move, but I don't care. I want to finish this already.

With each blow we take at each other, a gnawing sensation sprawls across my chest, making everything inside of me seize up. I'm invincible. No matter how hard I try to die, there's always someone stopping me. A cop trying to spare my life. A foster parent finally growing a conscience. A victim too afraid to fight back. Or Remedy, giving me a chance.

She has hope and faith in me that I don't deserve.

But fuck it all. I love her. And this is for her.

He darts toward me, and this time, I hold up my knife, using it to stab him in the arm, but the detective uses that moment to get the knife out of my hand. He punches my face, flattening me against the asphalt, and I go still. Remedy presses her eyes to the window, handcuffs binding her wrists. There's pain and destruction in her expression, and I can't let her life be ruined.

This can't be her end.

I spit a mouthful of blood onto the asphalt as the detective reaches for his handcuffs. "You're under arrest—"

I lunge out of his reach, but he gets one cuff on my wrist. I punch my free fist into him, then knock the gun from his holster. His legs buckle and I twist onto my hands and knees, reaching for that gun.

"If you touch that weapon, I'll have no choice," he shouts.

But the bastard doesn't kill me. He takes out a second gun from a hidden holster.

This is it. I'm gone.

But I don't care about dying. All I care about is her.

"You're under arrest for the murder of Cassius Winstone, and the—"

The headlights turn on, and both of us look into the light.

———

Remedy

Once I flick on the headlights, I switch back to the cuffs. The bobby pin slides between my clammy fingertips. "Shit, shit, shit," I whisper to myself. I'm drenched in sweat and desperate to figure this out.

The lock on one of the cuffs finally pops open, giving me one free hand. I let the cuffs dangle from the other wrist and reach for the steering wheel. I'm so damn lucky that Peter left the keys in the ignition, but I don't know what I'm going to do now.

I heard everything Cash said: *Remedy was a pawn. She doesn't mean shit in your investigation.* But I know that he didn't want me to get arrested too. I honk the horn incessantly. It screeches like a bat and the two men flinch, but Peter stays focused. *We did you a favor,* Cash said. We. *Us.* Cash believes in us.

Cash is on his hands and knees like an animal, limping to get to the other gun, but Peter has a second gun and we don't have much time. Someone is going to die.

When Peter told Cash to drop the knife if he cared about me, Cash let go of the knife instantly.

Kill me. I'll keep killing, Cash said.

He wants to die for me.

We should both be arrested. It's the right thing to do.

But my hands find the key and I turn on the engine. The car roars to life.

Peter jabs the gun closer to Cash, and I don't think anymore.

I step on the gas, ramming the car forward. The bumper hits him first, then his body tumbles over the car. In the rearview mirror, lightning flashes in the sky like a jagged razor blade, illuminating the lumpy forms, but I don't take time to think. I put the car in reverse and fly backward, tumbling over his body. I go forward, then backward again, until I know there's no way he's still alive.

Cash's hands are covered in blood. His lip is puffy. There's dirt and blood on his shirt and jeans, and now there are three bodies in the parking lot. Handcuffs dangle from one of his wrists, just like me. But his spotted black eyes hold me, and there's a look I've never seen on him before. He's swaying slightly, but his gaze settles on me, and that shock melts into possession. I've chosen us.

This is in my hands, and now, we're safe.

CHAPTER 22

REMEDY

I KILL THE ENGINE, THEN RUN TO CASH. AS I CUP HIS FACE, I glance quickly back and forth between each eye, focusing on those dark spots, the murky circle and the line, the bait luring me in, as if it's proof that he's still here, still alive. He pulls my hands down, then yanks me into his arms. A thunderclap crashes across the sky, and the storm clouds pour open, raining down on us.

"Did he touch you?" he shouts through the rain.

I blink, trying to focus on his words. *Touch me?*

Tears fill my eyes. The only time Peter touched me was when I resisted arrest. Peter was a good man, and I killed him. The pain tightens my throat then stretches behind my eyes, threatening to explode.

"Are you okay, little cure?" Cash asks, his voice quiet. His mouth is slack, like he's confused about how to help me.

I can't answer. I shake my head, and then it happens: the sobs rake through my body, tearing me apart, and I can't control it anymore. My breathing rasps in and out of my chest and no matter how hard I try, I can't calm down.

Cash has done so much for me. I had to kill Peter, or Cash would have died. *I had to do it.*

Didn't I?

"If the bastard wasn't dead already, I'd kill him for making you cry like this," Cash says. His voice is low and full of vibrations. Snot stuffs my nose, but I snort and try to catch my breath. He strokes the top of my head, trying to comfort me, and I want to laugh. It's such a sweet thing to say, and yet it's completely demonic. Guilt seeps into me everywhere.

I killed an innocent man to protect a serial killer. There's no way anyone in this world can forgive me for that.

But I'm so damn relieved.

"He was just like your stepdad," Cash says. "Another predator who needs to be erased."

A laugh escapes from my mouth, because I know Cash is just saying that. He's trying to make me feel better, but even if those rumors that he drugged that girl in high school are true, Peter always respected my boundaries, even if he didn't keep his promise to take care of my stepdad. I want to focus on the horrible things Peter has done, but I can't.

He's gone, and I'm not sure if I did the right thing.

But it's what I wanted.

"Wayne Cash," Cash says in a loud voice, breaking through the pounding rain. I look up at him, drops spattering my face. A gleam of moonlight flashes in his dark eyes. "But call me 'Cash.'"

He lifts me off of his lap, then he goes to his truck and digs around. For a minute, the rain pours, and my heartbeat rocks in my ears. Then old licenses and fake IDs land at my feet. Each of the plastic cards has a picture of Cash at various ages and styles. Shaggy hair. A shaved head. A thick beard reaching three inches past his chin. Always with those same dark eyes, freckled with a black cloud and a line.

And in the last ID, he looks the youngest. A cropped haircut. A scar from a zit on his cheek. Even though he's barely an adult, his eyes are the cruelest in that picture. Dark and full of menace.

Wayne Cash, the ID says. His birthday is on October thirteenth. He's over ten years older than me.

"Wayne Cash," I repeat. He blinks his eyes lazily in a show of disinterest. I raise my voice over the rain: "You don't like going by 'Wayne'?"

"One of the breeder's names," he says. That's why he doesn't use it, then.

"It's lucky you missed the 'junior' part," I say.

"Junkies don't remember suffixes."

I'm sure this isn't easy to talk about. I bite my lip, but a warmth fills my stomach. He's opening up to me about his past. I didn't expect that.

"Was Cash your dad's last name?" I ask.

"Neither of theirs. They just gave it to me. I was told they were big fans of Johnny Cash." He shakes his head. "Fucking addicts."

I gather the plastic cards into a pile, then wipe each of them off on my dress before stacking them for Cash. They're still wet, but he throws them in his glove box, then we both climb into his truck. We close the doors and it's quiet. The rain patters the metal exterior, and the bodies look like piles of rocks in the darkness. Cash stares out at the dark ocean, and I follow his gaze.

"What do you want to do now?" he asks.

"You're the pro at this," I say. "Aren't you supposed to tell me?"

"Us," he says. "What do we do about us?"

My chest tingles and I smile to myself. *Us. We.* He's acknowledging that I mean something to him.

He's acknowledging that *we* mean something to him.

"You don't have to be with me," he says, tossing his head to the side. "You can still go. I'll take the blame. All of it."

He thinks I don't want to be with him?

"Are you lying?" I ask. I'm not sure if I'm teasing him, or if I'm serious. It just seems like a strange thing for him to say. I literally just killed for him, and he's questioning me?

His eyes meet mine. "Not about this," he says.

I look down at my lap. "It's pretty safe to assume that we're in this together."

Cash takes my hand and holds it. It's such a small sign of affection, and completely unlike him, but I like it. He's being vulnerable with me. My heart swells, and I know this is right for us.

"He has the surveillance footage?" he asks.

I nod. "He hacked my computer or something."

Cash laughs. "That's not legal without the proper warrants."

"He didn't seem to care."

Cash bows his head, thinking it through. "I'll get rid of the evidence. After that, we run wherever you want."

It seems surreal. Getting rid of the evidence. Going on the run. The fact that I'm even considering all of this is strange, like I'm settling into a new life. It's crazy. Just like Cash and me.

"I know someone in Central Florida who can get rid of these cars for us, but we still gotta clean them up before we can take them there," he says.

"And the bodies?"

"You let me worry about that."

I open my mouth to question him, but he shakes his head.

"Don't worry, little cure," he says. "You don't have to worry about any of that anymore." He elbows me in my shoulder. "Trust me."

I swallow hard and Cash squeezes my hand. So much in my life has been about never trusting anyone. But somehow, I trust Cash.

Those dark freckles beam down at me, holding me up, and it's like I'm crawling toward him all over again.

"We're going to go somewhere else where we can forget that this ever happened."

Tears well up in my eyes, but I blink, holding them back. I'm scared. I don't know what the world is like when you're a fugitive, and no matter how hard I try, I know I'll never forget everything that happened here. *And I don't want to.* I want to remember every moment here. When Cash choked me with a noose. When he made me crawl until my knees bled. When he fucked me with a knife, so desperate to make me come that he cut his own hand. The same place where I chose Cash over everything right in the world. Just like he chose me.

Cash kisses me on the lips, a softness lingering in his touch, and for once, I don't feel dread. I feel relief. And that holds me up.

Cash

Back at the estate, we shower, then I hold her in Winstone's giant bed. I don't close my eyes until I hear her heavy breaths. The only way I can let myself relax is by making sure she's relaxed first. She calms me.

In the morning, I leave a note on the side table: *Unfinished business. Back soon. —C.* I kiss her forehead, and I'm gone.

In the parking lot, I shoot the detective's guns a few times, debating whether to make it look like a shootout occurred between him and the hostages. But the detective's body is bruised to shit, and that won't pass with the other cops. Luckily, most of the blood washed away with the storm. I chop them all up, throwing them into garbage bags. I'll get rid of them on the way out of the Keys. I clean the rest of the detective's blood off of his car. Winstone owns the property, so there's no reason for anyone to know that this spot is here.

I pick the lock at the detective's house, then access his computer. His software connects to Remedy's laptop, giving him remote access, and it looks like he recorded some clips too. I smile to myself; Remedy must have watched our footage together, then. Next, I wipe his computer clean. I doubt what he did is legal, but as long as he didn't send the footage to anyone else, we'll be okay. *Remedy* will be okay.

Booting up his computer again, I access the dark web, paying for evidence that will link the detective to a human trafficking ring, then order a victim for rape and kill, using my own untraceable cryptocurrency. To everyone else, he'll look like he's a piece of shit who disappeared once he knew he was going to get caught. The police will never touch Remedy, and she'll believe that he deserved to die. I don't have any guilt, but for now, she still feels things. She doesn't like what she did to the detective, so this is the least I can do for her.

I dial the police on a burner phone, tilting my head as I wait for them to answer.

"Key West Police Department, how may I direct—"

"Your detective is a trafficker," I say.

The line is silent. "I'm sorry, sir, did you say—"

"He's buying women on the dark web and raping and killing them," I say emphatically. "He has had that track record since high school. You need to investigate him."

"Sir, if you could just—"

I hang up. The police will be forced to investigate, and once the information leaks, he'll be all over the news. Punishment like that always riles up the media. And when Remedy sees it, any doubts she has will be gone.

At the estate, I check in with Remedy, kissing her lips, full of tension and force. I scrape the hell out of her back while she melts into me, but I rip myself away before I get distracted. I make sure she's occupied upstairs so that I have time to work. In the down-stairs office, I remove Winstone and the stepdad. The white primer makes the stepdad look like a puffy balloon, but with Winstone, it's like a shriveled banana peel. I chop and toss them into the black garbage bags too.

In the evening, I rent a tow truck with cash. I can't get all the dents out of the detective's car, but most of the blood is out. It takes all night to make it to the center of the state. I stop at different veterinarian hospitals and funeral homes on the way there, picking locks when I can and starting the incinerators and crematories to take care of the remains. Eventually, the body parts will be ashes, and so spread out, no one will notice the difference.

In Central Florida, I drop off the detective's car at a scrap metal junkyard. It's a friend I've used from time to time; I like that he doesn't ask questions.

When I get back to the estate in the early afternoon the next day, Remedy is asleep by the front window, waiting for me. The windows are open like I always leave them, but now she's comfort-able, letting the breeze come in. The sun lights the deep tawny skin on her neck and her open, purple lips. I've never cared for kissing, but finally kissing her creates this urge inside of me to make up for never doing it. I need her mouth on mine all the time, even if I can't breathe.

I sit by her side. The cut on her face is healing rapidly, but I make a plan to peel the scab later, to make sure that it scars. It's fair, considering the damage she did to my back. I'll even let her scar my face too. Seeing her like this, she reminds me of an angel of darkness. She brings blood into the world, and with my last breath, I'll make sure that nothing ever hurts her again.

No one can hurt Remedy, but me.

I move a black tendril of hair out of her eyes, and she stirs, but she doesn't flinch away.

"You're home," she says in a drowsy voice. *Home.* I've never had a home. But if home means I'm with her, then yes. I'm home.

She rubs her eyes and sits up, letting out a yawn. The corners of my mouth lift; she takes my breath away.

And I'm going to protect her darkness with all of my fucking soul.

"We should talk," she says.

"We should."

"If we're going to do this, *together,*" she uses a strangely stern voice, almost as if she's joking, though I know she's not, "then you need to admit that you have feelings for me."

"I know."

She presses her lips together, stunned for a second. "You know?"

I shrug my shoulders slightly. "Finish your speech."

"Is this love, or is it obsession?" she continues. "I need to know. Either way, you have feelings for me, but as long as we know where we stand, we can figure out what our future means. If that means we're together or not."

I killed her boss, killed her ex-boyfriend, killed her stepbrother, *helped* her kill her stepdad, watched her kill a cop, then covered up those deaths so that she'll never be found. And if I need to, I *will* sacrifice myself. As long as she's safe.

Love *is* an obsession to me. Everything is dull, given to the same predictable tendencies, but Remedy isn't. There's a darkness inside of her that draws me in. And I know we'll be the end of each other, but I also know I'll die happy.

"Does it make a difference?" I ask.

"Yes," she snaps, crossing her arms. "It lets me know where I stand with you. And like I said, Cash, I'm *done* with your bullshit. If you're obsessed, then you'll lose that obsession over time, and we have to figure out a long-term arrangement that works. But love? *Love stays.* Love doesn't give up just because you lose interest. So I need to know." She stares at me with that fiery little gaze, and I want to fuck her into oblivion. To show her exactly how obsessed *and* in love with her I am. "Do you love me?"

"Come here."

She hesitantly inches closer to me and I cloak her in my arms until she's completely consumed by my touch. She lays her head on my chest and I nuzzle the top of her head.

"I'm not sure what this is. This feeling," I say. I stroke her hair, the silky strands mixing with my bumpy fingers. "But it's warm and it tingles and it consumes me whenever you're near. And I've never felt it before." I position her until we're looking into each other's eyes, and I search her, making sure she knows that I'm here for her, and only her. "I'm not sure what love is, but I know I will die for you. I will kill for you. And if you have to, I want you to kill me too."

"Cash—"

I put a finger to her lips. "I love you," I say.

Finally, her shoulders drop, and she melts into me, both of us relieved.

"I love you too," she whispers.

I scoop her into my arms and bring her to the downstairs office for the last time. The sunlight glitters on the broken glass covering the floor. The room is empty without the newspaper, and knowing that Winstone and Remedy's stepdad aren't dead in the crawl space anymore makes it bittersweet. I imagine it's like visiting an old home; there's familiarity and comfort in everything you know, but it's not yours anymore, and it will never be the same.

But I still have her. Remedy is my home.

I lay her down on the rug over a few small shards of glass, then I remove the blindfold and earplugs from the desk. She tenses, but I hold her down, not letting her move, and her eyes soften like it's comforting to be surrounded by force. Once the blindfold and plugs are in, I undress her, kissing every inch of her body until she shivers with anxiety. This is gentle, the kind of touch that repulses her. And that's why I need to do it. I need to show her that she can trust me, no matter what we do. I need her to know that I'm only doing this for her.

And maybe, somewhere inside of me, I need to know that she trusts me too. She needs those three words, and I need this. This is my proof.

I drag a finger between her pussy lips, her arousal wetting my fingertip. But I take out my pocketknife and drag it along her inner thighs until white lines paint her skin. *I'm still here,* I say through those knife lines. *You can trust me. You're lying on broken glass and I'm using this knife. This is gentle, but I'm still here.*

She relaxes, and those shivers stop. One day, she'll be able to have pure pleasure without pain again, but it'll take slow steps like this. I remove one of her earplugs.

"Do you want me to stop?" I ask.

"No." Her chin trembles, but she shakes her head. "Please, don't stop."

The plug squishes back into her ear and the tears roll down her cheeks. I keep kissing her, teasing her with the spiked end of the blade, and kissing her lips and skin, softer than before, and she writhes her hips into me, wanting more. And as I press a finger in between her pussy lips, those sobs unleash. I drop the knife and pull her into my arms, covering her with my body like a giant blanket, to let her know that this is okay. Whatever she needs, I'm here for her. Even if she needs the knife. Even if she never wants me to touch her like this again. Even if she just needs to cry. But she wraps her arms and legs around me and thrusts her hips forward, and I know what she wants.

I undress quickly, then rip off her blindfold and earplugs. I want to see her face. Every twist of pleasure. Her sweet agony. And with every moan and growl that forces itself out of my soul, I want her to hear what she does to me.

"I love you," I say, my voice hoarse. Her lips move to say it back to me, but I can't wait. I plunge inside of her, my dick filling up her tight cunt, each press of my hips deliberate, and her three little words turn into succulent screams. The tears finally stop and pleasure builds up inside of her, her skin flushing from head to toe, and that's enough for me. I don't need those words; I just need to see her lose herself in us. I rock my dick inside of her until the orgasm crashes through both of us, and we're lost in pure bliss.

Epilogue

Cash

one year later

"Happy Unbirthday!" Remedy shouts as I open the door. She pops her hips to the side, pointing to a cake stacked with an insane amount of candles on the kitchenette counter. The pink scar on her cheek stretches with her smile, mirroring the fresh scar on mine. A new, skimpy black dress shows off the new lace pattern on her upper thighs, her onyx wedding ring glimmering with the candlelights. "Guess how many candles this time?"

"One hundred?" I ask.

She tilts her head. "One day you'll get your triple digits," she smirks.

Bones's new collar jingles down the hallway. I need to take off the bell—we're not supposed to have pets in this monthly motel—but right now, I want Remedy. I grab her ass and kiss her deeply. This is our pattern: the three of us, Bones included, never stay in one place for long, and we make 'friends' in each area. If Remedy has a preference—usually someone she thinks 'deserves' it—then I kill that person, stealing their money along with it. No one misses a foreigner. But if she doesn't, I pick the one who will last the longest. It's more entertaining that way.

And every once in a while, it's my birthday or unbirthday or whatever Remedy wants to call it, and I beat her ass and choke her until she comes so hard, she passes out. I don't care for the cake—I've never been into sweets—but I do like the beatings.

This unbirthday has us on a little island off the coast of Mexico. I blow out the flames and Remedy squeals, immediately taking the candles out in handfuls.

"Hey," I say, stopping her. "Count them."

As she counts, her eyelids flutter, knowing that I'm going to make her count again later too. I dip my finger into the cake, then lick the icing off of my finger. She watches me swirl my tongue, knowing that's exactly how I'm going to feast on her clit later. A coppery taste comes through the sugar; blood is still stuck in my fingernails, and my dick hardens for her. The last time I watched Remedy kill a man pops into my mind. Blood covered her hands and stomach, and in the chaos, blood even smeared her pussy, and I licked it off of her. I've still got her beat by plenty of bodies, but she's slowly building up her count. She's at four now.

What we have is rare, but that's what makes it special. We're alike in so many ways, but I like that she's different from me too. She needs a reason; I don't. But I like that about her.

Her burner phone vibrates, and when I see the phone number, I motion for her to take the call. It's her mom.

She mouths, *Sorry.*

"Gives me a chance to make sure you're not skipping candles," I tease.

I count them all—this time, it's thirty-nine, only a few years older than my real age—and by the time she comes back, her expression has changed. Her shoulders drop, her mouth loose and sullen.

"You all right?" I ask.

She nods to herself, but I can tell she's trying to play it off like it's nothing. I move the hair out of her green eyes.

"I feel bad," she says.

I know it's about her stepdad. Her mother hasn't taken his disappearance well, even though they had been divorced for years. I guess they kept in contact anyway, and now, she thinks he's ghosted her.

"You shouldn't," I say.

"I know, but my mom, she's so—"

Remedy stops and the words disintegrate in her mouth.

"You did what you had to do," I say. "For all you knew, I would've killed *you* if you didn't kill him."

She huffs through her nose, her nostrils flaring. "You wouldn't have killed me." She rolls her eyes, a sassy grin on her plump lips.

"You don't know that."

She laughs. I wrap my arms around her, stuffing my mouth with her neck, biting down until she squeals. "Cash!" she shouts. "Oh! By the way," she lifts her burner phone, "Jenna's got a new boyfriend."

Remedy catches up with Jenna by making fake social media profiles and searching her pages for new information. If anything bugs her about leaving Key West, it's losing her best friend. But we both agreed that this is the best way to keep Jenna safe.

"Do we need to take care of this one too?" I ask. Her last abusive ex was Remedy's number three.

"No," she says, feigning reluctance like she's disappointed that we can't kill him. "As long as he doesn't hit her, I honestly don't care."

A few months after we left, we mailed Jenna a picture of a very dead-looking Mr. Winstone. *Movie Props*, Remedy wrote on the back. She left it unsigned and without a return address.

I swing Remedy around until she's leaning on the counter, pinned between my arms. I press my lips to hers, growling as her tongue searches for mine. Her lips are like satin, and I know I don't deserve her. I can't give her back her best friend or her mom, but I can give her a life like this. We're traveling the world, one place at a time, meeting and destroying people we meet. We even have matching onyx wedding rings to symbolize our union. We can't get legally married without leaving a paper trail, but we know we are our *chosen* family. That's what matters.

I bend her over the counter, pulling up her thin black dress. She stands on her tiptoes, waiting for me to strike. I take out my gun, still faintly warm from the last bullet, and rub the barrel against her pussy. She grinds back onto it like it's a dick, and fuck,

I hold my cock in my other hand, ready to trade it for the gun. I love playing games with her, but I want inside of her now.

One day, our love is going to kill us. But I've never been scared of death, and Remedy isn't afraid anymore. We're in this together.

THE END

ALSO BY AUDREY RUSH

DARK ROMANCE

Stalker

Standalone

Dead Love

Grave Love

Hitch

Assassin

The Feldman Brothers Duet

His Brutal Game

His Twisted Game

Mafia

The Adler Brothers Series

Dangerous Deviance

Dangerous Silence

Dangerous Command

Secret Society

The Marked Blooms Syndicate Series

Broken Surrender

Broken Discipline

Broken Queen

Secret Club

The Dahlia District Series

Ruined

Shattered

Crushed

Ravaged

Devoured

The Afterglow Series

His Toy

His Pet

His Pain

Billionaire

Standalone

Dreams of Glass

———

Erotic Horror

Body Horror

Standalone

Skin

Psychological

Standalone

My Girl

ABOUT THE AUTHOR

Audrey Rush writes kinky dark romance and erotic horror. She currently lives in the South with her husband and child. She writes during school.

TikTok: @audreyrushbooks
Instagram: audreyrushbooks
Reader Group: bit.ly/rushreaders
Threads: @audreyrushbooks
Reader Newsletter: audreyrush.com/newsletter
Banned Account Info: bit.ly/bannedsupport
Amazon: amazon.com/author/audreyrush
Website: audreyrush.com
Facebook: fb.me/audreyrushbooks
Goodreads: author/show/AudreyRush
Email: audreyrushbooks@gmail.com

Acknowledgments

Thank you to my husband, Kai, for helping me think like a serial killer, *and* for designing all of the things; your support means the world to me. Thank you to my dad for your critical feedback on the blurb. Thank you to my ARC readers for your honest reviews and your continued support; I always learn from you and relish your encouragement. And thank you to my daughter, Emma, for tolerating my writing sprints and being such a great kid during quiet time.

Thank you to my amazing beta reading team. Chelle, you helped me think of ways to incorporate Cash's backstory and motivation, as well as how to make Remedy spunkier. Johanna, you helped me think of ways to develop Remedy's strength and Cash's persona. Lesli, you pushed me to level up the descriptions in this book and to stop holding back so much. Meagan, you helped me make this book hot as hell. Michelle, you showed me where Remedy could be more feisty and strong so that the story made the most sense. You are all truly brilliant, and I value your feedback so much!

But most of all, thank you to my readers. You are the reason I love to turn my daydreams into stories. Thank you for coming on this journey with me.

Made in United States
Orlando, FL
29 March 2024

45253110R00148